Hunt

Add a little bit of body text

The Aurora Marellup Saga Book 2

Written By:

Serenity Rayne

Adult Supervision Required

Reverse Harem Romance / Why choose?
True / Fated Mates
Medium—Fast Burn
Multiple Points of View
Blood and Gore

Musical Inspiration Provided By

A7 ~ Hail to the King
Metallica ~ Sanitarium
Megadeth ~ She-Wolf
Metallica ~ Of Wolf and Man
Shinedown ~ Devil

Also by Serenity Rayne

Ascend

Fight

Attack

Welcome home

Princess Lost

Destiny Found

Once Upon A Raven

Heart Shaped Box

A Very Klaus Christmas

Tiamat

Discovered

Innate

Balance

Destroyer

Stalker Links

Readers Group ~ Serenity's Den
IG: Serenity Rayne
TicTok~ Serenity Rayne
Other Author Links

Prologue - Alaric

Yakuita, Russia, Ice Dragon Fortress

I sit at my crystalline desk reviewing the maps available for the Bering Land Bridge between Siberia and Alaska. According to what Ellis told me previously, Tomas has the Polar Bears waiting for Aurora and her troops on the island in the ice bridge center. The Diomede Islands, located in the dead center of the soon-to-be land bridge, seem to be where the attack will occur.

I quickly take out my cell phone and text Alex what I have discovered, so hopefully, he can relay the information to Aurora and her people. Almost immediately, my phone dings, and it's a text back from Alex.

He's been in contact with his brothers, who happen to be two of Aurora's mates. They are currently training with Lycans as well as the old Ice Dragon King. Within Alex's compound, he's presently training his people to be ready to join Aurora in her final fight.

I look back through messages I've been exchanging with Alex, and I finally find what I'm looking for. The video in question shows Aurora shifting for the first time in the middle of the arena. I replay the part where her fur and body are blanketed in frost. I watch as the frost crystals form on her coat and on the ground around her. It's truly a vision to behold. The uniqueness of her existence brings a whole new level of wonder to her theatrical display.

Aurora appears to be a very proud and dominant female with how she handles herself in the arena. To be quite honest, I've watched this video of her far too many times for it to be considered research anymore. My dragon is beyond obsessed with her and her shifted form. He wants to feel her talons rake across his scales. My dragon wants to bathe her in his frost fire. If I'm to be honest with myself, I want all those things too.

I sigh and close the video, returning my gaze to the maps before me. I have to calculate the distance from the Lycan camp in Ferdig, Montana, to Wales, Alaska. It's approximately twenty-three hundred miles on land. I already know that most of the trip through Alaska will be on foot for them. If they are able to drive or fly, they are looking at about a fifty hour trip just to get to Wales. Sadly, most of the flights will be grounded when they are attempting to travel due to unpredictable weather.

I quickly look through my resources to see if I can somehow send aid to her. My dragon's instinct is pushing me to help and protect her. He wants her for himself. I pause when that revelation is made.

Shit... my dragon has chosen...

I breathe deeply before getting up to walk to my balcony. Pushing open the double doors, I step out into the blizzard. Without hesitation, I leap off of my balcony, shift, and take flight. I need to investigate the islands for myself and then meet up with Ellis.

The miles melt away quickly with every beat of my wings. Hundreds of miles of ice and snow separate me from Ellis. I scan the ground and sky around me to make sure I'm not being followed. A couple of hours pass before the Polar Bear Camp becomes visible.

Carefully, I land about twenty miles away from the camp and head to the cavern Ellis and I use for our meetings. I shift back to my human form and enter the cavern. Quickly, I move to the far back towards my hidden crate and remove spare clothes and my cloned phone. I power up the phone and text Ellis, alerting him of my arrival. Slowly, the clone phone catches up to where my other phone is.

I'm experiencing an emotion I've never dealt with before. It's rather disturbing to think I'm currently feeling anxious. My right hand raises and starts to rub my sternum. Anxiety is something I don't know how to deal with. I am an Ice Dragon Prince—I'm battle proven with many victories under my belt, but I fear failure for once. *Shit*. I'm actually afraid of something. I ponder this thought for several moments.

Eventually, I arrive at the conclusion that I'm not scared of something, but for Aurora. I don't want to lose the princess before I've even met her. I start kicking rocks and ice chunks around the cavern because I can't deal with what I'm feeling. I wouldn't say we hit the end-of-the-world danger level, but inside I feel like my world is in danger of ending.

While I have my moment, Ellis arrives and bears witness to my mini flip out. "Whoa, bro, settle down! What's wrong?" Ellis crosses his thickly muscled arms over his chest, appraising my temperament.

"I'm fine, Ellis, just dealing with some heavy shit." I reach up and run my fingers through my long, blonde hair. After settling myself down, I decide to speak again.

"I started calculating the time and distance for the princess to travel. It's a minimum of fifty hours if they can drive and fly to Wales." I begin to draw the map out for Ellis in the snow between us using a stick I found.

"We both know in the next couple of days all flights will be grounded until the spring thaw." I look up at Ellis, and I know he can fucking read me like a book. I'm deflecting hardcore, trying not to deal with what I'm feeling at the moment.

"The plan is solid, man, but what's eating at you? You never throw a temper tantrum like you did when I walked in." Ellis cocks his head to the side. He's staring at me with that knowing look.

Fucking hell. Maybe I should have just texted him. I begin to pace. *Fuck.* Dead giveaway that something's bothering me. Quickly, I turn to face Ellis. My eyes are the silver-gold color of my dragon.

"My dragon has chosen." I drop my gaze quickly.

Finding a mate is so very rare for a dragon—those picky bastards. I should be elated, be shouting it from the mountain tops. Instead, I feel like a child who got caught with his hand in the cookie jar. Honestly, I feel like a thief because no one else even had the chance to meet the princess, and my dragon has called dibs. Ellis looks frozen in his state of shock. His mouth hangs open and his eyes are wide as he stares at me.

"Hold up! Back that mother fucking train up! Your dragon has chosen? Seriously?" Ellis moves quickly and wraps me up in a tight bro-hug.

"Horrible timing, but excellent news, man! I'm so happy for you! Let me guess, the Fire Princess? It's gotta be her, she's got curves for days!" Shaking my head, I place both hands on Ellis's shoulders to get his attention.

"It's none of the females my father has been parading around the castle." I reach over and grab hold of his cell and find the message from Alex, then I fast forward to where Aurora shifts. Understanding flitters across Ellis's face. He watches the full shifting sequence before looking up at me.

"Oh? Oh boy... You can't be serious. For real, bro?" He throws his arms up in the air dramatically.

"I mean, she's hot, but she's not a dragon. Your father will have a fucking cow if he finds out! It's bad enough he wants her dead." Ellis stands there shaking his head and even starts pacing.

"How loyal are your boys to you?" His eyes lock with mine, searching my face for answers.

"Very loyal. I was planning on tonight's training flight to detour away from our normal route and tell them of my recent development." I walk to the back of the cave to retrieve a skull I had hidden there. It's a skull from a Tizheruk, the snake-like sea creatures that hunt the village fishermen.

I stare at my prized possession, then offer it to Ellis. "Please send this to Aurora for me." Ellis takes the skull from me with an odd look on his face. I shift my left arm to that of my dragon gauntlet, pluck off a single armored scale, and place it on the line where the skull plates meet.

"It is of utmost importance that the scale remains with the skull. She'll understand it, trust me," I plead with Ellis for understanding. I hope against all hope that she accepts my prized skull and knows the value of the scale I send her. It's a promise of forever and a far deeper bond than a mate bite could ever create. Scale exchanges between dragons mean forever; this life, and into the great beyond. Ellis's facial expressions clearly convey his dislike of my gift.

"You dragons are fucked up with your customs. What happened to sending girls flowers? Instead, you send her rare ass skulls? No worries, bro, I got you! I'll box this bad boy up and ship it off." Ellis sets the skull down, then takes his phone and texts Alex for the address. A few moments later the reply is received. Ellis fucking smirks at me and screenshots the address.

The next thing I know, my phone goes off and it's the screenshot. I nod slowly and stick the message in my hidden folder in my phone. I also move her video and any other photos of her there and delete all my text messages.

"Just let me know if you hear anything. I have a shit ton of arrangements to make." When Ellis's phone goes off again, he bursts out laughing, causing me to look over at him and tilt my head at his reaction.

"Man, you two are perfect together. Sick fucks." Ellis holds up his phone as the video starts playing. Aurora is looking at the bones of her enemies displayed on the walls of her home. She's smiling and laughing—excited, happy, and proud. Apparently she has a lot of dragon tendencies.

I must have that love-sick puppy look on my face because Ellis is shaking his head at me. "You've got it bad. Damn, I never thought I'd live long enough to see this day come to pass. I'm gonna jet and get this mailed to your girl. I'll let you know if she sends anything back." One brief bro-hug, and he's off on probably one of the most critical missions I've trusted him with to date.

I turn to leave and stand at the mouth of the cavern. The snow is just starting to fall here, and it's a beautiful sight. I wait long enough for the snow to begin falling harder before I prepare to leave. I shut my spare phone off and leave it and my clothing hidden in the cavern. The snow is cool upon my skin as I walk out far enough to shift back to the form of my dragon.

I take flight and decide to follow Ellis for a bit, making sure he's safe. He's heading to the nearest town with a UPS store in it. I can only imagine the look on the poor attendant's face. I circle several times before heading back to my home. There's going to be lonely days and nights ahead of me. My dragon won't let me touch anyone else now; he's chosen, and his word is final. The most frightening part is, I'm actually okay with that.

CHAPTER 1

Sebastian

Going against my wolf's insistence to stay with Aurora, I slowly walk outside. Mentally, I know Jayce needs his time with Aurora to complete the bond. But fuck, we almost lost her, and all I want to do is hold onto her for dear life and never let her out of my sight again. I stand on the porch and look out across the compound. Dom slowly approaches me from behind and places a hand on my right shoulder.

"Scariest three days of my life. I don't know what any of us would have done if Aurora died," Dom says in a low, relieved tone. He looks around the central part of the compound, then back to me.

"Which direction do you want to start the patrol?" Dom, a potential alpha, waits for my command. It's a nice change for once.

"I mostly want to stay close to the main part of the community. If there will be another attack, they will focus on Aurora again. We can't afford to be too far away with her in such a weakened state." I honestly half expected a fight over my decision, but Dom nods in agreement.

"I figure we'll start at the furthest house and walk clockwise around the perimeter." I step off the porch and head in the direction

I just indicated. Dom catches up to me and begins fiddling with his phone. Apparently, it was shut off for the last few days.

"Hmm, Alex sent several texts. Apparently, we have informants in the Ice Dragon and Polar Bear Compounds. Tomas is plotting to attack us as we cross the Bering Land Bridge on the two islands in the middle." Dom's eyes lift to meet mine, then shift back down to his phone as more texts come through.

"Apparently, the Dragon Prince and one of the Polar Bears are part of the resistance. We are assured assistance, protection, and shelter along our journey." More messages come through, and Dom reads through them quickly.

"The prince has shipped a package to Aurora, but Alex has no clue what it contains." Dom goes back to texting back and forth with Alex, informing him of the recent attack and Aurora's near-death experience.

Dom felt that the prince and the bear needed that information. "Alex said he'll pass the news along once he hears from them again."

"Shit. Well, we should start planning for the battle on the ice then." I pull out my phone and bring up my mapping program and search for the Bering Land Bridge. It's not fully intact yet, but it should be when we are ready to cross. I see the islands in question and show them to Dom.

"If your brother's information is correct, here's the attack zone." I don't doubt Alex's integrity, but I don't know the other males involved to fully trust them yet. As we stop in the middle of the road, we draw the attention of Aurora's father, Nicodeamus. Silent fucker almost scared my wolf white with the way he seemed to materialize before me.

"Holy fuck, Dad. You just scared the hell out of me!" I pause, my skin becoming paler. I just called Aurora's father *Dad*. Nicodeamus smirks at me—like father like daughter.

"It happens, son. What has drawn your attention to the phone? Is that the correct name for the magic information box?" His brows are furrowed in concentration, much like his daughter when she's in deep thought.

"Yes, Father, it's a phone, and we've received intel from Alex about where Tomas is setting up to ambush us." Dominik takes this moment to show Nicodeamus the islands' map and shows him the text messages from Alex. Nicodeamus starts to smile and lets out a slow breath.

"Wonderful news!" Nico says in probably one of the most jovial tones I've heard him use since seeing his daughter.

"Alaric was just a hatchling when I last saw him. He was such a good boy. His mother is a Golden Dragon. They are known for their sense of justice." His eyes light up as he reads further. He glances between Dominik and me, then back to the message.

"Can you find out when and why the prince is sending Aurora the present?" Nicodeamus's dragon is so close to the surface that scales randomly ripple along his flesh. Dominik looks up at the king, a little spooked by his behavior.

"Of course, Father. I'll question my brother immediately." Dom takes the phone back from Nicodeamus and fires off several questions to Alex, then begins pacing, waiting for the answer.

I'm not used to seeing Dom rattled, but you can feel the anxiety coming off him in waves. Several pings of incoming messages fire off in quick succession. Dominik's face goes pale as he passes the phone to Nicodeamus. Dominik locks eyes with me, and the look he has on his face makes me worried. On the other hand, Nicodeamus has that Cheshire Cat smile on his face, making him look like a deranged serial killer.

"Alex heard from the bear that it's a Tizheruk skull with one of the prince's scales." Nicodeamus hands the phone off to Dominik, then grips my left shoulder tightly.

"Do you know what this means?" He gives me several shakes. Nicodeamus's excitement level is turning frightening at an alarming rate. What kind of a shit storm is about to hit the fan for us?

"No, Father, I don't. Remember, I'm not a dragon, and we're all trying to get used to and learn dragon customs." Okay, now I'm genuinely getting concerned. Either the news is really good or really bad. I'm going to safely assume it's okay because he's still smiling.

"Forgive me, boys. I forget you have no clue. A male dragon bestows his prized skull to a female he swears fidelity to. In short, it's a promise of protection and an offer to become mates." He quickly snatches me up in a one-armed hug before turning and doing the same to Dominik.

Nicodeamus takes off shouting for Dimitri and pretty much anyone else who will listen to him. Dominik and I stare at each other, absolutely gobsmacked at the information relayed to us. Game changer, yes. On the positive side, we possibly have a legion of dragons on our side. However, we have a Dragon Prince—another alpha—to contend with. *Fuck...* Dominik finally comes back to his senses and looks at his phone, then back to me.

"Okay... um, back to planning for the attack. We should probably find Dimitri and speak to him. Maybe he can shed some light on how the Polar Bears think and operate." At least Dominik isn't shaken by the revelation that the prince is now involved.

"That's probably a good idea, Dom. Let's go back toward the center of town." We start heading back, and as we approach the Alpha House, what do we find? My mother and Nicodeamus jumping up and down, hugging each other like they won the fucking lottery.

Both Dimitri and Andre look just as gobsmacked as Dominik and I did at the news. We both pause to take in the scene before us. I personally feel like I'm in the middle of a shitty episode of *The Twilight Zone*.

We start to walk toward the group again, and we can hear my mother and Nico discussing where and how to place Aurora's skull collection so it may impress the prince. I facepalm, and my mother looks up after hearing my hand hit my forehead. Before I can react, my mother plows right into me and attempts to hug me to death.

"Isn't it wonderful news! A Dragon Prince on our side for the battle!" She quickly releases me, then proceeds to take Dominik hostage next.

"Nico and I decided we're going to build Aurora a Throne of Skulls. Imagine it: walking into the Alpha House, and next to the fireplace is Aurora sitting on her Throne of Skulls. Her hands are shifted to her hybrid's with the dragon scales, talons gripping the Strigoi skulls." Mom has that dreamy look in her eyes, pleased with her idea even though it's creepy as fuck.

With the way my warped mother describes the scene, I could easily visualize it; my beautiful mate, her eyes pools of mercury. The dominance pouring off her in almost oppressive waves, forcing the weak to be subjugated before her. Her dragon scales coating her forearms and hands in their partially shifted state to look like armored gauntlets. Her long, white, hooked talons digging into the skulls of the Strigoi.

Yet, she's a vision of beauty in her blood-red gown, legs crossed at her ankles. Dominik and Jayce, in their wolven forms, are sitting on either side of her throne. Their large, heavily muscled black Dire Wolves ready to attack at her command. As for myself, I stand at her right as her first mate, prepared to advise her or quell her rage. I blink my eyes rapidly, then look at Nicodeamus. The fucker is smiling at me.

"Did you just share that vision with me?" He starts laughing.

"Yes, I did. I also shared it with Dominik. With both of you fully bonded to Aurora, I had to test my theory. Soon, you will all be able to share visions as well as talk without sound. It's a dragon thing. You'll get used to it." He smirks.

"She is a vision of beauty on that throne, wasn't she?" Dom and I nod our heads, and I turn to my mother.

"So, what do we need to do to make that vision a reality?" My mother looks to Nicodeamus, then goes up on her tippy toes and kisses his lips before leaving the room. What the fuck just happened? When the fuck did this happen? I fucking quit. I drop my head and follow my mother. Dom chooses to remain behind to catch Dimitri and Andre up on what's been transpiring behind the scenes.

I follow my mother back to her workshop. Apparently, she has already abducted every able-bodied male she could find. Mom is standing by the men, directing them as they carefully stack the skulls in crates. Another group is picking up the containers and carrying them through the back door of the house.

"Mom?" Slowly, my mother turns to face me. By the look on her face, she knows the question I was about to ask.

"Don't look at me like that, baby boy. You look at me as if I am wrong to have any kind of relationship with anyone besides your dead father. I've been alone for the last hundred and ten years. I deserve to be happy too." Unshed tears finally break free and silently roll down her cheeks.

Okay, I absolutely feel like shit for making my mother cry. I move quickly and wrap my arms around her and hug her tightly. Gently, I press a kiss to the crown of her head.

"I'm sorry, Mom, I was just shocked. I'm glad you're happy." I smile as I look down at her. Hopefully, she can see that I'm sincere. Mom's eyes eventually find mine, and she smiles at me.

"I had a crush on Nicodeamus when I was a young woman. He was such a brave and selfless warrior." Her eyes glaze over, and I can tell she is lost in a memory.

"My sister and I were sent as emissaries between the clans. We were the ones versed in the most customs. On one visit, I had the chance to watch Nicodeamus sword fight a Red Dragon Prince," she sighed softly. I look up and see Nicodeamus approaching, and I motion with my hand to halt him.

"That was probably one of the most epic battles I had ever seen. Unbeknownst to the Red Dragon Prince, Nicodeamus was equally dangerous fighting with the sword in either hand. In probably one of the most unforgettable moves I've witnessed, he dropped the sword from his right hand to his left. He thrust it into his opponent's chest, ending the battle." Mom giggled like a schoolgirl at the memory.

"I was instantly smitten with him. It's amazing how quickly a crush is forgotten when your mate stands before you. The sun rose and set according to your dad. No one will ever take his place, but I can care for another." Mom kisses my cheek, then walks into the house. Nicodeamus's face is priceless. Apparently, he had no clue mom ever had a crush on him. I take a page out of his playbook and smirk at him before moving to grab a crate.

I move through the Alpha House, carrying the crate of skulls and come to an abrupt halt. Apparently, the throne idea didn't just happen. By the looks of it, they are halfway done with their little project. Now that I look at it, the throne seems kind of wicked. I place my crate close to where the guys are working before walking around the throne to study it. My mom honestly had a brilliant idea, and I know Aurora will love it. Dimitri enters through the front door with Dominik following closely behind. They both stop dead in their tracks and stare at the half-way done skull throne.

"It's a brilliant gift for Aurora, isn't it?" Maybe I'm becoming just as daft as the others, but I'm starting to see the need for the throne. Dom looks to Dimitri, then back to me.

"Um, yeah. It's a great idea, and I'm sure our mate will love it, but don't you think planning our strategy is more important than home decor?" Dominik and Dimitri assume the same stance, crossing their thick arms over their chests. I look at the two of them and realize they are fucking dead serious, so I text several more young pack-mates to come assist with the project. I pull myself away and head toward the office off the main chamber. Dimitri and Domink follow me, then close the door behind them.

"Here's a map of the area we'll have to cross." I pull the map out of the tube, which arrived this morning. Carefully, I spread it out on the large meeting table and use the crystal paperweights to hold it down flat. I move back to the desk and take little pewter wolf-shaped figurines out of the drawer. After, I open two small boxes on the corner of the desk. One holds little bear figurines, and the other has dragon figurines. I start placing the figures in the proper places near the Bering Land Bridge.

"Okay, this is what we're looking at; according to intel, the dragons will be waiting on the Siberia side, the Polar Bears on the islands, and we're here in Alaska." I slowly push our wolves and Dimitri's bear toward the Polar Bears on the island.

"I'm not one hundred percent sure when the prince will make his presence known, but I'm assured of his intentions." I raise my eyes and notice that Nicodeamus let himself into the room and is now approaching the table.

"Very nice, young prince. Only one problem: where's my dragon on our side? I will be in attendance." He's quite firm in his declaration. Dominik reaches across the table without skipping a beat, grabs a dragon, snaps off the wing and front left leg, and then places it next to our wolves. Nicodeamus praises Dominik's work and gives him a nod of approval. Fucking picky ass dragon. Nicodeamus studies the map and figure placement, and you could almost hear the gears turning.

"It's times like this when I wish I still had both wings." His right hand comes up to absently rub where his left arm used to be.

"We need eyes on that island, or at least over it. I'm not sure how well Andre's eagle will handle that type of cold—all things considered." It's nice to think Nicodeamus is taking into consideration Andre's aging problem.

"Other than dragons, I'm not sure how many other flight shifters can handle that kind of cold." Dominik wears a look of complete concentration as he studies the map.

"If we really bundle Andre and he rides on Dimitri's back for warmth, maybe he can fly long enough to identify what we are getting into." Dominik's eyes search mine, then Dimitri's and Nicodeamus's.

"That's a question only Andre can answer. I, for one, am not willing to risk his life for a peek." Dimitri wins the prize for the best resting bitch face of the night. He is deadly serious and unwilling to budge and sacrifice Andre, and I can't say I blame him. Other than the Dire Wolves, other species really can't handle that kind of cold.

"I propose we send the Lycan forces as well as Andre overseas by plane. There's a rogue faction of Lycans in Germany that my mother has been friendly with over the years. According to her, they will house our troops and aid in the battle. Andre can fly from there and do recon on the castle itself." I return to the closet and pull out the map of Europe.

"The Lycan pack is located just outside Wegscheid, Germany. It's almost a straight flight to The Carpathian Mountains section in Moldavia, Romania." I measure the distance between the two locations and write it down.

"It will take approximately sixteen hours by vehicle to reach the mountain. Then, who knows how long to scale it to get to the castle." To my surprise, Dimitri pulls out his phone, opens a satellite image app, and shows me precisely where the castle is located on the mountain. I study his program and spin it around, finding the main road that leads to the castle. Nope, we won't be going that way.

"There are the old tunnels the Strigoi used to invade the castle down over here." Dimitri pans and zooms the image to the stream that runs through the mountain.

"It's an underwater access. Not many alive now would know where it's at. I suggest sending someone to scout the entrance to see if it was closed off in the last two hundred years." My eyes fall back to the stream on the map before I look up at Dimitri.

"I'll have my mother call the other Lycan alpha and see what she can arrange for us." As soon as the words are out of my mouth, that devilish sprite of a woman enters.

"What are you having me do, boy?" Elena's eyes become the white-blue of her wolf as she stares at me, her hands on her hips. Fuck, I'm in trouble now. Yup, I'm going to be killed by my mother.

"Mother, Dimitri relayed information about a hidden escape tunnel that we can use to gain entrance to the castle undetected." I press my finger on the spot on the map where the entrance should be in theory.

"We were merely suggesting to get one of the Lycans from the pack in Germany to scout it. We need to make sure it's still viable before we plan to use it." I watch the anger slowly bleed away from her expression as she ponders the information.

She reaches into her pocket and pulls out her phone. I watch her scroll through the contacts and hit send. "*Hallo, Gustav. Es ist Elena. Sie müssen einen ihrer besten späher auf mission schicken. Ich werde ihnen die Einzelheiten schreiben sobald sie fertig sind. Danke, alter freund.*" Mom looks between us and shrugs her shoulders.

"They'll go in the morning and look. No worries, as you kids say. I have a throne to build. Have fun storming the castle." Mom waves over her shoulder as she departs the room. What the actual fuck just happened? And since when can mom speak German? I look at Dimitri and Nicodeamus. Both guys shrug their shoulders at me.

"We both speak multiple languages. It's like traveling between states here, over there. Except every time you cross a border, you're speaking a different language," Dimitri says like it's no big deal. I guess to them, it really isn't a big deal. They were raised that way.

"Okay, so the tunnel exploration problem is being handled. We're flying the Lycan team to the other Lycan pack. What else do we need to plan for, Dad?" I look to Nicodeamus for guidance because he's had the most direct contact with our enemy out of all of us. Nicodeamus moves slowly around the map, studying it, then heads over to the whiteboard on the wall.

"First thing we need to do is educate your pack and the Dire pack about the Strigoi. Then, we can train both packs on how to kill them. The European packs have been dealing with them for generations. We will employ the same tactics here for training purposes." Nicodeamus begins to list the strengths and weaknesses of the Strigoi on the board. It's kind of frightening to think they have far more strengths than weaknesses.

"Question: will the Dire Wolves' toxic bite have any effect on the Strigoi? It works by rupturing platelets and degrading the cellular integrity of muscle fibers." I look at the notes on my phone that Alex sent me this morning. Making sure I don't miss any important questions, I raise my eyes again to Nicodeamus, watching him closely. I see several different emotions flitter across his face before he smiles.

"I believe their bite would be most effective. Dominik, do you or Jayce possess this toxic bite that Sebastian speaks of?" Dominik snaps out of whatever little bubble he's in and looks up.

"Jayce does. He took after our mother in that sense. He possesses one of the strongest toxins in the entire pack." Dominik's eyes widen in realization of what he just said. Panicking, he looks between us and then the door.

"Aurora... Oh God's no.." Tears well up in his eyes as he bolts for the door. Nicodeamus, one-handed, stops him in his tracks.

"Fear not, son. You already bonded with her. She will be safe from your brother's toxins. Besides, if my daughter is like me, she will bite him first," he says with a cocky smirk. Dominik and I look at each other, knowing we both bit her first. In unison, we close our eyes and concentrate on the bond, reaching out to sense our mate. So far, she's good, real good.

Dominik reaches out to her gently. *Bite Jayce first. His bite is toxic.* His voice echoes in my head; it's a pleading tone. We both hope she listens to him.

I know! Go away! she answers back, booting us both from the connection. Nicodeamus is still smirking at us, then shakes his head slightly.

"She does pack a punch, doesn't she?" He laughs at his own statement before looking to the whiteboard again.

"What special combat gifts do Lycans have?" Nico turns and looks at me. I move to stand next to Nicodeamus and start writing on the board.

"The two advantages I feel stand out the most are bi-pedal and able to grip things. We each have different gifts; some have speed, strength, agility, the list goes on. We can easily separate the pack according to abilities." Sebastian's eyes move between the three of us, then come to rest finally on Nicodeamus. Dimitri and Nicodeamus are both nodding slowly as they absorb the information I just gave them. Dimitri is the first to speak up.

"I believe that would be a wise move, young prince. Let's set up a pack meeting for tomorrow night and address this idea." Dominik moves forward and pulls out a small notepad from his back pocket. He flips it open and turns the pages until he finds what he's looking for.

"There's still the matter of the ferals and rogues to be dealt with." Dominik looks back to his notes again.

"With both groups being packless for so long, there's no telling where their loyalties lie. There's no definitive answer if they will fight with us." Dominik's concerns are valid. If the two groups join us, that adds another twenty to thirty fighters to our cause.

"We agreed to let Aurora sort the bodies out. It's better if she plays judge, jury, and executioner than any of us. Who knows, she may be able to save all of them." My eyes drift to Dominik, then Dimitri, and finally Nicodeamus.

"Or we're going to end up with a huge pile of skulls that Elena will have to prepare for Aurora." Nicodeamus's spot-on assessment of his daughter's all or nothing mentality is kind of frightening. Dimitri chooses this time to speak up.

"What can we expect from the Ice Dragons? Are there any weaknesses we can exploit?" You can tell that Dimitri's question rattled Nicodeamus because his eyes flicker to that of his dragon, then human again.

"Very few, old friend." Nicodeamus looks down, almost sad to relay that information.

"Dragon versus dragon would be best. I can't fly, so I'm a target, but I can help with the ground troops." He looks back at the whiteboard again.

"When we get Jayce's venom, we can test it on dragon blood to see if the cells explode under the microscope." Nicodeamus draws in a deep breath before speaking again.

"If that works, then we need to get ahold of some sniper rifles with armor-piercing rounds that are hollow points. We can turn the toxins into a gel and fill the hollow points." Nicodeamus sighs then turns back to face us.

"It's my only suggestion. Unless the prince helps, it will be lambs to the slaughter." Well, that revelation just shot the meeting straight to hell.

"Dimitri, what can you tell us about the Polar Bears?" Dimitri moves to the whiteboard and doesn't bother writing on it.

"They will be smaller than I am. So, we train the wolves to fight me. If they can defeat me, they are ready for the Polar Bears." I move slowly and place my hands on Dimitri's shoulders.

"Are you sure you want to do this?" There are more wrinkles around his eyes and more grey hair dusting his temples. Granted, time isn't catching up as fast as it was, but it's still progressing quickly.

"It's for Aurora. I swore my dying breath to her. If I die training troops to protect her, then it was worth it." I can see the tears he's fighting to restrain. I give him a curt nod and a brief bro-hug and move back. Nicodeamus full-on hugs Dimitri, both of them blubbering like babies. Nicodeamus keeps thanking Dimitri for all he's done for his daughter.

I look over at Dominik, and he has silent tears rolling down his cheeks. Slowly, I move to his side, wrap my arm around his shoulders and remove him from the room. We move to sit in the kitchen. I grab two beers and pop the tops. Dominik takes his and downs half of it in one gulp. His emotional state hasn't improved, but it hasn't gotten worse.

"Wanna talk about it, Dom?" He shakes his head but starts talking anyway.

"His love for our mate knows no bounds. She's not just a job to him." Tears hit the tabletop as he keeps his head hung low. Slowly, he raises his head. His eyes are bloodshot and that of his wolf.

"You know, if it's anything other than time that kills him, Aurora is going to be a force to be reckoned with. Her thirst for vengeance will know no bounds. Her pain will turn to rage that will burn brighter than a thousand suns." When Dominik puts it that way, I'm terrified of Dimitri and Andre's death. I honestly don't think the world will survive Aurora's pain.

"Mother plans to sit and talk to Aurora about it. Mom thinks, all things considered, they may live another year at most. It could be a lot less with strain and exertion." I gently rub Dominik's shoulders, and I look up to see my mother watching us. She, too, is grieving right alongside us.

"There's only so much that can be done, boys. We have done all that we can. Time is a bitch." Mom goes to the fridge and pulls out three beers, and opens them before passing them around.

"Nicodeamus feels horrible that his scale isn't helping. If my sister was still alive, I could find out what spell she used and bind them to Nicodeamus. Her journals may still be in her room in the castle, if we can find them before it's too late." Mom's look is pensive as she studies the beer bottle as if searching for answers.

"I don't know what else to do for them." She downs her beer quickly before abruptly standing and leaving the room. Everyone in the room is in some semblance of pain this afternoon. We just have to hope and pray our fearless leader has a better plan in mind.

I reach forward and use my claws to slice the nightshirt free from her. Aurora looks a little shocked, but it's totally worth it. There it is, the fabled black lace thong she favors. I drop to my knees before her and grip the lace with my teeth. My hands rest on my thighs as I slowly begin to pull the thong down. I slowly move it down over her bare mound, my hot breath caressing her flesh as I move. I get to her knees and release my hold on the thong, letting it fall to the floor at her feet.

Her hands rest carefully on my shoulders for balance as she steps out of the thong. I remain on my knees before her, staring up at her for a moment before I place a feather-soft kiss right above her clit. Her sharp intake of breath tells me I'm on the right track.

I run my hands slowly up her calves to rest on her thighs. Gently, I urge her thighs apart so I can have an unobstructed view of her glistening wet pussy. The scent of her arousal is driving my wolf and me insane. Lightly, I lick the tip of her clit, teasing her. Aurora's fingertips dig into my shoulders before one hand moves up to grip the back of my head.

"Jayce, please... please, my love... I need you." Her breathy pleas almost cause me to cave. Aurora attempts to move her mound closer to my mouth, wanting to grind upon my face. I sit back on my heels and look up at her. I'm not dominant by any means, but for fuck's sake, a man has to take a stand at some point.

"Be patient, my love. I'll make you come so hard you'll be begging me to stop." Without warning, I stand and scoop her up in my arms to toss her onto the bed.

Aurora squeals upon impact then goes into a giggle fit. I move as slowly as I can toward her. She's my prey today, not the other way around. Sadly, that idea doesn't last long. By the time I have one knee on the bed, she flips me onto my back and sits on my chest, looking down at me. Aurora's eyes flicker back and forth between the steel-grey and molten mercury of her wolf.

I now know what a deer feels like when it's stared at by an apex predator like her. My best bet is to give the lady what she wants. I hook my arms under her knees and move her, so her dripping wet folds are over my waiting mouth. I start to tongue fuck her pussy while both my hands begin to tweak and pinch her nipples. Aurora starts to ride my tongue with reckless abandonment.

I know I got her when the first orgasm rips through her, as she pulses and throbs around my tongue. I remove my right hand from her breast and coat it in her slick, sticky juices. As she's coming down, my index and middle finger start exploring her tight rosette. Based on her gasp and sudden bucking, I know I'm doing something she likes very much. I wet my fingers again as I begin the assault on her clit with my tongue. She's back to grinding down hard on my face, so I apply pressure to her rosette and gain entrance. I'm easily two knuckles deep in her ass as I begin to time my thrusts with her rhythm.

I swear to the gods I feel her squirt all over my face when she comes. Aurora curls forward, bracing herself on her forearms and using the headboard for support. Slowly, I withdraw my fingers from her backdoor and wipe them on the covers. I caress her ass and slide her down my body, leaving a snail trail in her wake.

We're finally face to face when I notice her eyes are back to human. Apparently, the wolf has been appeased for now. I watch Aurora slam her eyes shut for a moment, a low growl escapes her lips before she opens her eyes again.

"Your brother just warned me about your bite." She leans down to kiss my lips as she wiggles her hips, attempting to line my cock up with her entrance.

"I'm going to bite you and make you mine, Jayce. Now and forever together." I take the hint and scoot up the bed a bit, using pillows to support me. When I scoot up, my cock finds what it's looking for, and I sink deeply into her welcoming embrace. Aurora sits up straight and smiles at me. Apparently, she's quite pleased with what she's feeling.

I stay as still as I can even though my balls are begging for release. Aurora begins to move ever so slowly, and it's the single most exquisite feeling I have ever felt in my entire life. Every wet slap of skin on skin, every slip and slide, magnifies as the bond begins to slip into place. Aurora's muscles start to twitch and spasm around my thick cock, and I know she's getting close. Aurora lowers her head and begins to kiss my neck and shoulder.

Without warning, her canines pierce my shoulder muscle and her pussy begins to milk my cock for all that it's worth. I'm not going to last much longer. I start meeting her thrusts, driving up into her harder and harder. I feel my mating knot form, locking me in place as my seed erupts into her.

Quickly, I lunge forward and sink my canines into her shoulder, opposite of where Sebastian and Dominik claimed her. I feel the final bands of the bond snap into place as I taste the coppery tang of her blood in my mouth. We remain locked, both of us still biting each other.

A content sigh eventually escapes Aurora's lips. Carefully, she withdraws her canines and proceeds to clean the wound. I follow suit, being extra careful that I don't accidentally release my toxins into her. Slowly, I tend to her wounds and make sure I promote her healing. Eventually, I lay back and look up at my beloved mate.

"Are you okay, my love? I didn't hurt you, did I?" I search her features for any sign of pain or discomfort, and I see none. Aurora smiles at me and gently kisses my lips.

"Everything is perfect, Jayce. I feel you in here." Aurora brings her hand up and touches over her heart. I can completely relate to what she's saying. I feel her in every fiber of my being. I also feel the relief from my brother and Sebastian that the bond is fully intact, and we are truly bonded. I pull Aurora down to lay beside me as my mating knot releases, and I make sure she's comfortable before extracting myself from the bed.

"Stay here. I'm going to get you some food and drink." I'm very anxious to please her in every sense of the word.

I walk into the ensuite bathroom and retrieve a washcloth and a dry towel. Carefully, I clean Aurora's nether regions, staying mindful of the fact she may be tender. I pat her dry, then look up to see her smiling at me. I can't help but blush at the look of affection on her face. I smile back as I finish cleaning her up.

Slowly, I lean forward and kiss her lips before I head downstairs to gather some food and a drink for her. As I make it into the kitchen, I find the full crew passing around drinks and having a freaking party without Aurora and me.

The world seems to stop for a moment as they all notice that I've seen them. The high fives and bro-hugs ensue for what feels like forever. I get passed around from Dominik to Sebastian, then over to Dimitri and even Andre. Finally, right when I thought I was safe, I end up in front of Nicodeamus. Just what I fucking need. I look up into his eyes and attempt to smile. Nicodeamus reaches up and pulls my collar to the side to inspect Aurora's bite mark. He smiles and gives me a brief hug.

"Get her food and go back to her now." Dimitri shoves a platter with food on it into my hands, then turns me and smacks my ass, sending me on my way. I don't even have the chance to say a damn thing to anyone.

I head back upstairs with a bounty of food to find Aurora curled up on her bed, asleep. I set the platter down on the small table next to the window. Carefully, I lay out all the food, trying to set the perfect spread for her. Once I'm absolutely sure it's as perfect as it's going to get, I return to the bed and sit beside Aurora. My hands slowly massage Aurora's back, trying to wake her up gently. Her eyes flutter open and, initially, they are pure mercury before they fade to her human steel-grey.

"Hey, baby, do I smell bacon?" Aurora asks with a sleepy, raspy tone to her voice. She smiles as she looks at me. I choose to just wink at her, answering her question.

I lean down and kiss her forehead, then offer her a nice, soft terry robe. Aurora gently takes the robe from my hands and slips it on. I offer her my hand and walk with her to her lunch spread. The look on her face is thanks enough. You would think that no one had ever taken the time out of their day to do something so simple. Aurora devours the meal that I set before her, but halfway through, she stops and moves to sit on my lap.

She gently begins to feed me the food I brought up for her. I've never been pampered in my entire life, and yet here is my alpha—my mate—feeding me her food. Aurora is so happy; she's softly singing to me as she feeds me. This gentle side is almost as frightening as when she's in a full-blown rage.

My phone dings, and it's a text from Sebastian. Apparently, a package is downstairs and it's imperative that Aurora comes downstairs to open it. I show Aurora the message, and the look of puzzlement on her face is worth it. Aurora goes over to the walk-in closet and slips into a blood-red bodycon dress that drapes to the floor.

"Let's go, love. I'm super curious what was sent to me." Quickly, she grabs my hand and drags me down the stairs behind her.

I am really starting to fear what she's going to be like come

Christmas time. We make it to the kitchen, where everyone seems to gather. When I say everyone, I mean our entire bond, extended family, and some of our closest pack-mates. On the preparation island in the middle of the kitchen sits the box in question. Aurora pads slowly across the floor silently as she cautiously approaches the box. It's not like the damn thing will bite her, but her wolf makes her investigate everything before proceeding. Once she and her wolf are satisfied that the box isn't a threat, she looks closer at the labels.

"Do we know anyone in Wales, Alaska?" Most of us shake our heads no—all except Dominik and Sebastian.

"Alex's contact sends intel from Wales when he's able to get into town." Sebastian approaches the box and studies the label.

"It's from the same man. I think his name is Ellis. You can trust him." Sebastian kisses the top of Aurora's head before backing away.

Aurora looks to her father, who gives her a single nod to proceed. Without a second thought, Aurora shifts one finger and extends a talon to cut down the sides of the box. She then cuts the top off, and the sides fall flat to the table. Packing popcorn goes everywhere and exposes its precious cargo. It appears to be a giant snake skull at first glance, that is until you really look at it closely. The skull plates are heavily armored and its jaw is thick, heavy, and hinged like all snakes. There are a few significant differences, though. Not only does it have fangs, but it also has rows of razor-sharp teeth like a shark.

Aurora gently brushes the last of the popcorn off and suddenly stops. Scales ripple up her forearms as well as the fur across the rest of her body. It's almost as if she is fighting for control over her body. Her pure mercury orbs are locked on the top center of the skull. I move closer to see what caused such a reaction from her, and then I see it: a heavily armored, silver and gold scale placed in the center of the skull.

"Nicodeamus, you may want to look at this... I don't understand what it means, and Aurora won't budge." I look up to see my brother recording Aurora's reaction, no doubt a request from the sender.

Nicodeamus approaches and sniffs at the scale, and a low growl escapes Aurora's lips at her father's intrusion. Her lips curl up defensively, exposing her descended canines.

"It's as I suspected. It's a mating offering from the Ice Dragon Prince. His prized possession, along with one of his scales. By the looks of it, Aurora's animal accepts the gift." No sooner do the words leave his mouth than Aurora reaches out and takes possession of the skull and scale.

Aurora turns to leave, heading toward the main hall to look for a good place to display her new prize. We quickly follow behind to find Aurora sitting on her skull throne while petting the giant snake skull.

"Dimitri, do we have anything left from the Wendigo?" Her eyes haven't left the scale on top of the skull. Dimitri moves forward and drops to one knee before her.

"We do. We have its skull and both horns." She nods, slowly running her fingertips over the bony plates of the skull. I move to rest beside her, leaning on the arm of the throne to look at her new prize.

"Please bring me the skull. I feel compelled to send a skull back to him." Her eyes raise, and she looks at Nicodeamus.

"Is that the correct protocol, Father? I don't understand why my animal is pushing me to do it." Nicodeamus moves forward and looks at the offering, then back to Aurora.

"The dragon half of your nature accepts the offering. It wishes to send something of equal value to the sender. Even if this only ends up as a political marriage, at least he did it the proper way and offered your animal a prize." Nicodeamus leans forward and kisses the top of Aurora's head before moving out of the way. Shortly after Nicodeamus moves, Dimitri returns with the skull and a box to ship it in.

Aurora slowly stands and places her prize on her seat before moving over to the Wendigo skull. Gently, she picks up the skull and hands it to me. I start to worry that I might fuck this whole thing up for her, so I remain perfectly still. Before my very eyes, she shifts her left hand, and it's covered in armored scales. Her eyes search for the perfect scale to pluck. After several times of flipping her hand back and forth, she finally removes one. Carefully, she places the scale on the center of the Wendigo skull—in the exact same spot as the male's scale on her prize. She does something a bit different, though.

She reaches up into her hair, finds one of her small braids, and cuts it close to her skull. Andre offers her a small rubber band to tie the end off with. Aurora takes the braid and sticks one end into each eye socket, so the braid rests on the nose plate. Dimitri stands stock still, holding the box out to her. Gently, Aurora lowers the skull in. Andre comes from behind her to refill it with the packing popcorn.

Meanwhile, Dominik texts his contact in Wales and asks for a return address, then writes it on a label. Dimitri leaves the Alpha House with Andre in tow, heading out to send Aurora's offering to Alaska. Aurora moves back to her prize and removes the scale from the top.

"What do I do with his scale, Father?" She turns the scale several times over in her hand as she inspects it. The flesh on the back still looks relatively fresh. Damn, freaky dragons and their crazy-ass shit. Nicodeamus moves forward to remove the scale from Aurora's grip.

"Your animal accepted the gift. Proper protocol would be to place the scale above your heart. Either Sebastian or I will cut your flesh and insert the flesh on his scale into the wound. If it takes and lives, it's a good match." Aurora slowly nods her head and moves the skull off her throne and into Dominik's waiting hands. Aurora then guides me to sit on her throne. Yeah, I'm so not comfortable in this position of power. Aurora climbs up and sits upon my lap without warning, then turns sideways so her head is on one arm and her legs hang over the other.

"Sebastian, I'm ready to see if you can place the scale." Her hands rest on her stomach, and I can't help it, I have to hold one of her hands through the procedure. Aurora calls Sebastian's name, drawing his attention away from his phone and back to what is going on.

"Are you sure about this? I don't wish to hurt you," Sebastian says as he leans down to gently kiss our mate's lips and stare deeply into her eyes.

A single nod is all she gives him before looking at me. A soft smile crosses her lips before she winks, then she closes her eyes and waits. Sebastian approaches with the scale in his right hand, which is partially shifted. Now, his own claws look more similar to Aurora's talons just not as long. He takes a few moments, staring at them, before moving into position. His talon moves swiftly, cutting deep into our mate's chest. Blood oozes out of the wound and pools between her ample breasts.

Quickly, Sebastian shoves the fleshy side of the scale into the cut he just made, and almost instantly, the area begins to frost over and the wound starts to knit shut. Once Aurora senses that Sebastian is done, she sits up and remains in my lap. I gently lick the blood from her chest and in between her breasts. A sharp intake of breath catches my attention. I turn to see Dom, who looks quite shocked.

"What?" I ask, confused. He immediately holds his hand up and turns away. I guess he didn't expect me to be so openly affectionate with our mate. I examine the scale closely; it appears to be healthy and vibrant. It most definitely survived the transplant.

"Sebastian, do you think we ought to send a close-up picture of the scale on our mate's chest?" Gently, I run the back of my finger past where the scale is implanted, accentuating my point.

"I mean, so the prince knows we're allies and all?" I'm honestly not sure what the correct thing to do is at this point. Aurora looks between Sebastian and me before readjusting her top, so the scale is evident. Aurora then decides to shift both hands, so they are covered in her armored scales, and her long white talons are on full display. She angles her left arm, so the spot where she removed her own scale is visible.

"Jayce, pull my top down. I'm going to use my scales to cover my chest." As soon as her tube-top pools around her waist, she brings her right arm up to cover and support her breasts. With the way she is posed, the prince's scale is on full display. Her eyes bleed liquid mercury as she stares at Sebastian.

"Take the picture before you come in your pants." Sebastian snaps several pictures, with Aurora making several minor adjustments.

When she is sure that Sebastian has at least one good shot, she shifts her arms back and pulls her tube top back into place. Quickly, she snags the phone out of Sebastian's hands and starts going through the pictures he took of her. She is angled in such a manner that I can see all the images on the screen. When Aurora notices me looking, she turns so I can look along with her.

Out of about fifteen pictures, we narrow it down to three. I send all three to me and then to Dominik. Within seconds, there is a crash in the kitchen, and Dominik comes running out into the main room. The look of disappointment on his face is totally worth it. He looks back at the images and forwards to his favorite. Without a word, he turns to leave, visibly adjusting his cock in his pants.

Aurora gives a single nod, and I send the image and the video off to Alex, so he can forward it to the prince. After handing Sebastian his phone, I return to mine and set Aurora as my new wallpaper. Aurora couldn't help but giggle before she grabs her phone as well.

"Take a picture of us," she says it so softly, it sends butterflies straight to my stomach. I immediately obey, and I go into her camera to set up selfie mode. Aurora presses her lips to my cheek and I snap the picture. I don't think I've ever had such a genuine smile in my entire life. I'm finally happy. I'm truly loved and in love for the first time in my life. Best day ever.

CHAPTER 3
Aurora

Everything's right in my world at the moment. I just spent a full thirty-six hours in and out of bed with Jayce. I definitely understand why his ex was fighting so hard to keep him. Hot damn, can that man move! And the things he can do with his tongue, holy fuck...

Now, there are several things on my agenda that I have to investigate. First on my list is the rumor that Alexis tried hitting on Sebastian while I was at death's door. To find out the truth, I decide to hunt down my most reliable source of information in the pack.

I approach Elena's house, and there's an argument going on. I don't like people going against the chain of command. Her word is my law and to go against her is to challenge me directly. I don't even bother knocking. I walk right in the front door and stand behind the female who's yelling at Elena.

I'm easily a head taller than this little firecracker, and I'm definitely built for war. Elena looks up at me and smirks. Apparently, I arrived just in time. I shift my hands into my taloned gauntlets and tap the wall next to the female's head. The scent of fear instantly fills the air as she stares at my talons. I don't budge, nor do I say anything.

She whips around and tries to stand behind Elena. I don't recognize this female, and that's a problem. I narrow my eyes as I feel my beast surge to the surface.

"Who do you fucking think you are, yelling at an Elder One? She is the Packmaster," I growl out while I stare the female down. Suddenly through the bond, I can feel the guys closing in fast to my position. She bows slightly and then extends a hand out to me. About the same time, the guys barrel into the room.

"I'm Alexis. I'm the nurse that helped save your life." Recognition barrels through the bond, and I knew in that instant that the rumors were true.

I stare at her hand, refusing to accept it. At that moment, she realizes I know what she did. "I thought you were going to die, I swear it." She's panicking now and searching for a way out. I'm having a hard time restraining my wolf, and the boys know it.

They move as one and attempt to restrain me. Elena yells for the girl to run. Yeah, that wasn't going to save her and Elena knew it. Reason four thousand, eight hundred and seventy-two of why I love my mother-in-law: she knows my Lycan loves the thrill of the chase.

Once Alexis is clear of the house, the guys relax, which is a huge mistake. The second I know I won't harm any of them, I bolt out of the kitchen and run through the house. The hunt is on. I shift fully to my Lycan and give chase. I can feel the guys hot on my trail, but they won't be able to save her.

Father, stop my mates. I'm hunting the bitch that hit on Sebastian while I was ill. I continue running, knowing my father will aid me in my quest for revenge. Nico reaches back out to me as I hear the roar of his dragon.

Consider it done, is all daddy dearest has to say. I know he's probably putting them in an ice bowl to stop them.

Once I realize her scent is weaker, I slow down. Hmm, she's hiding somewhere nearby. I take in the scenery around me; there's a pond and a muddy bog, both of which can hide someone's scent quite easily. Out of the boys, only Sebastian's Lycan catches up to me. Apparently, our bond gifted him my talons.

Aurora, nothing happened. She desired me and I rejected her in front of everyone. Mother removed her from the house. I look at Sebastian as his words attempt to quell my rage. Then, it dawns on me: she's hiding in the bog somewhere. I turn to face Sebastian and start backing up toward the marsh. Oh yes, I'm going to turn Alexis into a bitch-cicle.

So, you expect me to forgive her trespass? To forget she tried to take what's mine when I was unable to fight? How would you feel if a lesser pack-mate attempted to take me from you while you healed? I allow Sebastian to feel the pain and anguish I was in over the fact that a pack-mate who knew we were mated attempted to take what was mine.

I don't hold back; no, not this time. They all need to know just how much I love them and the lengths I will go to defend my claim. Through our bond, I feel understanding, acceptance, and a flood of love from Dom and Jayce. From Sebastian, I feel instant rage pulse through the bond at the idea of another male trying to take me from him. I have him now. His great, black wolven head lowers slightly.

Do what you must, love. I wouldn't let the fucker live if someone tried to take you from us. I dip my head slightly to him before I sink my talons into the mud at the edge of the bog.

I watch as the ice spreads rapidly across the mud and water. Eventually, Alexis flushes from her hiding spot, the look of absolute terror on her face adding to the excitement. My father and the twins eventually catch up to us as the ice begins to blanket everything. Frost clings to my fur and, in spots, small icicles hang off of me. Elsa, eat your fucking heart out! It's quite entertaining, watching Alexis jump as she tries to escape the ice that's chasing her.

When she's finally herded into the deepest part of the bog, I begin to walk out across the ice after her, each step freezing the ice thicker as I approach. I simply crouch down, staring at her before I lunge at her. I open my great wolven maw wide, taking her head into my mouth and crushing her small, human skull like a cantaloupe. I howl my death song into the wind, alerting the pack that justice has been served.

As I return to my mates, the ice slowly recedes behind me. In a sense, I feel better, one less internal threat to worry about. For now, everything is in the clear. Tonight, we feast and celebrate the return of my father. But before anything, I really need a shower and a toothbrush.

We walk in relative silence back to the central part of the compound. I refuse to shift back to my human form. There are still things to be done. As we approach Elena's house, she comes out of her front door and stands on the porch. She smiles gently, noting that my snow-white fur is splattered with the blood of my enemy.

"The ferals need your attention first, Aurora. For everyone's safety, I fear some may need to be put to death. They may be too far lost to their animals." Elena walks with a single hand on my heavily scaled forearm like it is perfectly normal. For us, it is the status quo.

"Mother! She can't go around killing every time things don't immediately fall into place!" Sebastian has no trouble walking around the compound with his dick swinging in the breeze. He also has no sense of self-preservation either.

I stop dead in my tracks, feeling the frost creep across my flesh. I'm already shifted, armored, and in a rather foul mood. Is he seriously going there right now? Elena releases my arm and moves far away from what may end up being an impact zone. I turn my head slowly, a deep guttural growl escaping my lips as I stare at my Lycan mate. He's really trying my patience today. He feels my eyes on him and freezes in place. For once, he actually looks scared as he assesses the situation. Bad mood? Check. Already shifted? Check. Talons clicking on scaled forearms? Check. The look of actual terror on your alpha mate's face? Priceless.

I stand locked in a staring contest with him for what feels like forever. Eventually, he makes a smart move and averts his gaze and lowers his head, then exposes his throat to me. I huff out a large puff of frost before turning and heading to where the ferals are being held. Personally, I think I handled that well. I didn't harm my mate, and I didn't lose my temper. I'll chalk that up as a win.

After some walking, we arrive at the feral's pen. I call it a pen because it's a ten-foot-tall, electrified fence that keeps the ferals isolated from the rest of the pack. Elena moves alongside me and looks over the last fifteen that haven't shifted back to their human form independently. I begin to pace back and forth along the front thirty or so feet of fencing. Let's be honest here, it's not easy to miss an eight-foot-tall, snow-white Lycan with dragon scales on its arms and muzzle. The ferals begin to gather, curiosity getting the better of them.

Most of the rogues are smaller than I am and quickly break eye contact. Like always, there's one mother fucker that has to be complicated. He's a rather large male, about the same size as Sebastian's Lycan. The fact that he's feral makes me extra wary about allowing him to continue to live. As soon as I shift back to my human form, he attacks the fence and is hit with ten thousand volts. He flies backward and lands on his ass before getting up to charge again. The stubborn son of a bitch doesn't learn after getting shocked the first time. I stand there, watching him charge at me over and over again until I eventually have enough.

"Let me in there... He's either going to submit or die." My voice is gravelly with the aggressive tones of my wolf.

Reluctantly, Elena opens the gate. Dominik and Jayce restrain Sebastian from coming after me. My father uses his ice to hold the male back so I can enter safely. As I walk into the pen, my shift comes quickly; bones and tendons break and realign at an alarming rate. In all these years, I can't remember a transformation as fluid as this one. The male now notices I'm inside the pen and charges, so I evade him and slice his side with my talons. Honestly, I'd prefer to force him to submit rather than to kill him. He's an extraordinarily resilient male, and to lose him would be a detriment to the Lycan kind.

I evade several of his attacks, slicing at his flesh as he goes past me. His blood is making his fur slick and lay flat against his sides, and the scent makes my beast want to go for the kill. At this point, it's becoming more difficult for me to resist the urge to kill him. One last charge and I grip him tightly by the throat, sweep his legs out from under him, then slam him to the ground. Quickly, I kneel on his left arm and grip the right to restrain him. Blood loss has tired him out enough that there's not much fight left in him. Lowering my muzzle, I growl into his face with my canines bared at him.

He's fighting a losing battle for control, and he has a hard time keeping his eyes locked with mine. I press harder on his throat, still growling and snapping at his muzzle. Eventually, I say fuck it and quickly move my taloned hand up his jaw, turning his head to the side just before I sink my canines into his soft flesh. My growls rumble against his delicate throat as the crushing pressure reminds him of the dire situation he's in.

Suddenly, he shifts back to his human form and cries and begs me not to kill him. He begins to thank me for saving him from his animal between sobs, explaining he had been trapped as his beast for years. I snort a plume of frost before I release him and stand at my full height.

My eyes lock on the remaining fourteen Lycan ferals in the cage. I stalk forward in full attack mode, growling and baring my canines at them. I'm hoping self-preservation will free their human from the hell they are in. One by one, they drop to one knee and shift back to their human forms. I assess all of them, noting they are all malnourished and worn out. However, after suffering for so long, the packless are finally home. I look back, and Jayce holds out a robe for me to put on. I motion for him to approach, and he moves to my side and flings the robe over my shoulders. I turn away from the ferals to shift back to my human form, my gaze once again falls on the ferals.

"Pledge your life to me and I will fight for you and beside you. We will return to our ancestral home and return it to the glory it once knew in my parent's time." I raise my right arm and show them my brand. My father, who's right behind me, also raises his arm to show off his brand. All at once, they say they swear their lives to me.

Fifteen lives are spared, all because I can show mercy. Hmm... perhaps Sebastian may be right. I ponder this odd occurrence for a bit. I step out of the pen, and each of my mates check me over, making sure I'm okay. I smirk while looking at Sebastian.

"You were right this time, love. Please, don't ever mess with my train of thought before a potential battle again. It may cost me my life one of these times. Doubt is a killer." I stand on my tippy toes and kiss his forehead, and he hugs me tightly to him, whispering he's sorry.

We snuggle tightly for several moments before we're joined by my other two mates. I look over at my father and he's smiling at me. I'm happy that he's proud of me and how I was able to handle the ferals. Gently, I break away from my guys and move to hug Elena. "Please find them a place to stay and make sure they are fed." Before taking her phone out to call down to the main camp, Elena nods and kisses my cheek. I turn back to the cage and look at the men standing there.

"Welcome home, my brothers. Please, follow Elena back to the compound and she'll make sure you're fed and clothed." In a sweeping motion, I point at Elena and she waves at the men.

"You'll be housed in the meeting hall until the dorm is completed. Take your time to get settled today, and sleep well tonight. Perhaps tomorrow you can help with the construction. You know, to find a purpose again." I smile after seeing how excited these men are with the prospect of starting over.

This is definitely the difference between a tyrant and a benevolent leader. You can tell by the change in their stance that they have never been treated as if they have value. I'll be damned if any of my people ever feel worthless on my watch. My father approaches me once the crowd thins out and my mates are escorting the new pack members home to make sure they are accepted.

"You did well today, daughter. You chose to rule with your heart and mind and not just your talons." Nicodeamus gives me a hug before we start heading back to the compound behind the others.

We walk in relative silence as I'm tucked up under his arm, much like you would do with a child. It's fitting, really; I am his only child. To be quite honest, I'm actually enjoying having one of my birth parents around. Andre and Dimitri are great, but they're not part dragon or Lycan. They did the best they could for me, and I'm forever in their debt. My right hand absently comes up to rub at the implanted scale on my chest.

Dad catches the movement and stops walking. "May I see it? I wish to make sure it took properly." Nicodeamus tilts his head as he moves to stand before me. Slowly, I move my robe to the side so he can examine the scale over my heart. Nicodeamus shifts one finger so he can touch the scale with his talon. I watch in wonder as frost coats the tip as soon as he makes contact. Nico smiles, then shifts his finger back to human and touches the scale again. This time, no frost, just pressure where my father is touching.

"Very good! Your body has accepted his scale." Nico lets out a short laugh. "I honestly don't remember the last time the scale trading tradition was done. It's been several hundred years, at least. I believe I was only a young boy back then. My own parents didn't share scales since their marriage was political." I'm quite puzzled by what my father tells me.

"Why wouldn't your parents share scales?" I had to ask—there's only so much he's able to teach me while I sleep. He whispers in my mind so the others wouldn't hear. *Scales only live on true mates.* Nicodeamus smiles at me, and everything starts to click. My eyes widen, and my mouth drops open from shock. Ladies and gentlemen, I have officially been rendered speechless.

The guys must have sensed my inner turmoil because they all stop dead and look back at me. I keep looking from the scale, then back to my father. Jayce, who was sent back to investigate what's happening, looks at my scale, then over to Nicodeamus. Realization dawns on him and, slowly, a smile creeps across those perfectly plump lips of his. Ever so gently, Jayce kisses my lips then looks deeply into my eyes. "I'll love him like I love you. The others will just have to get over themselves." Jayce winks and kisses me again.

He's the perfect mate. Then again, I think he secretly wants another hot male to ogle over. I couldn't help but smile at Jayce. He's definitely the most light-hearted one out of my mates and brings balance to my rage. Without warning him, I run behind him and jump onto his back for a piggyback ride.

"I wish to get a cold drink and rest. Take me home, love! Giddy up!" I reach down and slap his ass, which makes him squeal and laugh.

My omega mate would move Heaven and Earth to make me happy, and my two potential alpha mates would rain fire and brimstone upon the Earth to protect me. One protects my heart, the other two, my body and my life. I wonder what role my dragon mate will play. Sometimes I believe that I see him in my dreams; it's so faint, so distant, I'm not sure it's even real. I lay my head down on my arm as Jayce carries me home. I have a lot to think about over the next few weeks. So much to do, so many Strigoi to kill. What's a girl to do?

We return to the Alpha House, and Jayce makes me comfortable on the porch swing. While I watch Dom and Sebastian supervise the ferals' care and the dorm's construction, Jayce disappears into the house. Housing here on the compound was insufficient, considering the size of the pack we're building.

Sebastian, make sure the dorm has a central kitchen and individual bedrooms with bathrooms for the single males. Sebastian makes eye contact with me as he listens to what I have to say. Like most packs, the male to female ratio is completely screwed. Not many males are willing to share their females, but from what I can see, there are more and more menage pairings than before. Perhaps my guys and I are setting a positive example and breaking enough barriers that others will follow in.

Way ahead of you. I'm putting a gathering place with a large TV in the central kitchen, so no one feels isolated. I smile and nod while listening to Sebastian. His idea will be a tremendous help as we integrate new members into the pack. These were his people long before they became mine, so he knows what they need far better than I do.

Jayce appears at my side with a tray of drinks and hands me my pomegranate juice with vodka—he knows me too well. I watch my gentle mate go and offer our other two mates cold drinks before he comes back to sit with me. He sits on the far side of the swing and pats his lap, offering it to me. I quickly finish my drink and move to lay my head on his lap. Jayce gently runs his fingers through my hair, working out the knots. Perhaps a nap will do me some good. After all, I've had quite a busy day today.

I don't know how long I napped for, but I wake up feeling refreshed and with my head still in Jayce's lap. I slowly roll over on my side so I'm facing Jayce, and I notice that he's asleep, leaning his head against the back of the swing. He looks so peaceful; his face is so angelic and innocent. Slowly, I rise from his lap and move so I can appreciate the handsome man before me. Yeah, it looks a bit creepy to an outsider, but my pack knows that I watch over my mates closely. They are my greatest treasure. For some reason that word resonates with me. I brush the thought aside before going into the house to retrieve my favorite blanket, which I use to gently cover Jayce.

Once more I go into the house and pull out my guitar and amp. I sit down next to Jayce and begin to play Pink Floyd's "Wish You Were Here." Technically, it should be an acoustic set, but I'm a bit too metal for that. Dimitri used to play a lot of Pink Floyd for me when I couldn't sleep, so I guess you can say I get my love of music from him.

Slowly, the pack begins to gather once they hear the melody coming from my guitar. I know there are dark days ahead of us, and I know the days of peace are limited now, so I do my best to enjoy every second. Just as Sebastian and Dom approach, Jayce wakes up. I switch it up a bit and start playing Metallica's "Nothing Else Matters." Although I sing it for the pack to enjoy, it's more so meant for my mates.

I make sure to hold eye contact with each one of them. I'm not like Jayce who wears his heart on his sleeve; I keep my feelings in, tight and protected. However, before this battle from Hell, my men need to know and feel what I'm feeling. I play the song in its entirety, all six minutes and twenty-something seconds of it. At the conclusion of the song, the guys swarm me. I feel the love they have for me, and I revel in it. I also fear for them with the battle to come.

In the distance, I spot Elena and my dad walking hand in hand toward the lake. It's about time both of them find happiness. Jayce is the first to notice that I'm staring at the hillside. He smiles and lets a soft *aw* escape his lips. Unfortunately, his cute reaction draws both Dominik's and Sebastian's attention. Dominik simply shrugs his shoulders and heads back to work, while Sebastian looks like he's beside himself.

He motions toward the hill and shouts, "Our parents! What the actual fuck!" He drags his hand down his face, then looks to me to do something. I can't help but start laughing. I'm not bothered by them being together, but apparently my big, bad—almost—alpha mate can't handle it. I give Sebastian a quick hug and pat his back.

"Don't worry, Bash. Dad's castrated, so there's no fear of any pups being born." I kiss Sebastian's cheek, then bound down the stairs and go for a walk to check out the new dorm the guys have been working on.

I turn back briefly and the look of shock on Sebastian's face is really worth it. Dom bounds down the stairs and jogs to catch up with me. He gently takes my hand as we enter the building. He takes the time to explain the upgrades and little, special features it has. It's everything I could have wanted for the single males and more: private quarters for sleeping, a large living room, and an open kitchen design.

"I'm so proud of you guys! Everyone has done a wonderful job." I kiss Dominik on the cheek as we finish the tour. Since Dires are apparently quite well off, Dominik and Jayce had extra funds to go into the project, and all of the planning fell on Domink.

We continue our walk back to the Alpha House. My throne has become the focal point of the main hall and today, I find flowers left on the table to the right of it. I can tell it's the pack children because there is a single flower from each child—about nine or ten flowers left for me. It brings a smile to my face, thinking about how thoughtful these little ones are. We run into one of the housekeepers, Anna, and her new baby, Lia, in her arms. I've never seen a baby before, so I'm quite curious. Dominik looks at me, puzzled.

"Babe, you act like you've never seen a baby before." I remain staring at the little one, then I turn to him.

"I've only ever seen them on TV. They never look this tiny." I lean down to sniff at the baby , and its eyes open. I pull my head back quickly because I wasn't prepared for the baby to look at me.

"Would you like to hold her, My Queen?" Anna asks, offering her precious child to me. I look at Anna then back to Dominik, tears threatening to fall.

I don't know what to do. I don't want to break it, I say to Dominik through our bond. Understanding flitters across his features as he guides me to sit on my throne. Gently, Dominik takes the baby from Anna, then comes to me next. I watch in amazement at how he looks so perfect holding the baby.

"Hold your arms like I am. Trust me, you'll be fine." I mimic the position that Dom's arms are in and he gently rests the child in my arms. I'm honestly frightened I'm going to accidentally hurt the baby. My other mates arrive quickly, sensing my anxiety and fear. They suddenly stop, watching me nuzzle the baby I am holding.

Lia grips a lock of my hair and pulls hard. I can't help but smile at this little being's strength; she dares to pull the alpha's hair. I nuzzle her again and make a low, comforting rumble at her. I look up to my mates, my wolf and I in agreeance.

"I want one." I immediately drop my eyes back down to Lia when I hear the thud of a body hitting the floor. Sebastian passed the fuck out. I guess he can't handle the day today; way too many changes in such a short amount of time. The twins take this opportunity to approach and stare at the child together.

"Soon as the war is over you can have as many as you want," Dominik proclaims.

Deep down, I know that's the smartest course of action. I keep sniffing and nuzzling the baby; she's such a precious gift. Fertility is becoming rare among the Lycans; to birth a daughter is nothing short of a miracle. I carefully shift my arm under Lia and pluck a single scale before shifting back. I look at Anna and hold the scale out to her.

"Give this to Lia when she's old enough to understand the boon I have given her. I will come for her no matter where or when. That is my promise to this baby." I lean down and kiss Lia's forehead before offering her to her mother.

"She is the first daughter born in a long time. She has my protection." Anna, practically in tears, looks from me to her baby. I have a gut feeling that she will be pivotal to the pack one day. I look up to see my father and mother-in-law have returned. Apparently, they witnessed the whole exchange.

"Child, are you okay?" My father asks softly. I know why he's asking; I feel the power of my beast pulsing. She tapped into some part of the dragon's ability that she can't access alone. I snuggle into my father's embrace and look up to him.

"I held the baby and felt that she has a part in the pack's future. I know it sounds strange, but my beast just knows." I search my father's features for answers. A slow smile creeps over his lips, and he nods slowly. Gently, my father kisses my forehead, then walks me back over to my mates.

"The first time I met Dominik, I knew he would play a role in your future. Our dragon side is very intuitive like that. I suspect once you mate with the prince, your dragon side will become better balanced with your Lycan side." My father briefly hugs me before letting go. I walk over to a prone Sebastian and decide to sit on his chest and stare down at him.

"Hey, Bash!" Quickly, I poke his chest several times before I receive a response.

He's still kind of pale, definitely looking off-kilter a bit. "What happened to you?" Dominik helps me off Sebastian, then passes me over to Jayce so he can help Sebastian stand up again. A quick look over and Sebastian is back to normal.

"Ever experience déjà vu? I mean, really experience it. I saw you, Aurora, with a baby nursing on each breast. One with white hair and one with black; one boy and one girl. It was really fucking surreal." I blink several times, looking at Sebastian, then back to my father. Nicodeamus walks closer to the group.

"I see Aurora's dragon side is gifting everyone with visions. It's a rather unique situation." The weight of my father's words hit me like a freight train.

My hand flies up to the prince's scale on my chest. Gently, I rub the scale, tracing the unique shape of it against my soft flesh. I have been feeling slightly different since it was implanted on me; a little stronger, a little faster. But the most significant change I've noticed is that I'm not as quick to go straight to murder anymore.

My gaze lands on my father, and he's smiling at me. He raises his finger and taps on his temple. Apparently, I've come to the same conclusion as he has. My eyes roam over my other mates, slowly assessing them one by one. Other than Sebastian, no one else has had any noticeable changes. I'll have to keep a very close eye on them. I love them too much to make them worry.

CHAPTER 4

Dominik

Watching Aurora with the baby and seeing the look of wonder on her face made my heart melt. I feel her desire for a family through the bond, along with another entity entirely. It's faint, but it's there. Just like her father pointed out, I believe it's the prince as well.

Sebastian and I have been working on training the Lycan troops day and night. We run drills and shift to fight against each other so they can see the difference in the species' approach in battle. Dimitri, against Aurora's wishes, has been fighting with the groups, so we are prepared for the Polar Bears.

In order for him to train the Dires before they head to Siberia with us, I'll need to sneak him out of the compound later today and put him on a plane to head to my brother. I don't know how anyone thinks going against Aurora's wishes is a good thing though. I mean, seriously? Do we all have a freaking death wish?

I never thought I'd say this, but the ferals are a godsend. Their animals are so primal that they can outlast the regular Lycans. It's definitely something to study for the future. I text my brother, Alex, to catch him up on all that's been going on here. I send him the videos of Aurora opening the present and the placement of the scale.

My phone immediately blew up since I'm now apparently in a group chat with my brother and some guy named Ellis. Ellis is beyond excited and can't wait to tell his friend the news. They are supposed to meet up before the attack and plan out what they can do to help. I remind Alex about sending Dimitri down later today. He, too, is concerned for Dimitri's health and doesn't want to face Aurora's wrath. Honestly, no one wants to face Aurora when she's in rage mode. I text over the supply request that Dimitri has for training.

What used to be the arena is now a full-blown training ground. Alex is trying to erase the years of fear the arena held by turning it into a positive place for our people. One of the most significant moves my brother pulled off, with the help of a video from Aurora, was the ending of the forced matings. It freed so many females from matings they didn't want anything to do with. The females were moved into a protected wing of the den and guarded twenty-four-seven. Several males have been locked up and await Aurora's sentences. Think of it as death row, where the death isn't a threat; it's a promise.

Apparently, my pacing has drawn my mate's attention. I look up to see Aurora, standing there and holding Lia again. I wonder to myself if Anna knows Aurora has her baby. "Hello, love." I gently kiss her cheek. "Does Anna know you have Lia?" Aurora smirks at me, then kisses the baby's forehead.

"Yes, she said she needed to ride the pony. It's been a while... whatever that means." Aurora shrugs and continues to rock the baby in her arms.

"Um, babe? It means she went to go fuck her mate." Aurora makes the *oh* face, then laughs.

"Anyway, I've been talking to my brother. We are doing well with preparations for the journey. Alex feels the Dires would benefit from seeing Dimitri's bear and learning how one moves." Aurora stops rocking Lia and stares at me, her eyes churning liquid mercury. Oh god, I pissed her off. Not good. Aurora cracks her neck and takes a deep breath.

"I understand where you're coming from, Dominik. I really do. But I worry about Dimitri's health and what the extra strain may do to him. I know he's willing to die for me." Tears break and roll down her cheek. I see Sebastian and Jayce come out of the dorm. I raise my hand to stop them, and thankfully, they listen.

"Is this what he truly wants, Dominik?" As Aurora looks up at me, Dimitri walks up behind her and kisses the top of her head.

"Aurora, I'll be fine. I've always done what's best for the defense of the family, haven't I?" Aurora nods slowly, with that innocent little girl look going on.

"I'll be fine, sweetheart. Besides, now that you've ascended, I think you can kick my ass." Dimitri smirks at her and gently caresses her cheek, forcing her to look deep into his eyes. Aurora whines softly as her eyes flicker between human and liquid mercury. Heartache echoes through the bond, almost like she's already in mourning for Dimitri.

"Be safe, old man. I love you!" She turns her head briefly and kisses the palm of his hand before backing away.

"Train the Dires well. I don't want any losses on our side if we can help it." Lightly she taps her chin as she ponders what to say next.

"Remember, there will also be dragons. Perhaps, you can take my father with you so he can work with the Dires as well." I could practically see the gears turning in Aurora's mind as she sorts out what needs to be done.

"Make sure you and father leave Sebastian and Dom a list of what needs to be worked on in your absence. In about three weeks, we'll be flying the Lycans to Germany and the Dires here. The second dorm will be completed before their arrival." Aurora's eyes turn toward me, and she notices I'm recording her directions. She gives me a curt nod. "Did I miss anything, Dom?"

I answer her from behind the phone. "No, love. I believe every-thing is sorted. I'll send this video to Alex and arrange transport for everyone." Aurora shakes her head no at me. I couldn't help but raise an eyebrow at her.

"No offense, love, but Jayce does much better at arranging these kinds of things. You get back to training the others, and if you're a good boy, I'll give you a massage later." Aurora places a hand on my forearm and kisses my cheek before walking away with Lia.

"Shit, that went better than I expected." I look over to Dimitri. Damn, that bear is a fucking huge man.

"Well, we have our marching orders straight from the princess herself. We better hop to it before she hands that baby back to Anna." Dimitri shakes his head at me and I see sadness briefly cross his features. I know the future isn't certain for anyone, but they are living on borrowed time for him and Andre.

Slowly, I move through the compound, watching all the citizens move about without a care in the world. I kind of miss those days, to be honest, but back in those days, I didn't have Aurora. So yeah, I wouldn't change it for anything, as much as I miss the simple life. In my wandering, I find Aurora leaning over Jayce's shoulder as he works on his laptop. It's nice to finally see my brother happy for once in his life.

Time seems to move in slow motion as I watch the events unfold before me. Sinclair comes out of nowhere, dagger in hand and heading toward Aurora. I start to scream when Aurora's sixth sense seems to kick in. She shifts rapidly to her beast, so fast it's terrifying. The blade hits the armored scales on her forearms and glances off, causing no damage. Aurora's taloned hand instinctually grips Sinclair by his throat and lifts him off the ground. He's kicking and thrash-ing, trying to pry her hand from around his throat. Aurora's Lycan beast walks forward with Sinclair dangling in the air like it's nothing.

Everyone starts gathering as soon as Jayce starts screaming at the top of his lungs, cursing at his ex-lover. I've never seen my brother so angry. Yellow-green toxin drips from his canines as he screams at Sinclair.

Fuck, Jayce is partially shifted, flailing his arms around. Wow, Hell has officially frozen over—Jayce is in a rage. All it took was him to find his mate and for her life to be threatened. Aurora throws Sinclair into the practice ring and stares him down. Jayce prepares to charge in, but Aurora grabs him and shakes her massive head no. Jayce only nods and steps back.

"Still doing the mix-breed bitch's bidding? She's going to bring death to all of you. Kill her now, and the Strigoi will forget this camp exists!" There's the reason for his boldness. Apparently, Tomas found the weakest link in the Dire camp and it's Sinclair. He hasn't realized he just signed his death warrant, and no one here will stand against Aurora.

Sinclair, in a move of absolute stupidity, shifts, and charges at Aurora—our mate looks positively bored until he moves. Sinclair leaps into the air, his mouth wide open and toxin dripping from his mouth. He latches onto Aurora's armored forearm, attempting to bite through the dragon scale.

You can see the look of *you've got to be fucking kidding me* on Aurora's wolf's face as she watches Sinclair attempt to harm her. Suddenly she whips her arm up, then drops to one knee as she brings the arm with Sinclair on it down hard and fast. The thud of his body and the audible crunch of bones breaking sends shivers down my spine—Sinclair's smoke-gray wolf whines, its body broken on the ground and unable to stand or move.

Aurora shifts back to her human form and stands over Sinclair, her head tilting from left to right. Her eyes lift to Jayce as if waiting for his judgment. Before he's even at Aurora's side, Jayce shifts into his enormous black Dire Wolf.

She threads her fingers through his thick fur and says, "I can end him for you, love. You don't have to do this." Shockingly, Jayce growls and snaps at Aurora, making her jump back a bit. Her eyes widen in shock staring at her gentle mate. Jayce suddenly lunges at Sinclair and bites into his throat, starting to thrash his head violently from side to side. The sound of flesh tearing and tendons popping is almost sickening; chunks of flesh and blood spray out from Sinclair's throat.

Eventually, Jayce severs Sinclair's head from his body, tendons and blood vessels twitch as if still alive as they dangle freely beneath his skull. He bites into Sinclair's fur one last time to lift his head up and carry it to Aurora. He drops the bloody mass at her feet, then stares up at her. Aurora touches the offered head, then wraps her arms around Jayce's thick neck, hugging his wolf tightly. I've never seen my brother so violent, but then again, he's never had someone he's loved so much to fight for. Aurora slowly stands and grips the fur of Sinclair's head to pick it up.

"I'm going to go take care of Jayce. He needs me." Aurora's tone rings with sorrow and heartbreak.

Watching her sweet, innocent Jayce kill someone he once loved must have hurt something in her. I'll talk to her about this later to see where she's at emotionally. I know my brother isn't in a good place either, having to kill an old love to save his mate. It's a sight to see: Aurora holding Sinclair's head in one hand and her other hand on Jayce's back. It's confusing to feel Jayce's anger and Aurora's sorrow. It's very odd for the roles to be reversed with them. I move over to where Sebastian and Dimitri are standing. We're still shocked over what we just witnessed.

"Dominik, what got into Jayce? That was way out of character for him." I know Sebastian feels what I am, but Dimitri can't.

"I'm guessing watching Aurora with Lia made something snap in him. He's always loved and wanted children of his own. I guess the threat to Aurora's life and the possibility of him losing the chance at pups pushed him over the edge." I shrug my shoulders. After all, I'm only speculating at the moment.

"I can see that," Dimitri says, not missing a beat.

"He constantly worries he's not strong enough to protect his mate. He completely forgets he has the toxic bite that, by itself, makes him lethal." The matter-of-fact way Dimitri says it is kind of frightening.

"Sebastian, can you do me a solid and drive Nicodeamus and Dimitri to the airport? I really need to make sure Jayce is okay with everything that just happened." Sebastian nods and claps Dimitri on the back.

They head toward Elena's house to collect Nicodeamus. I head back to the Alpha House and go straight to Jayce's room, and I'm not particularly shocked to find it empty. I arrive at Aurora's room, where I find candles lit and soft music playing. Then I hear the water running in the shower. I decide not to waste any time and strip before I enter.

Slowly, I push the door open to find Aurora washing my brother under the hot water from the twin shower heads. Jayce has his forearms on the tile, letting the water run down his back in streams. Aurora is gently washing every inch of his body, and it's probably the sexiest thing I've ever witnessed. Aurora slides down between Jayce and the wall before leaning forward to lick his cock from base to tip.

My own cock is rigid and pulsing as I watch our mate lick my brother's. The soft, pleased rumbles of her beast echo off the tiles, calling to the more primal side of me. Jayce lowers his left hand to grip Aurora's hair as she sucks his cock into her mouth.

I watch her head bob slowly as Jayce gently thrusts his hips forward, fucking her mouth. I feel my balls draw up tight from listening to the moans escaping my brother's mouth. When Jayce finally comes, he roars out his release while Aurora slurps down every drop greedily.

Without skipping a beat, Jayce lifts Aurora up, quickly hooking his arm under her left leg and holds it up before he thrusts his cock into her. I gasp at the force he drives his cock into Aurora and watch as my brother fucks our mate hard against the tiles.

The wet, slapping skin mixed with their moans... I'm damn near ready to blow my load without being touched. Aurora screams out Jayce's name as she comes hard, and Jayce's first instinct is to bite her shoulder, marking her as his again. His bite causes Aurora to come once again, only this time, she bites him back.

I honestly can't help it; I blow my load like a randy teenager. I moan through my orgasm as strings of come coat the nearby wall. Jayce and Aurora slowly turn to look at me, smiling.

"Um, hi? I just wanted to, um, make sure you're ok and stuff." Gods, I sound like a bloody idiot. Jayce slowly lowers Aurora to the floor and waits for her to regain balance.

"Learn anything, Dominik?" Jayce says without missing a beat. He walks over and grabs a towel for Aurora and one for himself.

"When the hell did you get aggressive, Jayce?" I was kind of speechless at the moment. My usually soft-spoken brother has developed a set of brass balls. Aurora decides to answer as she walks toward me.

"You should know by now, Dominik. I love it when you guys get all dominant with me. I don't always like being in control." She stands on her tippy toes and kisses my cheek.

"To be perfectly honest, I kind of want a twin sammich before bed. That is, if you two are up for it?" Aurora runs her hand over my abs as she passes me, heading back to her bedroom. Jayce simply starts laughing and follows after her.

"You heard our woman, she wants a twin sammich. Let's give it to her!" Jayce briefly grips my shoulder as he moves past me. I swear to the gods, I'm in the fucking Twilight Zone.

I walk into the bedroom to find Aurora already sliding Jayce's cock back into her waiting pussy. How the actual fuck does he still have an erection? I move onto the bed behind Aurora, and she sits up to lean back against my chest. She holds out a bottle of lube.

"You do know what you're doing, right, Dom?" I blink at Aurora as I take the lube from her.

I place a hand between her shoulder blades and push her down onto my brother. Then I lube up her rosette and work the tight muscles until they loosen up. Jayce does his part by distracting her while I stretch her to fit me. I slowly insert one, then two fingers into her tight ass. Oh, my gods, she is going to feel amazing when I finally get there. Several minutes pass before I lube my cock up real good. I squirt an extra glob of lube right onto her rosette.

Slowly, I push the head of my cock past that tight muscular ring. I pause for a few moments and rub Aurora's lower back to get her to relax more. Jayce reaches forward and grips Aurora's ass cheeks, spreading her wide for me. I push forward steadily, until I'm fully seated in our mate's tight ass. It feels like fucking heaven.

She's so tight and full, especially feeling my brother's cock in her pussy. We all release a sigh before Aurora starts trying to move. "If someone doesn't fucking move soon, I'm going to get pissed off."

I can't tell if she is joking, so I pull back first. When I seat myself deep within her, Jayce pulls out. It takes several moments before Jayce and I find our rhythm. Aurora seems to let out one constant moan as she nips at Jayce's chest and my forearms. I lean forward and bite her shoulder blade and release a low growl. Aurora quickly stops her biting nonsense, allowing Jayce and I to pick up the pace a bit. We're thrusting in and out as fast as we can until Aurora's orgasm rips through her. Her muscles milk our cocks hard in a rhythmic, pulsating motion. It takes all the willpower I could muster to not come with her, and I see my brother is fighting the same battle.

I decide to switch it up and pull Aurora up to me and off Jayce, then I lay down with her back flush with my chest. Jayce rises up on his knees and thrusts back into our mate's soaking wet pussy. I wrap an arm above and below Aurora's chest, holding her tight to me as I thrust up into her ass. Jayce and I find our rhythm again, but this time much harder than before. My balls are drawn up tight, and I feel my mating knot starting to form. I look up to see Jayce's wolf present in his eyes, and his thrusts are getting as erratic as mine. Aurora cries out as her orgasm crashes over, and like a chain reaction, Jayce and I cum within seconds of each other. Both of us bite Aurora on her shoulders again, sending her into a second orgasm.

Several moments passed before Jayce and I release Aurora. We lick her wounds clean before moving her so she's more comfortable. Jayce gets up to grab wet washcloths for us while I merely stare in wonder at our beautiful mate. Aurora is such a powerful, unique being, yet she submits here in private. It's a thing of beauty to think she trusts us enough to release control, if even for a little while.

Gently, I run my fingers through Aurora's hair, untangling the knots we made tonight. This was the first time I have ever shared anyone with my brother, and I get the feeling tonight will not be the last. Jayce returns with some washcloths, and we clean ourselves up first before we consider waking Aurora.

"I think we should do what we can without waking her. I'd like to keep my balls attached to my body," Jayce says with a smirk. Aurora has been a significant influence on Jayce, she's really brought him out of his shell.

"That would be our safest move. I think she's going to be asleep for a while," I say, nodding slowly. We take turns lifting Aurora's limbs while we clean her. It kind of reminds me of that game, Minesweeper, we used to play as kids—one wrong move and we'll have one pissed off she-wolf on our hands. To be honest though, I think a minefield would be safer than our sleeping mate. Once I'm sure Aurora is adequately taken care of, I motion for Jayce to follow me out of the room.

We head to the study across the hall from Aurora's room, that way we're close enough in case she wakes up early. I move to where the maps are spread out behind the desk and consider what lies ahead of us.

"There's going to be a lot of casualties going across the Bering Land Bridge," I state very matter-of-fact. I can't candy-coat this at all. It's going to get ugly real quick, and not much can be done to stop it.

Jayce looks up to me as he speaks. "Have we heard more about this prince? I feel a faint presence, but I can't put my finger on it." So, I'm not the only one sensing the new entity. I release a measured breath before texting Sebastian to join us.

"I know what you mean, Jayce. I just messaged Sebastian to join us. He's been bonded to Aurora the longest, so he would know better than me." Speak of the devil, that smirking, arrogant asshole is now standing in the doorway with his arms crossed over his chest.

"Ask, and ye shall receive. What's the secret meeting for?" Sebastian closes the door behind him, then flops into the chair behind the desk and hangs his legs over the arm.

"Have you been feeling another presence beside us?" I get straight to the point. If Aurora didn't love this fucker and have that "no hitting the other mates" rule, I'd love to beat his ass. The arrogant fuck acts like he's in charge when Aurora isn't present. I can't wait until the day someone bigger and worse than him knocks him down a peg or two. Sebastian quickly sits up and looks between Jayce and me.

"Yeah, it's different than when she acknowledged you two. This feels stronger, almost more primal." He shakes his head, looking at his hands.

"Whatever it is, it's fucking strong." Sebastian looks worried, which is a first.

Nicodeamus's voice fills the hall after apparently hearing part of our conversation. "The *it* in question is an Ice and Gold Dragon mix. Alaric's mother is a Golden Dragon, and his father is an Ice Dragon, both of which are very powerful in their own rights."

Nicodeamus breathes in deeply before continuing. "One sides

with justice, the other with his horde and power. I, being an Ice Dragon, know the temptation of treasure. Treasure, when it's physical, can corrupt—in this case, Alaric's father." Nicodeamus strides into the room and shoos Sebastian from the office chair to sit behind the desk.

"If you three are starting to feel the prince, imagine what Aurora is feeling." He tilts his head to the side, looking at each of us in turn.

"She has his scale implanted in her flesh." Nicodeamus taps the area over his heart.

"He will always know where she is and how to find her, no matter the distance. Until they are mated, it will be faint, almost ghost-like—a whisper in the back of her mind, and his." A sly smirk creeps across Nicodeamus's lips as he looks at us.

"Be prepared for a battle of wills between Aurora and the prince, as they are both true-born alphas, unlike you three." His smirk turns into a sadistic grin as his eyes lock with Sebastian to drive his next point home.

"Sebastian, you and Dominik are maybe betas in the pack; you'll never achieve full alpha because your animal will put survival over dominance." His almost feral look softens as his gaze turns to my twin.

"Jayce, you already know you're an omega, and you're fine with your role. You are the safest of the three when it comes to the prince's arrival." Nicodeamus, with his ancient wisdom, literally told us that Sebastian and I may be fucked. We will not stand a chance against the prince in a physical battle. Kind of a bummer to hear, but at least Nicodeamus put Sebastian in his fucking place. I start to pace the room a bit, pondering everything that Nicodeamus said.

"So, if I understand this correctly, if Aurora's in a very high-stress situation, she may act like a homing beacon for the prince during the battle? Similar to how the guys and I sense Aurora's distress?" I stop my pacing to look at Nicodeamus. I've put a lot of thought into this, and I want to make sure my theory is sound.

"It's similar, but not the same. A dragon's bond is blood deep—spiritual, in a sense. It transcends time and space; distance means nothing to a dragon's bond." Nicodeamus sighs softly before stroking his beard a moment.

"As Aurora grew and her beast became stronger, the easier it was for me to dream walk and teach her things in her sleep. I believe in time, the prince may be able to reach out to Aurora." My body tenses, and Nicodeamus holds up his hand to stop me from speaking.

"However, we won't know how powerful he truly is until he attaches her scale to himself." Nicodeamus taps his index finger on his chin, then comes up with an idea. He rises up from the chair and goes to the lamp, shifting his index finger and using the talon to cut through half the electric cord. He bends the halves apart, so the power never passes through.

"Okay, so to make it simple, here's an example: the solid wire is Aurora, having attached the prince's scale to herself. The broken wire represents the prince on one side and Aurora's scale on the other side. Until he implants the scale, the connection is half-assed. Once he implants the scale..." Nicodeamus pushes the halves together and the light blazes to life. Across all our faces, realization dawns. Their connection may be the strongest out of all of ours. Sebastian seems to be taking this the hardest as he begins to pace the room, stress pouring off him. Besides, when we almost lost Aurora, I've never seen Sebastian look so terrified.

Suddenly, the door explodes, sending splinters and chunks of oak flying everywhere. Aurora, in all her hybrid glory, is ready for battle. A low growl rumbles in her chest as frost coats her fur and yellow-green toxin drips from her canines. Her beast looks around the room, talons clicking together as her mercury orbs search for the threat. Apparently, Sebastian's stress triggered Aurora's shift and attack mode.

"My love, it's okay, there's no threat. We're sorry Sebastian's anxiety woke you up like that." Jayce approaches Aurora with his hands held in a placating manner, trying to soothe her enough to shift back. Aurora shakes her massive wolven head, snarling before slowly regaining her human form. Jayce quickly removes his T-shirt and gives it to Aurora. Reluctantly, Aurora pulls the T-shirt over her head and stares Sebastian down.

"What the fuck are you drama queening about now? I was sleeping, fucking sleeping soundly until your dramatic pansy-ass woke me the fuck up. What's got your man panties in a bunch?" Jayce and I give each other the *oh shit* look before watching the train wreck that's about to happen. Don't get me wrong, I love Sebastian like only a bond-mate could, but he's an entitled, royal pain in the ass.

"Drama queening? What the fuck, Aurora! You're not about to be usurped by an unknown male who's not even here yet!" Sebastian flails his arms like a girl on the flag squad at a football game. Nicodeamus is trying like hell not to laugh out loud, but it's challenging, to be honest. Sebastian is being ridiculous.

"Usurped? Who the fuck do you think you are, the fucking king? The only king in this pack, is my father. Goddess fucking help me, if you ever try to usurp him—mate or not—I'll kill you myself." She growls and freezes the ground around her as she stares Sebastian down. Now is not the time to interject, but of course, Jayce does.

"Love? I think Sebastian is trying to say that we feel the Dragon Prince, even though he's not here, and we know you must too." He raises his eyebrows and smiles, putting his dimples she loves so much on full display.

"We're just concerned since all of our bonds are so new. Some of us suck at expressing our feelings though." Jayce took that moment to smirk at Sebastian as Aurora steps up and snuggles into his side. She holds onto Jayce tightly and kisses his throat before looking at Sebastian and me.

"Guys, I love you, even when some of you drive me bloody mad with your insecurities. I feel the prince, but he's like a whisper in the back of my mind. I feel his anxiety, like something is going on behind the scenes." Aurora raises her hand to rub the prince's scale lightly.

"Jayce, Dom, has Alex said anything new? Something's up. I just know it." Her eyes turn liquid mercury as she looks between all of us, and I watch Nicodeamus's eyes also change to that of his dragon. I'm not sure what's going on, but it has their animals on edge. While I text our brother, Jayce gently runs his fingers through Aurora's hair.

Motherfucker, something is up. My phone blows up with messages from Alex as he fills me in on everything that's going on. I hand the phone over to Nicodeamus so he can catch up. I watch his eyes fly over the messages, then he hands the phone over to Aurora and leaves. Aurora nods along as her eyes pass over the screen, then she hits call and starts pacing.

"Alex, it's Aurora... Yeah, I'm good. I see we need to adjust our tactics. My father and Dimitri will be there tonight. Yeah, I saw that. Hopefully the prince receives the skull sooner than later. I may need to summon him when the battle starts." Aurora goes silent as she switches to video call to show Alex the map. Her fingers glide over the map as she explains her plan for the attack. Her brows knit tightly together.

"Yes, I know there's going to be dragons! I'll handle them, and you train the Dires to evade them. I'll bring the fuckers down." She sighs softly. Through the bond, I can feel the idea of killing possible kin is tearing her apart.

"I will do what I have to, to keep our people safe. Get a hold of Ellis; he needs to get to Alaric and secure a dragon force. The bears may or may not be enough." Aurora looks exhausted—more emotionally and mentally than physically.

Possibly as his smartest move, Sebastian goes over to hold her. Aurora rests her head on his chest and sighs again, still listening to my brother. "I get that, Alex. We are going to be fucking lambs to slaughter if Alaric doesn't bring reinforcements with him. My father can't fucking fly, and he's going to be a fucking sitting duck. If you think I'm going to lose him now, you're sadly mistaken!" Aurora hands the phone over to me and starts crying on Sebastian's chest. Okay, this now ranks in the top five scariest Aurora moments on record. Aurora plus emotions usually equals rage and destruction.

"Jayce, can you please take Dimitri and Nicodeamus to the airport? I'm currently being held hostage by a potential nuke." Sebastian kisses the crown of Aurora's head and holds her tightly. He's correct in thinking this can go bad really quick. I watch Jayce nod and kiss Aurora on the cheek before leaving on his mission. I motion for Sebastian to follow me. He carefully scoops Aurora up and carries her bridal style down to the kitchen. I decide that pouring her a glass of wine and giving her ice cream is probably an excellent idea to help calm her down.

Aurora won't release Sebastian for anything, like he's her own personal woobie. Watching him try to maneuver so he can sit with her on the stool is comical. However, I'm not used to seeing our mate in this state. She is by no means defenseless. Sebastian picks up the spoon and starts feeding Aurora the ice cream. Hesitantly, Aurora takes the ice cream from the spoon, and her eyes slowly fade back to their normal steel grey. Softly, she smiles at us and starts feeding herself instead.

"I'm sorry I lost it, guys. I don't want anyone to die because of me. I just got all of you, and I'm not even remotely close to consider being ready to lose any of you." Aurora sighs softly, then looks between the two of us.

"I'm almost thinking a small force will be easier to hide than a large mass of black bodies moving across the tundra. Number wise, it puts us at a disadvantage, but it may give us the element of surprise." Aurora taps the spoon to her plump lips, pondering what move to make next.

"Dom, get your brother to put together a group of the absolute best fighters in the pack. We're going to go in hard and fast. We'll break into alpha and bravo teams and converge on the Polar Bears. I'll run straight up the middle since my white fur will cloak me the longest. I'll head straight for the leader and rip his head off," Aurora says, so matter-of-fact it's almost scary.

Sometimes, her gaining Sebastian's battle strategy is a blessing and a curse all in the same breath. I don't like the idea of her charging alone into battle while we attack from different sides. The Polar Bears also have the white fur advantage as well. I began to pace as I notice Sebastian grab the notepad on the island and draw a mini version of the large map we have upstairs. Aurora looks as well, making small adjustments to his drawing."Her plan is solid, Dom. The only problem I see is that the Polar Bears and Ice Dragons are also white. It will be tough for us to spot them in time." Sebastian states.

"Gee, ya think?" I say under my breath. Captain Obvious strikes again. I roll my eyes. Seriously, does Sebastian think we're stupid? With the way he speaks to everyone, he must think we are at times. Aurora spots the faces I'm making while Sebastian is busy. Aurora rolls her eyes at me, then slides off Sebastian's lap. He's so engrossed in what he's doing, it barely registers that she moved. Aurora goes behind Sebastian and starts making some of the silliest faces I've ever seen her make.

Sebastian must sense something is up because he turns to catch Aurora sticking her tongue out at him. He quickly grabs her tongue between his index and middle finger and growls at her. Aurora simply smirks at him. I look down to see she has shifted her hand, and her talons are millimeters away from his cock and balls. Realizing his family jewels are endangered, he quickly releases her tongue and backs away. Aurora clicks her talons together and looks them over before shifting her hand back to normal.

"Just remember, love, you may be my first mate, but I am still alpha." She pats his cheek and smiles at him. Aurora winks at me, then grabs her empty bowl and dumps it in the sink. I could tell she has a lot on her mind by the way she stared at Sebastian's drawing.

Just about any way we slice this mission, there's going to be a high body count.

"Sebastian, I want to go swimming at the lake. Mind taking me?" Aurora smiles when Sebastian agrees. Slowly, she stands before me and gives me a soft kiss—one that could set your loins ablaze.

Gently, she rests her forehead against mine and says softly through our bond, *Don't fear, my love. Call your brother. Make the arrangements. All will work out.*" Her terse sentences don't fill me with comfort. They do, however, give me something to do while they are off swimming.

CHAPTER 5
Elena

Jayce is the one who comes to gather up Dimitri and Nicodeamus. I give Jayce a questioning look and he only laughs. "Aurora had a mini-meltdown, and Sebastian volunteered to remain at ground zero if she loses her temper." He shrugs and goes back to loading the luggage into the car's trunk.

"Come to think of it, Elena, he's been pissing her off more often than not lately. Do you know why he's pushing her buttons?" It's times like this when I wish the boys thought more with their heads than with their hearts. I know Jayce means well, but if looks could kill, Sebastian would be dead. To be honest, I'm not sure which of her two father figures would do it first.

"I believe, Jayce, it's because he's afraid of losing Aurora, be it in the war or because of this new male. His dad wasn't exactly the best example of how to be a good mate and father." I lower my head for a moment and give it a brief shake. Nicodeamus is by my side in a second, lending me his strength. His arm bands around me, tightly holding me to him. I smile up at him to let him know I'm ok.

"Let's just say I wasn't sad when he lost the alpha fight to Angus. Sebastian believes it's his birthright to be alpha. My son isn't alpha material. He doesn't have the same commanding presence that Aurora has. In a sense, I believe he's jealous of his mate. Correct me if I'm wrong, Nicodeamus, but First Mate's title is just that: a title. He may think it gives him dominion over the others. Aurora would be wise to set him in his place," I say as Jayce nods slowly, taking in all that I've told him.

"Aurora has put Sebastian in his place many times. If he keeps his nonsense up, I fear for his safety that she may tear him apart one of these days. He likes trying to keep her for himself, and it's not right," Jayce says, looking down sadly.

You can tell he's trying to keep his emotions under control. I fear the damage my son is doing to his bond mates, especially this gentle one. I wiggle out of Nicodeamus's grip and go to embrace Jayce. He snuggles into me tightly, needing the emotional security. I run my fingers through his hair in an attempt to soothe him. The guys continue loading the car while I take care of Jayce.

"Son, don't worry about Sebastian. It may do him some good if Aurora kicks his ass and makes him submit. He might actually get the silly notion he's an alpha out of his head." I smile at him as he stares at me in disbelief. I kiss his temple before patting his bottom in a motherly move, sending him on his way.

"You need to get going. You don't want to miss your flight. May the Goddess watch over you and keep you safe." I hug Dimitri next and thank him for what he's doing. My heart breaks for Aurora every time I look at Dimitri and Andre. Time is catching up to them far too fast for my liking. Nicodeamus steps up to me next and kisses me passionately. He stirs the fire deep within me, making me wish he wasn't leaving. Reluctantly, I pull back and look up at him.

"Elena, I will make sure the forces are prepared properly. We have too much at stake to accept anything less than perfection. Only the strongest will run beside our children. We shall not fail you." The strength of conviction in Nicodeamus's voice soothes my nerves. I stand on my tippy toes and kiss him once more. I back away, watching the guys get into the car. I trust in Nicodeamus's judgment completely, but as a mother, I still worry.

I approach the training ring in measured steps, where Dominik is sparring with the other pack members, honing their skills for the battle ahead. However, something makes me stop and start looking around. Something isn't right. My eyes scan the area quickly, trying to find what's causing this uneasy feeling.

"Dominik, get Aurora and Sebastian back here! Wolves, prepare for battle! Something's coming!" It's been ages since I last shifted and even longer since I actually had to fight as my wolf. The familiar snapping and cracking of bones is almost music to my ears. My body slowly shifts forms as my bones, muscles, and sinew shift alignment and grow in size. It's been years since the pack has seen me like this. I tilt my head back and howl, calling all the wolves that can hear me. Dominik's Dire joins in, our blended tones carrying far and wide. In the distance, I hear Aurora's bone-chilling howl soon joined by Sebastian's. I know whatever is coming doesn't stand a chance. I raise my eyes skyward to find Andre circling, calling out, and flying toward whatever he sees. Now that we know the direction of the attack, we adjust accordingly.

The first Strigoi breaks through the trees, followed closely by a Black Bear. Damn, now the local bear dens are involved in this mess. Strigoi and bears clash with our wolves. The once white gravel of our town center is painted crimson and black in a matter of moments.

One of the bears comes straight for me. I quickly dodge to the left and sink my claws into his side, rending flesh from bone. He turns, now favoring that side, and charges again. I never repeat a move, so instead, I leap up and land on his back. My canines sink deeply into the back of his neck as my claws rip out his throat.

Aurora bursts through the tree line, leaving a trail of frost in her wake. The air around her is supercharged with her rage. I've never seen her Lycan look this angry and aggressive. She charges into the fray, swiping left and right, ripping throats out, and severing heads as she goes.

Her growl is so deep, almost demonic , you can feel it as if she's standing right next to you. Sebastian finally makes it to the party and stops next to me. We watch in wonder as she goes on a rampage. Sebastian leaves my side to assist Dominik, who happens to be surrounded by five bears. He makes quick work of the first bear by ripping his head clean off. The rest of the pack is doing quite well holding their own against the Strigoi and bears. I'm watching them work as a well-oiled machine. Everyone is looking out for each other, making sure to fight in pairs like we trained.

Suddenly, Aurora leaps up on top of a building and closes her eyes. She shakes her head several times before jumping back into the fight. I wonder what that was all about? She looks a little shaken by what happened. Her rage lessens as she finishes off the last few Strigoi.

One large Black Bear moves toward me and shifts back to his human form; it's the leader of the bear's den. He drops to his knees before me and says, "Please, stop the slaughter. Tomas lied to us, told us that we had to kill you to save ourselves. Please, call them off. Bears! Stop! Submit and live!" The leader yells, and all the bears immediately obey him.

Aurora stops and shifts back to her human form. Dominik and Sebastian flank her side. Anna runs out of the Alpha House with Aurora's robe and quickly assists her with putting it on, then scurries off. Aurora raises a single hand and, through the pack bond, she sends everyone home. Her eyes fade to that of her human.

"You beg for mercy after attacking my people because a leech said so?" She tilts her head to the side, assessing the leader of the bears. He's not that big of a man, but he's slightly bigger than your average human male. Aurora's fingers run through Dominik's thick, coarse, black fur. Her eyes dart to Sebastian, and he moves back toward the

Alpha House. Slowly, Aurora reverts her attention back to the scared man before her.

"They took my daughter. If we didn't attack, they would kill her." His head hangs low as he begins to cry. I watch emotions flicker across Aurora's face, then vanish almost as quickly as they came. Her eyes narrow on the man before her as she turns her right forearm out to face him. Once he sees her family brand, his eyes widen. As soon as recognition hits him, Aurora turns and heads back to the Alpha House.

"Follow me," she says without turning around.

Inside the house, Sebastian helps her get cleaned up and dressed in her blood-red, floor-length gown. By the time the leader of the bears and I enter the house, she is perched on her Throne of Skulls. In her left hand is a glass of red wine, Dominik's wolf sits at her right side, and Sebastian—dressed—stands to her left. Aurora looks majestic as she sits there, and quite frightening, to be honest.

The bear leader drops to his knees before Aurora, and Dominik growls in warning, not liking how close the man is. Aurora's right-hand goes to rest on his head to calm him. "How long ago did the Strigoi kidnap your daughter?" Slowly, Aurora raises the glass to her lips and takes a sip of her wine.

"Two nights ago, My Liege." He keeps his eyes lowered. I'm guessing he realizes how badly he fucked up today.

"Sebastian?" Aurora turns her head to regard my son.

"Take a team and scout the area around the bear's den. The weather is in our favor. Now, bring back his daughter." Sebastian leans forward and kisses Aurora's lips before heading out.

"Go with my mate. He will find your daughter. In repayment for this boon, I require your people to guard my people in my absence when we go to war. There shouldn't be any attacks. The Strigoi are after me, and with me gone, there's no reason for them to even think about coming here. Do we have a deal?" Aurora's eyes churn liquid mercury as she watches the leader of the bears. Her hand is extended to him, waiting for him to accept. The man quickly moves forward and takes her hand without a second thought. He shakes her hand firmly, then kisses her knuckles.

"I swear to you, on the last beat of my heart, I will not fail you. We will fight beside you and guard your people as you command." Aurora nods and looks at me.

"Elena, we seal this the old way: a blood oath." Aurora's canines elongate, and her hands partially shift to talons. I bring her a wine glass and hold it out to her, then she quickly cuts her left wrist and drips blood into the glass. Aurora's tongue darts out and licks her wound, sealing it instantly. She grabs the man's arm and slits his wrist over the glass. I watch his blood mix with hers. Aurora grabs her other glass and pours some wine into the blood mix, then stands up, holding the glass high.

"I hold my blood and the blood of the bear's leader in my glass. On this blood, I swear we—the Lycan clan—will help find your missing child." Aurora takes a sip of the blood wine, then holds the glass out to the bear leader. He takes the glass and raises it up before those gathered.

"I swear on my blood and on the last beat of my heart to serve the last Lycan Queen and to protect her people in times of war without question." He too, drinks the blood wine, then hands the glass to me. Aurora gives him a nod, and he proceeds to follow Sebastian. She returns to her throne and runs her fingers through Dominik's fur.

"I heard the prince mid-battle today. He's placed my scale, and the bond is slowly growing. Dominik, shift back, love. I'd like to talk with you." She smiles softly, caressing his muzzle, and kisses his wolven lips. She shows such reverence to all of her mates. I have yet to see her favor one male over the others. Dominik seems to be her voice of reason. Jayce is the peacemaker and the one that helps her deal with emotions. My son, Sebastian, seems to be her sword and shield, her guardian and protector. I reach back and grab the spare robe I keep near the throne, just in case. I hand it to Aurora, who takes it and waits for her mate to shift. She offers him the robe and he slips it on.

"You can hear him? It must be the dragon bond the scales have forged." Dominik begins to pace, but Aurora grips his forearm, stopping him in his tracks. She backs him up until he's sitting on her throne. She smiles, admiring him sitting on her throne. Aurora's gaze meets mine, and I smile and nod at her. Slowly, she looks back to Dominik.

"You do look rather handsome on my throne, like a conqueror." I watch Dominik sit up a little straighter, a little prouder, at his mate's assessment of him.

"Each of you have a strength and a weakness. Dom, I have to say your thought process is the most similar to mine: use force only when needed but destroy my target utterly." Aurora is walking around the throne, watching Dominik. She is studying him closely. His pride isn't getting in the way, and he just smiles and nods at her words.

"My love, I will be whatever you need me to be. I wish only to be at your side and to be seen as an equal." His eyes flash to that of his wolf, then back to his human hazel. Aurora smiles, then sits on Dominik's lap. Her fingers thread through his thick, black hair while her eyes are searching, studying him up close.

"Elena, I wish for you to announce to the pack that we have dragons on our side." Her eyes close quickly, and she pauses her breathing. Dominik tightens his grip on her, studying her features for any signs of distress. Her eyes suddenly open, and they are the liquid mercury of her wolf.

"He has eighteen loyal only to him. Do not mention the numbers. He's in flight to the court of his mother's birth to petition the Gold Dragons for help as well." Dominik kisses Aurora's cheek and nuzzles her jawline. Unlike my son, when the dragons are mentioned, I don't sense any anxiety from him. He's calm and measured in his thoughts and actions.

"That's fantastic news, love! The prince seems to be very generous and concerned for your safety. That means the world to Jayce and I. I'm not too sure if we should fill Sebastian in on how strong the bond is yet. Elena, he's your son. What do you suggest?" Dominik and Aurora turn as one to face me.

"I believe your assessment is correct. I don't think my son can handle the idea of the bond growing stronger. We'll have to break it to him slowly when it gets closer to the start of the war." Sadly, I feel the need to hide things from my son, especially the role I play in this scenario.

Honestly, he's a bit immature with this whole situation. He knew from the start that Aurora was destined to have a harem. I know he secretly dreamed of his mate as only his. But if he keeps fucking up and pissing her off, Aurora just might add his skull to her collection—mate or not. I sigh softly. My poor son always feels like he's on shaky ground with Aurora. He doesn't realize she treats them all equally, that no one is favored over the other.

My cell phone pings, alerting me to a message. I look down to find a text from Nicodeamus saying they are at the airport. He felt a shift with Aurora and is wondering if she's okay. I text him back, filling him in on what has transpired. He sends back a heart and a thumbs-up emoji. I guess he's almost caught up with everyone else.

"The guys have made it to the airport. Jayce is on his way back." Aurora nods slowly and turns to look at Dominik; her eyes bleed liquid mercury as their gaze locks. His eyes are now the gold of his wolf. I'm not sure what I'm witnessing, but it's impressive as all hell to watch.

"Jayce is stopping at the store to get me more ice cream. He says everything went fine at the airport. It took him almost twenty minutes to explain to my dad what a plane is though." Aurora shakes her head and rolls her eyes, laughing softly to herself. "My dad wants to know what enchantments are on the metal beasts to make them fly. Since they can't use their phones on the plane, I told him I'll watch a video about it in a bit so he can watch too."

"Wait a second, you can speak to your father as well as your mates?" This is exciting news to me. I've heard of dragons dream walking, but communication on this level is scary. Scary, but useful.

Aurora shrugs her shoulders, but Dominik says, "It freaked me out in the beginning as well. It comforts Aurora's wolf in stressful moments when her father's dragon can reach out and soothe her." Dominik smiles and brushes a lock of Aurora's hair behind her ear.

"The communication thing is definitely a dragon gift. For years, her father was dream walking to train her before seeing each other for the first time. As mates, if Aurora concentrates hard enough, we can see through each other's eyes." Aurora's smile turns gentle just before she kisses both of Dominik's cheeks.

"We were talking to Jayce together and planning dinner. He wanted our opinion of a cut of beef, so we took a look," Dominik says like it's the most natural thing in the world. I guess for them, it has become that way. I never experienced that with Sebastian's father. Ours was a true mating, but not a fated mating. Only the animals loved each other; the humans, well, we barely tolerated each other. Deep down, I have to admit I'm a bit jealous of Aurora. She knows and feels precisely what her mates are feeling. In her lifetime, she will never have to question where she stands with them. Honestly, it's a thing of beauty.

I look outside, and the sun is beginning to set, painting the sky in so many vivid colors. Tonight is the first night of the Hunter's Moon. It's a beautiful, crisp October evening, and soon the moon will rise high in the sky and illuminate the ground. The Hunter's Moon is typically when the pack goes to hunt elk on the ridge. I watch as families gather and prepare for the hunt. Young ones, finally into their teens, prepare for their first hunt with the pack.

Aurora and Dominik walk onto the front porch to send off the hunters tonight. It is tradition that the stag head is returned to the alpha in offering. This kind of ritual is right up Aurora's alley, especially with her impressive skull collection. Aurora and Dominik share a look, then lean their heads back and howl, signaling the start of the hunt. The pack splits into three teams and runs off in different directions. Both of them watch as the last of the pack members disappear from sight. Aurora stops moving rather suddenly and looks at Dominik. In the distance, the sound of a car crash can be heard. Smoke rises up into the sky, marking the area of the impact.

"Jayce!" Aurora screams before shifting to her beast to run toward the accident.

CHAPTER 6
Aurora

The sudden burst of adrenaline that sets my blood on fire is unlike anything I have ever felt before. One minute I get to appreciate the beautiful sunset with Dom, the next, I'm running as fast as my wolven form can carry me. My shift came so quickly, the fear for my mate overtook any sense of self-preservation I had. Anger begins to flood my thoughts. The fucking bears, they had to have set this up as a last-ditch effort to please the Strigoi.

As I get closer, I see the Strigoi and bears circling Jayce. Oh yes, all those fuckers are going to die. Quickly, I break through their ranks, using my talons to rend flesh from their bones as I pass. Blackened blood and fur from the bear's pelts fly through the air as I battle my way through their ranks to get to Jayce. I am of a singular focus, destroy anything that comes between Jayce and me.

Dominik, Elena, and several other Lycans are in the distance. I lay a taloned hand on Jayce's side before I start freezing the ground around us. Jayce leaps up onto the hood of the car as the ice spreads, rooting some of the Strigoi in place. Through the bond, I warn Dominik not to get too close. He obeys and steers Elena and the other Lycans to fight on the edge of the group.

After I make sure Jayce is safe, I systematically shred and rip the heads off the Strigoi closest to me. I'm in a rage, betrayed by the bear clan after swearing a blood bond. There would be no bears left standing after tonight. This I swear on the blood of my mother. I know Jayce is injured from the accident; his jerky movements are a dead giveaway.

With most of the Strigoi dead, I move on to the bears. The largest Black Bear charges at me—a fatal mistake on his part. I know this particular one is the leader, but if he's here, where is Sebastian? When the leader gets close enough, I sink my talons into his pelt and encase him in ice. I need him alive for now.

Once he's neutralized, I move on to the next bear. He charges as well, yet another idiot in the group. I show no mercy and sink my talons deep into his chest and wrap my fingers around his beating heart. The bear is clawing at me, fighting for his life as I stare into his eyes.

Slowly, I tighten my grip on his heart, making it harder for the muscle to beat. Blood pumps out around my arm and down to my elbow before dropping onto the ground. The light in his eyes slowly fades away as the blood pumps out of the hole in his chest. Violently, I rip the still-beating heart from his chest and drop it to the ground.

Several bears still live, but not for long. Jayce is off the car now and fighting a bear with his brother, Dom. It's interesting to watch the two of them fight together. A second bear joins their fight, and now I see the change in Jayce: toxin drips yellow-green from his canines as he charges the bear. Because I'm distracted from watching the twins, I get blindsided by another bear. This fucker is going to die.

I roll onto my feet and remain low with my hands flat on the ground. The bear attempts to circle me, but I mirror his movements easily. I watch how he favors his one foreleg, and I realize he has a weakness on his right side. He goes to charge, and I leap out of the way only to land on his back. I sink my talons deep into his pelt until I feel his ribs.

One by one, I start snapping them. I feel no remorse as it becomes harder for him to breathe. My wolven muzzle comes down and clamps onto the back of the bear's neck, applying as much pressure as I can. I listen to the tendons snap, and bones crack under the pressure I'm exerting. A quick twist of my head snaps the bear's neck. I call it a mercy killing.

My eyes turn back to the leader, who—in his only smart move— has shifted back to his human form. Jayce, Dominik, and Elena have him surrounded. I shift back to my human form with every step in his direction. I leave only my hands and forearms shifted, so my gauntlets and talons are at my disposal.

"Where is Sebastian?" I practically growl in his face as I press the tip of my talon into the soft flesh under his chin.

"He's safe, I swear! I have him knocked out and tied up in a cave near our den." The leader of the bears looks at me, fear radiating off him like a bad cologne. I tilt my head left and right, studying him. I know my silence is only frightening him more.

"You swear? That's fucking funny. You swore a blood oath, yet here we are!" I dramatically throw my arms out to encompass the remnants of the battle.

"You attack two of my mates and one you actually tried to kill. If Sebastian is dead..." I laugh; it's a borderline unhinged kind of laugh. Am I crazy? Maybe just a touch.

"If Sebastian is dead, you will know exactly what Hell on Earth is. You will be begging for me to take your life by the time I am done with you." I pull my hand toward me, slicing my talons through the soft flesh under his chin.

His ice prison starts melting around him. "Start walking. If there's even the slightest hint of a trap, you die. And know this: at the end of tonight, none of your clan will be left alive. I cannot take the chance of them betraying me again." The color drains from his face as he finally realizes he just caused the extinction of his people. I'm not joking, nor am I one to play games or make empty threats. Betrayal isn't something to be overlooked. It's not something to be forgotten or forgiven.

The walk through the woods is in relative silence. I had shifted back to my Lycan form before we entered the forest. I don't want to be vulnerable, just in case this is a trap. Jayce and Dominik flank my sides as we move deeper into unfamiliar territory. Part of me wants to call my Lycan pack to join in the hunt for Sebastian. The other part doesn't want the pack to watch what I feel I need to do.

In the distance, the cave in question comes into view. Elena prepares to bolt toward the cave, but Dominik and Jayce move to block her path at my command. I give her a short growl to warn her of the possible danger that lies within the cave. As we get closer, the first scent I pick up is blood and Sebastian.

A menacing growl escapes my lips, and my hackles stand on end as I stare at the bear's leader. My lips are curled back, exposing my long canines and sharp teeth. I motion for the guys to investigate the cavern since Dire Wolves can see in the dark better than Lycans.

Dom's voice appears in my head through the bond. *He's ok. He's bound and gagged, and it seems like he's been drugged. The blood isn't his; he must have killed the three bears in here before the drugs kicked in. Jayce and I will get him out of here.* I'm relieved that Sebastian is safe and sound. I am, however, still royally pissed off at the bear's leader. He knows he's in deep shit.

I shift back to my human form to address my mother-in-law. "Elena, I need you and Jayce to take Sebastian home and make sure he's really okay. Dominik and I have matters that need attending to." My voice is as cold as ice and as harsh as a hurricane. There will be no mercy; only women and children will survive this. Any threat to my people is a direct threat to the throne, and I must deal with it as such.

Dominik and Jayce walk out with Sebastian in their arms. I quickly create an ice prison for the bear's leader before I look Sebastian over. Slowly, I walk around the guys, looking at every inch of him. There's barely a bruise on his body; in that sense, I'm pleased.

"Lay him down and elevate his head." Carefully, Dominik and Jayce lay Sebastian down with his head on Jayce's lap. My beast is out for blood after seeing her mate defenseless.

"Tilt his head back and open his mouth." I watch as Jayce does as I've instructed. When Sebastian is positioned correctly, I bite my forearm, allowing my canines to elongate and pierce my own flesh and muscle. Rich, sanguine fluid drops slowly into Sebastian's mouth. My theory is since I heal faster than the guys, perhaps my blood will help remove the sedative from Sebastian's system. I watch the rivulets of blood slowly drip onto my mate's tongue, turning it vermillion. I observe as he slowly swallows the first gulp of my blood.

My hand tightens its grip on the other to squeeze more blood out and into his mouth. Sebastian's color slowly improves, and eventually, his eyes open. He reaches up with shaky hands and grips my bleeding arm. He gently licks my self-inflicted wounds, healing me. A soft *thank you* echoes in my head from Sebastian. I kiss his lips softly and lock eyes with Jayce.

"Get him and Elena home safely. Your word is my law. Anyone questions it, fucking bite them and let the toxins take them." Jayce simply nods; no words are needed at this point.

My eyes move to Dominik, he knows what I have planned, and he's completely on board. Without warning, I partially shift my arms. Thick, sharp, white dragon scales create gauntlets on my forearms and down my fingers to the long, hooked talons on my fingertips. I look over my weapons as I defrost the ice prison that's holding the bear's leader. He's begging for his life, begging for mercy. His pleas are falling on deaf ears, and I'm past the point of accepting any sorry from him.

I stand directly in front of him, my eyes turning the liquid mercury of my beast. My left-hand grips his throat, and both of his hands fly up, trying to loosen my hold on him. What he doesn't notice is that my right hand is aimed at his upper stomach. I slowly press my talons to his flesh about five inches above his navel.

The skin bends and flexes only so much before my talons pierce through his flesh, then through the thick muscle layer of his abdomen. His eyes lock with mine, shock starting to set in. I continue to press deeper, feeling his intestines slide along the back of my hand. I sense Sebastian shuffling behind me. I keep pushing until my talons touch the muscle of his diaphragm. His blood is slowly running down my forearm, leaving streaks of crimson along my scales.

I pause in my forward movement to watch the blood trickle along the various scale plates. It's almost a work of art. Then again, death can be beautiful if done properly. I look over my shoulder at Sebastian and smile at him. I'm happy to see him standing up. His hand grips my right forearm as he presses his chest to my back. Quickly, he thrusts my right arm up and through the diaphragm. I literally have the man's heart in my hand.

Sebastian places his left hand lightly around my throat and brings his full lips to my ear. His voice is low and sultry; it drips of raw, sexual power, hitting a tone that sets my blood on fire. Sebastian utters four words, and I honestly can't help myself. "I want his heart."

I comply immediately. The man's eyes go wide as I suddenly grip his heart tight and rip down. The wet, sucking noise fills the air as my arm comes free of his body. The bear's leader drops like a ton of bricks on the forest floor before me. Slowly, I turn and offer the heart to Sebastian. He kisses me softly and takes my offering, giving me that cocky smirk of his. If he wasn't so panty-melting hot, I'd probably be pissed at him.

Jayce comes up alongside Sebastian, and they begin to walk home. My gaze lands on Elena next. She looks at the man's body and begins removing his skull to add to my collection. She knows me too well. Dom places his hand on my lower back and tilts his head to the side, silently questioning what was next.

"The bear's main camp is to the north over this ridge. We shift and go in hot. Only sow's with children live." I may be heartless at times, but I refuse to kill children or leave them as orphans. We shift and take off in the direction of the bear's compound.

It's not as big as I initially thought it would be. We see Strigoi moving about the compound, but no bears out in the open. Part of what the leader said was true. He didn't, however, admit to the Strigoi using his compound as a base. I motion for Dominik and I to retreat. We need to plan this as a team, and a night-time strike is not the smartest move for us to make.

We return to the Lycan compound, and I send Dominik off to gather the others. I call Dimitri and tell him we need my father's wisdom. The guys all gather around, as well as some of our strongest fighters. My phone rings, and it's Dimitri and my father on the other end. Dominik goes through his observations from the attack and the hunt for Sebastian. Then Sebastian fills everyone in on what he overheard before he was sedated. I notice Jayce is writing everything down in bullet points on the whiteboard, making it easier to track where the conversation is going.

"Okay, so I'm going out on a limb here." I stand in front of the whiteboard to look over the notes.

"What if the bears have been involved since the beginning? For a group that recently arrived, the Strigoi have too much knowledge to hunt my ass down. At some point, we need to make sure there are no other moles in our ranks. For now, we need to plan the attack for the morning. Put the compound on lockdown. No one goes in or out until tomorrow night." My eyes search those that are gathered; none flinch from what I just said.

My father's voice cuts through my thoughts. "Good idea, daughter. Only one problem: more than likely, the Strigoi will have prisoners in the basements. How do you plan on handling that?" My father raises an interesting point. I ponder the idea further, then I slowly turn to Sebastian.

He steps forward and bows his head to me, presenting his idea. "We need to evacuate as many bears as possible and burn the main buildings the Strigoi are in. From what we have seen, they tend to bunch up, so I assume they do the same for sleep."

Sebastian turns on the smart TV in the office and hooks up his phone to it. I grab my phone and switch the call to video. I turn the camera to face the TV as Sebastian pulls up his map program to show the bear's camp. "Not every house will have a basement, so we can eliminate those houses first. I suggest we wait until the sun is high in the sky before we move in. Aurora and I can rip the roof off the houses we suspect have Strigoi in the basement. Worst case scenario, after that, we can rip up the floorboards as well." Sebastian keeps his back turned from the group as he explains his idea. I mean, most of it has merit.

"Okay, so let me get this straight: I'm supposed to use precious energy to rip a house apart when we're not even sure the Strigoi are there? Logistically, it doesn't make any sense to me at all. Dad, is there any way to track the Strigoi that would make pinpointing them easier?" Who knows how old my father is? Maybe, in all his years, someone had a stroke of brilliance and figured it out. It's a long shot, but worth asking. I watch my father pace while Dimitri rolls his eyes. I see now where my flair for the dramatic comes from.

"Nope, no easy way to find them other than the distinct scent of sulfur and rot," my father says like it's nothing. Has he been hanging out with Andre too much? Everyone in the room turns to Jayce and Dominik. The Dires have the best nose out of all of us. Compared to the rest of us—especially me—they are the closest to pure wolves. Jayce and Dominik look at each other, then back to me.

Dominik is the first to speak. "We've got this. Dimitri, have Alex send two enforcers and two wolves with toxic bite as soon as he can.

We'll need more help here in the future." Dimitri gives a short reply, then he ends the call.

"Let's get some sleep; tomorrow is going to be a long day." Dom immediately offers me his hand and I sigh softly, giving him a gentle kiss before hugging him tightly.

"I need to spend time with Sebastian. He may be an ass and an arrogant fuck at times, but he's still our mate, and I've been spending more time with you and Jayce than him. I don't favor anyone, and I don't want anyone to feel as if they don't matter as much as the others. Besides, if anyone is going to kick his ass first, it's going to be me." Dominik and I share a good laugh over that before I turn and leave him behind.

Upstairs, I find Sebastian sitting on the edge of his bed with his head in his hands. I feel the emotional rollercoaster he's on, and it's partially my fault. I walk past Sebastian and into his bathroom. I decide to fill his oversized tub, and I add in different oils and herbs as the hot water begins to rise. Curiosity must have gotten the better of him because, eventually, he joins me in the bathroom. After I shut the water off, I turn to him and put a finger to his lips, asking for silence. He gives me a slow nod. Tonight is about him, not me.

Deep down, I feel like I've been neglecting Sebastian. He brought some of it on himself, taunting the other mates. Sebastian always had the bad habit of trying to place himself above the others. This made me distance myself from him, mostly because I was continually trying to reassure the other mates of their place. After thinking I lost him, I know I need to set things right tonight and spend quality time with him. My hands grip the hem of his Henley, and I slowly lift it above his head. I drop his shirt to the floor and lightly run my fingers over his taut muscles. I almost forgot what it's like to appreciate what's before me with all that's happened lately. I reign in my desire for now. I must remember to stay on task.

I motion for Sebastian to sit on the edge of the tub. Carefully, I remove his shoes and socks, then go for his belt. Sebastian stands to help with his pants. Adonis has nothing on Sebastian's physique. He is pure, sculpted perfection; the definition of man-candy. Fuck, I got lucky in the mate department. I motion for him to get in the tub, and he gives me that look. You know, the one that makes you want to lick every inch of the person.

The look that makes your insides melt and your lady bits weep with joy. Sebastian steps into the hot water and lowers himself into the tub. His moan of appreciation makes my insides clench. I try to ignore my pussy, but the bitch is screaming at me. I grab the softest washcloth I can find and load it with the body soap I keep hidden in his bathroom.

I spend the next half hour washing every square inch of his body. My fingers trace every bump and ridge of Sebastian's muscles, his baby blue eyes locked on mine as I bathe him. I'd be lying if I said I wasn't turned on. Other females would kill to be where I am right now.

"My love, you don't have to bathe me, you know? I appreciate how thorough you're being. I'm okay, honest, Aurora." I move so I'm now straddling Sebastian's lap. My fingers roam over the rock hard muscles of his chest.

"Sebastian, I feel like I haven't been a good mate to you. When I thought you might have died..." My words fail me as tears slowly roll down my cheeks. Sebastian's hands come up and cup my face, using the pad of his thumbs to wipe away my tears.

"Shh, love. You haven't been a bad mate. Jayce needed a lot more attention than me. I'll always be right here waiting for you." He punctuates his statement by gently kissing my lips.

"As much as I want to bury myself deep in you and fuck you until dawn, we need sleep. And to be honest, I'm still feeling off." He's making sense, like always.

I look closely at Sebastian. Why didn't I notice how tired he looks? I'm so fucking selfish sometimes. Carefully, I remove myself from Sebastian's lap, then out of the tub. I quickly grab our towels and offer one to Sebastian. I can't help but stare at my sexy mate. Sebastian has a well-defined athletic build. His shoulders are thickly muscled, and his waistline is tapered in. My eyes roam hungrily over his chest, down to his defined abs. You know that *V* everyone talks about? The one at a man's hips that trails down to his groin? Sebastian blows that expectation out of the water.

"Aurora?" I snap out of my inner monologue to look up at Sebastian.

"Your wolf is showing," he says. He gives me that cocky grin that infuriates me, and turns me on more in times like this. Evil, evil mate. If he keeps looking at me like that, we won't be sleeping.

I grumble on my way back to the bedroom. I need to reign in my desire and put Sebastian's health first. My towel falls to the floor before I climb into bed, snuggling myself in and watching Sebastian move about his room. Honestly, I'm starting to get sleepy. I didn't realize how much the day has stressed me out. Sebastian climbs into bed behind me and pulls me flush against his chest. I fall asleep quickly. For once, no dreams disturb my slumber.

Sebastian and I are awakened by Jayce jumping on the bed. Have I mentioned I'm not a morning person? I grumble and growl at Jayce and try to hide under my pillow. The next thing I know, I see Jayce's face looking at me under my pillow.

"Love? Reinforcements arrived very early this morning. Alex sent us six Dire Wolves: three enforcers and three with the toxic bite. We need direction from our leader." He smiles before leaning forward to kiss me. Jayce extracts himself from my hiding place, and I toss the pillow to the floor. I turn to find Sebastian and Jayce lip locked. So, I do what any red-blooded mate would do: I grab my cell phone and turn off the flash to take several pictures of them kissing.

Ever so carefully, I extract myself from the bed to get changed in my room. I search through my clothing for something that says *I'm not going to take anyone's shit.* I find my black leather pants and a blood-red bodice. It's kind of a steampunk meets dominatrix look. After searching for what seems like forever, I finally find my knee-high boots.

I head down the stairs and into the main hall. The Dires stand immediately, then bow before me. I stroll toward my throne and take a seat. My eyes assess the Dires before me until, one by one, they slowly look up at me.

"Welcome to my home. Please, make yourselves comfortable. We'll have breakfast first, then off we go to take back the bear camp." Dominik comes up to my right side and offers me his hand. He guides me to the table and begins introductions for the reinforcements. All six of them are in agreement; the Dire compound has become a much better place ever since the alpha was killed. I sit and listen to them telling stories and cracking jokes at each other. Dominik remains on my right side as I watch everyone eat.

My beast is a bit on edge, and I can't place what's setting her off. *Dominik, something isn't right. Colin, the enforcer, watch his body language. He's nervous. His scent is acidic from fear. An enforcer shouldn't be afraid.* Dominik gives me a very terse nod and squeezes my hand. Sebastian and Jayce finally make it downstairs, and Dominik gets up quickly to pull Sebastian aside and fill him in. Jayce comes to sit on my left and takes my hand. He knows something is off by how rigid I'm sitting in my chair and the fact I haven't touched my bacon yet.

"Aurora, my love?" Jayce says in such a soft tone. The reverence in his voice warms my black heart. I slowly reach up and brush his cheek with my hand. I know, in that moment, my eyes shift and swirl liquid mercury. He feels the power flow through me, and his wolf's eyes glow in response to my agitation. Dominik and Sebastian stand behind me, each placing a hand on my shoulder in an attempt to calm me. I give the signal to my personal guards, and they leave the room, locking the doors from the outside. The sound of the locks clicking into place sets the Dires on high alert.

"I'm truly blessed to receive help so quickly. But it's come to my attention that there's a traitor in our ranks." Five out of six Dires are calm and looking directly at me. Number six—that fucker—is fidgeting and restless. I feel a little different, and I have a very bitter taste in my mouth. My eyes search Jayce's as I part my lips slightly and run my tongue over my canines. His eyes widen at the sight, thinking it's sexual in nature. Realization hits him, and he stares at my canines closer. My sweet, innocent mate smirks at me, then winks. I stand and walk soundlessly around the table, stalking my prey.

My fingertips lightly run over each of the guys' shoulders as I pass them. When I reach Colin, both of my hands come to rest on his shoulders. I lean down and nuzzle his cheek, freezing him in fear. I can hear his heart pounding in his chest, racing a mile a minute. My guys are standing on the opposite side of the table, watching with rapt attention. My tongue darts out and licks his throat, tasting the fear and salt in his sweat.

Without warning, I strike. My canines sink deep into this throat. The snaps and crunches of tendons and sinew breaking can be heard clearly—the sharp, metallic tang of his life fluid coats my tongue, spurring my beast on. I can taste the taint of the Strigoi in his blood.

Through the bond, I share my knowledge with the guys. Their growls fill the air, but it doesn't distract me from my task at hand. Colin starts to thrash and tries to throw me off of him. I sink my talons into his shoulders to strengthen my grip as I start pumping the toxin into his bloodstream. I've gained enough knowledge from his blood. The Strigoi taint has touched the Dire compound far worse than I had initially suspected. I jump off Colin's back and watch him stumble before he falls to his knees.

"How many more, Colin? Tell me, and I'll end it quickly." I'm on all fours in front of him on the floor, staring him down and trying to will him to answer me. Alpha powers, don't fail me now.

Colin shakes his head several times before spitting blood. Fuck, I wrecked his vocal cords. He uses his blood to draw the number three. His breathing is labored, and he's having a hard time keeping his eyes open. In one final push, he writes the names of the tainted. His green eyes plead with me for mercy. My resting bitch face game must be on point today because he looks panicked right before I slam my taloned hand into his chest and rip out his heart. His body falls to the floor with a wet splat into a pool of his own blood. Within seconds, Sebastian is at my side, offering me his hand to help me up. I rise to my feet, still holding Colin's heart. I turn my attention to Dominik.

"There are tainted ones within your pack. Call the other enforcers. Have these three dispatched and their heads sent to me." My voice has a wolven growl to it as I fight to enunciate the words. I'm so close to losing the battle with my beast when Jayce's hand slips under the back of my bodice. The simple act of him pressing his hand to my skin seems to soothe my beast. I draw in a slow, deep breath and then kiss his temple. Through the pack bond, I have the guards open the doors to the room again. You know it's pretty bad when they don't even blink after seeing a dead body or a puddle of blood in the house anymore.

Elena comes running into the room, chattering away with a phone stuck to her head. Suddenly, she stops dead in her tracks as she took in the scene before her. "Yeah, Nico, Aurora killed someone in the house. No, no, no, she's okay. She's got a heart in her hand again." Sebastian facepalms, listening to the way his mother describes the situation to my dad on the phone. I shake my head and start walking out of the room. I step over Colin's body and make my way out into the main hall. About another thirty minutes and it's go time. The Strigoi won't know what hit them.

CHAPTER 7
Jayce

It frightens me to think my pack-mates would turn against Aurora. The way she decided to handle the traitor was something my father would have done. However, there is one huge difference: he wouldn't have shown mercy and ended it quickly.

I'm not sure how the mate bond thing is supposed to work. Is Aurora supposed to gain a unique ability—a gift—from each of us or just each species? Personally, I know I've gotten stronger and faster since we've mated.

My phone dings, and it's a text from Alex. He's just as upset as I am over the betrayal. The three in question will get beheaded tonight. Alex also tells me the prince received Aurora's gifts, and he asks me to gather the others before he sends the video over to her.

It will be the first time she gets to see him. Part of me is scared. I'm not afraid of losing my place in the pack, but I'm so frightened of having a pure-blooded dragon in the bond. What if he has a bad temper? What if his bad temper makes Aurora's worse? So many questions bounce around in my head as I enter the main sitting room to find my other bond mates.

"Aurora, love, Alex has forwarded a video for you." Aurora scrunches her nose and tilts her head to the side as she studies me.

"Please cast it to the smart TV, Jayce," Aurora says. Sebastian turns the TV on and sets it up to receive. I send the video to the TV, and we watch as it pans from the vast white of the tundra to the mouth of a cavern.

A blonde man is standing inside; if I didn't know any better, I'd swear he was a Viking. He's easily three hundred to three hundred and fifty pounds of solid muscle. His hair is a light, golden blonde and hangs down past his shoulders. His face is rather rugged, complete with a full beard and mustache. Aurora is so focused on the video she barely notices Sebastian picking her up to sit on his lap.

Dominik and I share a look and watch as Alaric receives Aurora's box. You can clearly feel the anxiety through the bond when he starts cutting the top open. Alaric slowly removes the popcorn and stops dead, looking at the box's contents. He reaches in and pulls out the braid of hair she had stuffed in there. Sebastian turns to me and mouths, *When did she do that?* I shake my head at him. If he had been paying attention to our mate and not his phone, he would know when she did it.

Alaric brings the braid to his nose and sniffs it. His eyes become the gold of his dragon, slit and all. I know the look of recognition, and that was it. Aurora has gotten quite antsy in Sebastian's lap as she waits to see what Alaric thinks of the skull. A black man—I believe his name is Ellis—steps into the frame and reaches into the box. He pulls out the Wendigo skull and holds it out to Alaric.

I can tell the moment Aurora starts to hold her breath. Her heart rate picks up, and her scales begin to ripple up and down her arms. Alaric's eyes lock on the skull, then the silver-white scale that Aurora placed on top. Alaric rubs the back of his hands across his eyes, wiping away tears.

Ever so gently, he takes the scale from the skull and sniffs it. His right hand comes up quickly, and he cuts into his own flesh. Ellis freaks out and runs back behind the camera. Alaric pushes the fleshy side of Aurora's scale into his wound, and Ellis zooms in on how quickly the flesh knits around the scale.

Alaric gasps and whispers, "I can feel her."

As soon as he says he can feel her, Aurora's hand moves to touch his scale in time with him touching hers. It's times like this I wish Nicodeamus was here to explain exactly what the hell is going on. We watch the remainder of the video in silence. Alaric turns to the camera and smiles.

"My princess," he places his hand flat on Aurora's scale over his heart, "I am yours to command. I have gathered forces beyond my father's reach. We will take back what is rightfully yours. By my blood, I swear this to you." He draws in a deep breath as his eyes flicker between human and dragon.

"To the first mates of our princess, we will be brothers in arms. We will fight for her and protect her together." His flattened palm turns into a fist against his chest, signifying the difference in his promises.

"Dream of me? Aurora?" Alaric smiles one last time and winks at the camera before the video cuts off. All eyes are locked on Aurora, waiting to see her reaction to his video.

"Holy shit, he's hot!" comes from behind us. All of our heads whip around to find Sebastian's mother, Elena, fanning herself in the doorway.

"Hot damn, baby girl, that's a mountain of a man that's pledged himself to you. A dragon's word is worth its weight in gold. Don't forget his mate bond and offered scale. He's yours for life." Elena casually walks into the room and flops into the recliner opposite Aurora and Sebastian. Aurora's cheeks are cherry red, and Sebastian looks like he wants to kill something.

"Elena? I have questions. The wolf's mate bond seems to be much different than the dragon's." I figured I'd ask since I believe I'm the only one not threatened by Alaric's arrival on the scene.

"Jayce, to be honest, there's not a lot that's different between the two species when it comes to choosing a mate. It's exactly the same by sight and scent. To a dragon, its mate is its greatest treasure. A dragon's hoard means nothing to them once they find their mate." Elena draws in a deep breath before beginning again.

"Unlike wolves, there is no bite needed to forge the bond. Dragons offer a scale, a piece of themselves to their mate. That, and a skull, of course." Elena looks down to her phone, briefly types on it, then looks back up.

"Unlike wolves, dragons cannot live without their mate, except if there's a hatchling. The remaining mate lives only for that hatchling. Like wolves, dragons only get one shot at a true mate." Elena's phone pings again, and we watch her eyes scan the message. Her fingers fly over the screen before she looks up.

"Nicodeamus needs to explain a bit of history to everyone. We need to cast his video up on the big screen TV." I take the phone from Elena and pair it with the TV. Carefully, I balance the phone under the TV so Nico can see us. I hit dial and connect the call.

"What do you mean it's on video, you giant furball! All of them won't fit on this tiny screen." Watching how animated Nicodeamus can get is quite comical. In the background, you can hear Dimitri tell Nicodeamus to look at his phone.

"Oh! Hi! Umm, okay, so congratulations, Aurora, on gaining your dragon mate. Sebastian, stop being a grumpy ass! I see the faces you're making behind my daughter!" As soon as the words leave Nicodeamus's mouth, Elena gets up and slaps Sebastian on the back of his head. The growl that comes from Elena is enough to straighten him out quickly.

"Thanks, love," Nicodeamus says before clearing his voice to continue.

"You probably have a ton of questions. I've been answering them the best I can by messaging Elena. The past was a dark time—a lot of magic and mystery. The alpha Vladimir was an evil, evil man." Nicodeamus looks down as he gathers his thoughts.

"He possessed blood mages and kept the Strigoi on a leash. He used blood magic to subdue your mother's mates to have us all castrated. If it wasn't for Andre's spy network and Dimitri's quick thinking, you wouldn't be here." Nicodeamus reaches up to wipe a stray tear from his eye.

"Rumors spread a while back that Vladimir still lives. I'll be honest, I didn't check his body before I set your mother's body on fire. I also didn't get to watch the whole thing burn to ash." He ponders that thought for a few minutes, then looks back to the phone again.

"Elena, use your contacts with the European Lycans and see what they can find out. We need to be prepared for everything." Elena nods and leaves the room, heading off to make her phone calls.

"Anything else we need to know, Nicodeamus?" I ask as I watch my brother and Sebastian take notes. Only Aurora seems disturbed by the information.

Nicodeamus watches Aurora closely before speaking. "My beautiful, powerful daughter. Elena was correct when she said a dragon cannot live without its mate. You die, so will Alaric. Your wolven mates will be left behind to wish for death. You are a special case, and I'm not sure what will happen to you if one of your mates die." Nicodeamus's sadness is apparent as he speaks to Aurora. All I can do is move to Aurora's side and run my fingers through her hair. I feel my eyes turn wolven as I stare at Sebastian. He's not even trying to comfort Aurora.

"What the fuck is your problem, man! Can't you see our mate is in pain! Can you get over yourself for five fucking minutes?" I reach down to take Aurora from Sebastian and pass her off to Dominik. It's interesting to see my larger twin shocked by my actions. I'm not a fighter, nor am I even a beta, but our mate needs us, and Sebastian is being a self-absorbed jerk. Sebastian stands and goes toe to toe with me, looking down at me like I'm nothing.

"What the fuck do you think you're going to do to me, omega? You're weak and soft and can't fight your way out of a paper bag." Sebastian's sky blue eyes turn the white-blue of his wolf. I know I'm in trouble, but I won't back down. He's trying to use his power to dominate me. For once, it doesn't feel oppressive like it usually would. I hear Nicodeamus in the background start to laugh.

"It's about bloody time Jayce stood up for himself. Good for you, lad, good for you!" Nicodeamus is proud of me? Wow.

While I'm distracted, Sebastian takes this opportunity to strike. He grabs me by my shoulders and attempts to throw me. I squat down like Dimitri taught me and grab hold of Sebastian's forearms and use his momentum against him. I pivot and whip my body to the side, sending Sebastian off balance and onto the floor. I shift quickly and grab him by the throat. I hold him there, growling until I feel Aurora's fingers threading through my fur.

"Sebastian, love, what have I told you about picking on the other mates?" Aurora's power is oppressive as she speaks. Sebastian is squirming under me, trying to escape.

"Jayce, love, please release Sebastian. I believe you made your point that he cannot pick on you anymore." I release Sebastian as asked. When I look up, I see Elena in the doorway with tears streaming down her cheeks. Her son's actions disappoint and hurt her. I let out a huff of a breath and stand next to my twin. I don't bother shifting back. I don't want to talk to anyone at the moment.

"When did he get so fucking strong?" Sebastian is pissed off that I put him down. You know what? I can't wait for the dragon to get here and beat his bully ass. Aurora slaps Sebastian across the face to get him to stop.

"What the actual fuck did I tell you about fighting with the other mates? I'm really disappointed in you, Sebastian. You're starting to act like my mother's Lycan mate. I swear to the gods, you even start going down that rabbit hole, and I will fucking rip your throat out my fucking self!" Aurora is screaming and crying at the same time. This really isn't a safe state for her to be in. I look back at Nicodeamus on the screen, and he shoos me toward her. I place my muzzle under her hand and lift up, so her hand rests on my head. I gently place the weight of my wolven body against her hip, trying to comfort her.

Nicodeamus's voice booms through the speakers. "You have a village to liberate. Get your heads out of your collective asses and go free the remaining bears." We turn as one and nod. Nicodeamus is right; we got off task and forgot what had to be done.

I turn to walk out of the room and head toward the front door. I sense my brother, Aurora, and Sebastian on my heels. We are soon joined by the five Dire Wolves from our pack at the Alpha House's front. Everyone shifts, and we head into the woods, following Aurora and Dominik up north into the mountains. After crossing a few small streams and climbing up a hill to the cliff's edge, we can look down on the village below us. Aurora is the first to shift back and look at all of us.

"The center house is the only one with a basement of any size. From what my father told me about Strigoi, they tend to nest together and sleep in a pile during the day. The leader will be in the center of the pile. We will systematically search all the outlying houses first before we converge on the center house." We descend upon the town like phantoms, moving silently through the remaining shadows along the edge of the town.

Aurora moves directly to the center house and begins to freeze the wood, making it brittle. Dominik and I search several houses, finding nothing of interest in any of them. Seven Dire Wolves and Sebastian join Aurora at the center house, which now looks like a giant ice castle. I cannot sense nor find any signs of life anywhere in the compound. As far as we know, the Strigoi have eaten all the bears.

Aurora and Sebastian start moving as one, using their talons to rip the boards off the house. Sometimes, I think it must be nice to be a Lycan and be able to do shit like that. Several moments pass until they have all the walls ripped off the house. The stench of rot and sulfur fill my nose, causing me to sneeze. The Strigoi are definitely down there.

Sebastian leaps onto the roof and begins to rip the wood off of the house. Aurora watches closely as Sebastian starts to remove the rooftop. Movement can be heard below the floorboards. Aurora's beast smirks and raises an eyebrow as she cocks her head to listen to the movement. A few of the Dires shift back to human and start to remove the furniture from the house. Dominik and I move to flank Aurora's great white Lycan beast as we wait for the last of the roof and furniture to be removed.

Eventually, Sebastian leaps down and lands right next to us. I turn my face to the sun, which is directly overhead. Now is the time to rip up the floorboards. Aurora and Sebastian move as one and begin at the room's outer edges, ripping up the floor. Shrieks and screams can be heard down below as the Strigoi start to panic and try to hide from the sun.

The other seven Dire Wolves move into position around the house's perimeter, making sure none try to escape through tunnels. Aurora suddenly stops and tilts her head, listening to something I can't hear.

*There might be a child left down there."*Aurora is beside herself, thinking about the defenseless little one that could possibly be down there.

She also knows it could be a trap to lure her down. Her growls rattle the floorboards as her talons sink back into the wood. Her drive to destroy this house is fueled by her need to find the possible child below. Sebastian joins her in the destruction, and soon, only a three-foot-wide section is left. The scent of ash is thick in the air from the Strigoi, who couldn't get to cover. We all peer down into the basement. About a dozen are left, but no signs of the child.

Plank by plank, Aurora and Sebastian rip up the floor. Off to the side, I notice a small tunnel by the bookshelf. I don't think it's big enough for a Strigoi, but who knows, a small one could possibly make it in there. The last of the planks are removed, and the Strigoi are reduced to ash and bone. I leap down into the basement and approach the tunnel.

In the far back is a small bear cub—the last survivor of the bear clan. I whimper at the cub, and it slowly waddles its way out of the tunnel to me. I gently pick it up by the scruff of its neck and leap out of the remains of the basement. Aurora quickly comes to my side, sniffing at the cub. Her shift comes quickly, and my mate takes the cub from me. The little cub rolls onto its back, giving Aurora its belly. She smiles and starts walking.

"Our job is done here. Let's go home." Aurora doesn't even turn to look at us; she continues to walk, carrying her precious cargo.

We walk in silence back to the compound following Aurora. We arrive, and Sebastian's mother runs up to Aurora, looking at the cub in her arms. I didn't know cubs could shift that young, to be honest. I know Dire Wolves don't shift until we're at least five years old. Elena attempts to take the cub from Aurora, and she growls at her. I shift back and slowly approach the two of them.

"The cub may be hungry. We should probably take it to the kitchen and feed it." Aurora's mercury orbs land on me, and she gives me a gentle smile.

A slight nod of her head sends me into the house before her, opening the doors en route to the kitchen. Before raiding the fridge, I set Aurora and the cub up in her favorite window seat. I make bacon, eggs, and ham for them. I also thin slice some brown trout filet's I found in the bottom of the fridge from Dominik's fishing trip yesterday. I carefully arrange the platter and bring it over to Aurora and the cub. I can't help but laugh; Aurora is still naked from her shift and holding a bear cub against her chest, softly singing to it. Definitely not typical Aurora behavior.

Speak of the devil, Dominik comes strolling in with a pair of shorts and a T-shirt for me and one of our T-shirts for Aurora. He stops dead, watching her with the cub. I can bet that he and I have the same thought; we can't wait to see Aurora with one of our pups. Dominik slides in close to the window seat and offers to hold the cub so Aurora can put the shirt on.

She reluctantly hands the cub over and quickly puts the shirt on. Her eyes lock on the tray of food in my hands, and she waves me over. I wiggle a strip of crispy bacon at Aurora, and she lunges forward, biting the bacon strip in half. In the back of my mind, I fear for my cock's safety when she does shit like that. Dominik gives me the same look. Yeah, we thought the same thing.

Aurora tears through the platter of food like there's no tomorrow; the only thing left behind is the ham and the fish strips. Aurora makes the *give me* motion with her hands, and Dominik hands the cub back to her. I bring the fish closer, and you can see the cub's nose sniffing the air. He starts making a distress call and tries to scramble toward the food. Aurora makes a soft growl to correct the cub, and it immediately obeys and settles back down on her lap. Strip by strip, Aurora feeds the cub while Dominik and I watch.

As I look around the kitchen, something dawns on me. Where is Sebastian? He never detaches himself from Aurora for too long. My eyes scan the area outside the window that overlooks the backyard. Sebastian isn't there either.

I lock eyes with my brother and speak only to him. *Where's his royal ass-ness?* I know it's not nice to call names, but Sebastian is a royal pain in the ass. Dominik looks away for a moment, scanning the room and outside the nearby window.

Not sure. He's been acting rather suspicious lately, Jayce. Ever since he implanted the scale on Aurora, he's been off—even more so than usual. Dominik furrows his brows and shrugs his shoulders lightly. I catch the change in Aurora's eye color before she speaks, and I know we're busted.

"Guys, it's not nice to have private conversations in front of others. You know I don't like it." Her eyes lock with ours only for a moment before looking back to the cub in her lap.

"We're just concerned. Sebastian has been acting odd lately—even more so than usual." I keep my eyes downcast. I don't want to challenge my love. Dominik stays quiet as well, waiting for Aurora to speak again. The cub has fallen asleep on her lap as her fingers gently move through the baby's fur.

"I went to bed naked with him last night, and he didn't even try anything. Something is eating at him, and I don't think it's just the prince. I sent Andre off to investigate Sebastian's bloodline further." Aurora's eyes flicker between mercury and steel-grey. I can tell the subject is bothering her, but at least I wasn't the only one sensing it.

Before I get the chance to continue the conversation, Sebastian decides to stroll into the kitchen like nothing's wrong. He gives Aurora his usual megawatt smile and offers her a single flower. She regards the flower, then gently takes it.

"The baby just fell asleep. You missed all the fun, Bash." He just smirks at Aurora in typical Sebastian fashion before heading to the fridge to grab a beer.

"I bet," is all he says before returning his gaze to his phone and typing away on it. I hear the low grumble from Aurora. I honestly believe, one of these days, she's going to shove that phone so far up his ass the proctologist will call it a lost cause.

"Sebastian? I want dick," Aurora says, so matter-of-fact. His eyes never leave his phone. He mutters something incoherent, sounding almost like "we'll get it at the store" or something along those lines. Aurora shakes her head, scoops up the cub, and walks out the back door.

I can feel her aggravation clear as day through the bond. I'd love to find out what's so fucking important on that phone that would cause Sebastian to start ignoring Aurora. I motion for Dominik to follow me, and we head outside to walk away from the main part of the compound. Something isn't right, but I can't keep dwelling on it. Aurora already has one unstable mate; she doesn't need Dominik and I to follow the asshole down the same rabbit hole. We continue walking into the woods in silence, trying to figure out how to handle this mess.

CHAPTER 8
Dominik

My brother and I walk into the woods to clear our heads. I really want to believe our issue with Sebastian is just him trying to keep Aurora for himself. Now that his behavior has changed, I'm blaming it on the idea that a real alpha joining our ranks has him on edge.

"Jayce, did you notice how attached Aurora is to the cub already? I think her next heat is coming soon." I raise an eyebrow and wiggle it at Jayce. He shoves me and shakes his head.

"Really, Dominik? Though, you're probably right. You saw how she was with Lia. I'm concerned about Aurora and this battle. I know she's powerful, but none of us are immortal. I mean, she's going to protect her father, which may put her in more danger." Jayce brings up a valid point. We need Nicodeamus with us since his dragon's sight is far better than any other creatures on the battlefield —besides, maybe, Aurora's.

"He's going to be a sitting duck for the dragons. If we can keep the ground troops away from him, he should be able to defend himself enough." We keep walking, discussing little things here and there about how we should approach this battle. Our major concerns are to keep Aurora alive and to keep Nico from getting killed.

After what seems like forever, we arrive at the lake Aurora told us about. It reminds me of that lake in the movie where the giant alligator eats the cow. The water is perfectly flat like a mirror. The air is still and all you can hear are the birds and wildlife moving around. I can see why she comes up here to think things through. Jayce and I flop into the sand and watch the birds on the other side of the lake.

We remain at the lake for a few hours, catching up on different things. Hell, we even had time to call Alec who broke the news of his wedding next summer. Something positive finally happened for Alec. We're so happy for him.

As we get up to leave, we hear an eagle's cry that is cut off halfway through. Jayce and I look at each other before we head in the direction the noise came from. We find several golden-brown feathers on the forest floor mixed in with the moss when we reach the area. Tiny droplets of blood are splattered on random leaves here and there. We follow this weak blood trail until we find a crossbow bolt covered in blood and feathers.

Who would shoot a bird with a crossbow? That doesn't make any sense. There's what looks like a drag mark along the forest floor, and the blood trail is heavier here. It looks like someone took a paintbrush, dipped it in blood, and painted the moss. We follow the blood to its end, and over the edge of the rock face, we see what made the trail. An eagle lays prone in the valley below us. Jayce was the first to be able to form words.

"No!" He leaps over rocks and scales down to the valley below. I'm frozen in my vantage point, watching everything as if it were happening in slow motion. Every step, every noise is slower and drawn out as one of my worst nightmares came to life. If that's Andre down there, we would have to tell Aurora. Jayce looks up to me as he kneels by the body. His wolf rips free of his body, exploding into existence and howling its grief into the wind. It's as I had feared: Andre has been murdered.

I feel Jayce's pain and anguish through the bond, and Aurora's haunting tone soon fills the air. One by one, pack members join Aurora in her eerie howl. We know it's only a matter of minutes before the pack starts making its way here. Jayce anxiously paces the valley, whining and whimpering. His anxiety is understandable; our beloved mate is going to be on the warpath.

The sound of paws thundering through the forest can be heard long before the pack can be seen. My eyes focus on the pebbles near me as they vibrate from the paws' staccato rhythm hitting the ground. Aurora lets out a location howl, which Jayce promptly answers to give her proper bearings.

Soon enough, that great, white beast of a Lycan hybrid comes into view. She's clawing and shredding everything that gets in her way. Sebastian is right behind her, with his mother trailing close behind. The rest of the pack brings up the rear.

Aurora whips past me, launching herself across the divide to the other side. She repeats the leap back and forth until she reaches the bottom. Aurora's shift comes quickly as her human form falls to its knees, her wails and cries echoing through the valley. Her hand shakes as she hesitates to touch Andre's prone form. Aurora withdraws her hand several times before she finally rests it on his feathers.

Jayce shifts back to his human form and rests a hand on Aurora's shoulder. No one else dares to go down there with her. Aurora doesn't handle emotions well, and to interfere now would more than likely end in a death sentence. Sebastian comes to stand beside me and rests his hand on my shoulder.

"She's going to need all of us after this. Her thirst for vengeance is going to burn brighter than the sun. No more macho male bullshit, right guys?" Hopefully, we have a truce until we get this shit storm settled.

Sebastian moves to the edge and looks down at Aurora and Jayce. I'm not noticing any signs of remorse or sympathy for what Aurora is going through. Yup, I still don't like Sebastian. Aurora takes the shredded remains of Jayce's shirt and wraps Andre up like a bird mummy. Now, Jayce chooses to embrace her and hold her tightly. Thankfully, Aurora accepts his affection before she tells him what she's planning on doing.

"Oh, this ought to be interesting," Sebastian states flatly. I guess my brother will see what it's like to get a piggyback ride from a half-crazed, grieving Lycan hybrid.

Aurora shifts back to her beast's form and places the hoop of fabric in her mouth so she can carry Andre. Her eyes lock on Jayce and motion for him to climb on. Reluctantly, he climbs onto her back and wraps his legs around her waist. Aurora launches herself at the rock wall, sinking her talons into the sandstone to gain purchase on the almost vertical ascent. Foot by foot, she climbs steadily with Jayce on her back and Andre's death shroud in her mouth. Unlike my descent, she's not launching herself back and forth. I've never witnessed her move so cautiously before in all the time I've known her.

Before she reaches the top, Sebastian and I reach down to help them over the edge. I back up for a few moments to give Aurora and Jayce some time to breathe. Cautiously I move forward and hold out my hands, waiting for Aurora to either drop Andre into my hands or refuse.

I watch Aurora look between me and Elena, who gives her a somber nod. Aurora lowers her head and releases Andre's body into my hands. I'm almost overcome with emotion from holding our good friend's body. Gently, I cradle Andre against me and watch my mate as she shifts back to her human form.

"How'd it happen? Did you see it?" Aurora's voice quivers as tears roll down her face. Her eyes are locked on the death shroud in my arms. They shift between human and beast faster than I can keep track of. Jayce steps forward and lays a hand on Andre.

"We heard an eagle cry. The second time it called out, it was cut short. Dominik and I started walking in the direction we last heard the cry come from. First, we found feathers, then blood. Eventually, we found a bloody crossbow bolt with feathers on it." Sighing softly, I have to swallow hard, attempting to keep my voice from breaking. Aurora needs me to be strong for her right now.

"Further in, we found blood marks where we suspect the eagle dragged itself. When we got here, I looked over the edge and prayed it wasn't Andre. I didn't hesitate and got to the bottom as fast as I could. His body was cold when I got there." Jayce looks up, the raw pain evident in his eyes as he looks at Aurora. Not only was he feeling hers, but his own pain runs bone-deep. My brother is so comfortable with his emotions that his tears roll freely down his cheeks. Aurora grabs ahold of Jayce and squeezes him tightly. Her eyes are practically glowing with the raw power she's struggling to contain.

"We need to call my father and Dimitri home and gather the Dire Wolves. To strike at someone close to me is an act of war. There will be no survivors. I swear on my blood that he will be avenged, and the murderer will know pain like no other." Aurora closes her eyes for several minutes, then draws in a deep breath.

"Father and the prince know what happened. I've been advised on what to do. Let's go home. We need to build a funeral pyre for Andre in the customs of his people. Dad and the team will be here by nightfall. At midnight, we perform the ceremony." Aurora releases Jayce and kisses his forehead.

"Please, carry us back. Shift for me, my love." Aurora's eyes are all human, tears welling up and threatening to break free as she turns to take Andre from me. Jayce nods at our mate and shifts back to his wolf. Sebastian and I move to assist Aurora onto Jayce's back. Slowly, Jayce leads with his precious cargo. Sebastian and I shift next, following close behind Aurora and Jayce. The pack moves in sync as we head back to the compound.

When we reach the Alpha House, Jayce lays down so Aurora can get off his back easily. Our mate has one hell of a resting bitch face because I can't read what the fuck she's thinking or feeling at the moment. Our immediate family group is the only one that enters the house. We lock the doors behind us as we follow Aurora into the office. She grabs two pillows and lays Andre's body on them. Her eyes raise up and lock on to each of us in turn, sending a chill right to our bones.

"It goes without saying: I want vengeance." She slowly unwraps Andre's body to look upon his fallen form. Her fingers come up to close his golden eyes.

"I need linen, sage, arrowroot, and barberry. Sebastian, your mother should have these in her workshop. Please get them for me." Her eyes are haunting—almost dead looking—without her normal inner light. She's running on autopilot at this point, numb from the loss of a parental figure.

Sebastian moves forward and kisses Aurora's temple before leaving the room on his mission. Aurora watches Sebastian leave, then looks at the two of us. The gears are turning in her head, and I'm not sure we're going to like where she's going.

"When your pack arrives, catch them up on *everything*." We nod and remain quiet as she looks over Andre's body. She takes notes of the entrance and exit wound, her canines visibly pressing into her bottom lip as she does so. I can't tell if she realizes that she's doing it or if she's just so lost in her thoughts. I watch her eyes flicker between human and her liquid mercury. She's in conversation with someone.

"Aurora? Is there anything we can do to assist you?" I'm concerned about her bottling up her feelings over this. I watch her emotions flicker over her face, as well as a wave of scales and fur. She breathes in deeply, composing herself, before looking up to me.

"Don't leave me. I'm barely holding myself together." Aurora looks between Jayce and me. I can clearly see how distraught she is. I will strike down anyone who brings this level of pain on her.

"I know I speak for the both of us when I say we won't leave you. I will be your sword, and Jayce your shield. Stay with us tonight, and let us watch over you in your sleep." I move behind Aurora and wrap my arms around her waistline, trying to lend her my strength. I kiss the back of her head as she continues her work. I can feel through the bond that she's struggling to remain strong for everyone.

Sebastian returns with the ingredients Aurora asked for and sets them on the table before her. He looks at my positioning and then over at Jayce. "I've made arrangements for everyone at the airport. They should be here within the hour. Mom said the pyre is almost ready." Sebastian looks almost concerned for Aurora, which is nice for a change. Aurora smiles at him and nods before returning to what she was doing. Sebastian takes a seat by the door, watching Aurora work on Andre's remains.

I watch closely over Aurora's shoulder as she mixes the herbs and then starts tearing the linen. Everything is set for when the others arrive. I sit down in the office chair behind Aurora and pull her into my lap. She's trying to remain strong for everyone. Aurora slowly turns her head to look at me. I do my best to smile and be the strength she needs.

"Thanks, Dominik." She sighs softly before stopping her work.

"I think I'll take you up on your offer. It's probably not smart for me to be alone while this upset. Ask Dimitri what happened the last time." Aurora raises both eyebrows and rolls her eyes. I remember Dimitri retelling the story. We definitely don't have time to clean up a mess like that.

The crunching of rocks from tires in the driveway catches everyone's attention. Aurora looks at Sebastian, and he goes to retrieve Dimitri and Nicodeamus. Aurora slowly extracts herself from my lap and goes to stand in front of the desk. Eventually the knob turns, and Dimitri sticks his head in. His normally bright hazel eyes are bloodshot, and his cheeks are stained with tears.

Nicodeamus shoves past Dimitri and bands his arm tightly around Aurora. Her arms fly up and around his neck. Dimitri moves slowly toward the desk and stands there, staring at his fallen friend. He stays statue still for what seems like forever. Aurora comes up alongside him to wrap her arms around his waist. They stand there in silence before Aurora breaks away to start the binding process with the linens. Elena eventually enters and clings onto Nicodeamus, resting her head on his chest.

She whispers softly. "How does she know how to do this? She's not old enough to have seen it done." Nicodeamus smirks and kisses the top of Elena's head.

"I taught her while I was flying back here. Her dragon side is quite strong for being a hybrid." He rests his head on top of Elena's and continues to watch Aurora work. Sebastian returns and remains in the doorway.

"We are ready when you are." Sebastian raises his hand and offers it for Aurora to take. Ever so carefully, Aurora picks up Andre's body and holds it tight to her chest. She cradles his body like a mother would a baby as she approaches Sebastian. Her head turns quickly, first locking on the table, then on me.

"Dom baby, please grab the remaining herbs to bring with us." I nod in agreement, and her eyes land on Nicodeamus.

"Father, I need your fire." Nicodeamus audibly swallows, then nods to Aurora. Only when she felt everything was in place did she allow Sebastian to lead her out.

We walk to what would typically be the training circle. The sandpit will contain the embers and stop them from spreading. The heat alone will possibly turn some of the sand into glass. The entire Lycan and newly arrived Dire pack gather to witness a ceremony that hasn't been performed in centuries.

Elena runs up to where Aurora positioned herself at the top of the pyre. Carefully, Elena lays out the blood-red cloth with the embroidered Marelup crest as well as the symbol for the Golden Eagles. Aurora reverently places Andre's wrapped body on the fabric. She folds three of the four corners to cover him, leaving only his wrapped head exposed.

We watch her layout the spices as well as crystals that Elena must have given her. Aurora draws in a deep breath and raises her hands above her. As she does so, we watch her arms shift and become covered in thick, white, armored dragon scales. Her snow-white talons appear even more menacing by torchlight. Everyone falls silent and kneels before her and the great pyre.

"My people!" We hear and feel Aurora's words and power through the pack bond.

"One of our own was murdered right here on our land." Her eyes scan the gathered wolves, searching for any sign of the betrayer.

"He was sent on a mission for me that only he could complete. He died on his way back to me, to us." She keeps a close watch over everyone present.

"Andre and Dimitri were tasked with my protection from the moment I drew my first breath upon this Earth. For over two hundred years, they were the closest things to parents that I've known." Aurora's voice gains the familiar growl of her beast.

"A small piece of me died with him today." Her eyes move from Dimitri to Nicodeamus and gives him the signal to shift.

Nicodeamus moves behind the pyre and shifts to his Ice Dragon, his head adorned with a crown of horns—denoting his age and lineage. His great head is raised above Aurora, waiting for her next signal.

"I..." Aurora hesitates for a moment, overwhelmed with emotion as tears stream down her cheeks. It's then I notice the scale on her chest glows faintly. Her right hand rests over it, and she calms almost instantly, her mercury eyes returning to steel-grey.

"Today, I lay to rest a man I am proud to call a father figure. I lay to rest a man that has put his life on the line time and time again for my mother and me. Today, I lay to rest my best friend." Aurora shifts her right hand back to human and slits her palm over Andre's body. She lays her bleeding hand upon him.

"With my blood, I swear to seek out Andre's killer and rip his heart from his chest. I will not rest until it's done." Aurora holds her bleeding hand up to the crowd. She turns her head to look at her father and nods.

You can hear the clicks of the dragon's ignitor firing up before the roar of flames fills the arena. Most watch in horror as Nicodeamus bathes not only the pyre in flames, but Aurora too. We see her stand there, watching over Andre as he burns. Out of the corner of my eye, I catch Jayce on the phone. I can read his lips; he's reassuring whoever is on the other end that everything is ok. I return to watching the flames and the pyre burn brightly in the night.

A miracle happens: a smoke wisp shaped like an eagle takes flight straight up into the night sky from the flames. Gasps are heard around the fire. Apparently, that's what we were hoping and waiting for. Jayce switches his phone call to video just before Aurora walks out of what's left of the burning pyre. Neither a scratch on her nor a hair out of place. Sebastian quickly offers Aurora his fleece button-down, which she gladly accepts. Aurora smiles brightly at us and looks up into the night sky.

"Did you see? I freed Andre's soul and sent him off to be with his ancestors." She's beaming proudly at her accomplishment. I only heard stories of events like this when I was a child. I honestly didn't think things like this were possible. Then again, a Dragon-Lycan hybrid shouldn't be possible either.

Jayce comes over, back to talking on the phone. I can tell by the changes in his tone that more than one person is on the line. I tilt my head to the side, looking at my brother. Jayce holds up one finger, then ends the call.

"The connection is stronger than we thought. Alaric called Alex directly when he felt Aurora's distress. He was ready to fly here, which would have destroyed everything we've been working for." Jayce's eyes focus on Aurora and reaches out to touch Alaric's scale. He smiles sweetly at her before looking back at the rest of us.

"I need to get everyone settled. If you need me, call please." His eyes are glassy from unshed tears; he's trying to be strong for Aurora.

I know he's going to find a private place to cry. I turn to look at Sebastian, and the fucker is back on his phone again. What the actual fuck could be so important that he never puts that fucking thing down?

"Hey, Sebastian! Got a minute?" He slowly looks up from his phone and nods. He continues to type on his phone for several moments before he finally walks over.

"What's up, Dominik?" Sebastian says with that almost bored tone of his. If only Aurora didn't have that *no hitting the other mates* rule; I'd love to deck him with something hard. I have to admit, Sebastian has that swagger that makes him attractive. But his attitude? Shit, I can't wait for the dragon to get here and knock him down a peg.

"Sebastian, I need your help organizing the clean up as well as the training for the Dires who just arrived. Right now, I believe it's best for Aurora to take it easy and heal from her loss." The Lycans are his people, and now we're almost on equal footing with both of our species here together. Sebastian's sky blue eyes change to the white-blue of his wolf before he smirks at me.

"Finally accepted your place in the family, I see. It's about fucking time. I'll organize my people, you handle yours. Training starts tomorrow. As for the mess, give me ten of your people, and I'll get ten of mine to return the training grounds back to normal." His look is one of challenge, and to be honest, I can't fucking take it anymore.

My Dire Wolf rips free of my body, pissed off to all hell. I feel different; my vision is different. Most of my vision shows shades of colors that outline the beings before me like a light is cast behind them. My night vision has evolved. I watch the blood pump through the bodies before me. I hear voices around me, and even Sebastian looks stunned.

"Dude, your eyes are mercury like Aurora's! Fuck!" That explains it. I see the fear in Sebastian's eyes as I stare at him. I stalk forward, growling at him.

As I get ready to lunge, I feel Aurora's hand on my back. I immediately abandon my original plan to attack Sebastian. Carefully, I turn to look up at Aurora, her liquid mercury eyes looking back at me. The look of wonder on her face is worth all the aggravation that Sebastian caused. I would give anything to remain in this moment forever.

"I see you have my vision, Dominik. Use it wisely; it takes a bit to get used to." Aurora leads me away from Sebastian and sits down on a nearby bench.

I shift back to my human form and take a seat next to her. I turn my body so I'm facing her, gently taking her hands in mine. "Dom, my love, I know things are tense between you and Sebastian. I get it. It's a constant measuring contest between you two. I know Sebastian can get on your nerves. Hell, he constantly gets on mine." Aurora grips my hands tightly as she looks at me. I know deep down she's in Hell, but right now, she's more worried about me than herself. I look down to our joined hands, then back up to her. I can feel the moment my eyes go back to my human hazel; no more outlines and shining silhouettes.

"Thanks, Aurora. I'm not concerned about Sebastian at the moment; I'm more worried about you. Sebastian can go to fucking Hell for all I care. I want to make sure you're okay emotionally, mentally, and physically. Death of a loved one is never easy to deal with." Slowly, I lean forward and gently kiss her lips. Aurora lets out a pleased sigh and smiles at me. Then she cups my cheek and rests her forehead against mine. Through direct contact of the bond, I feel everything: her love for me, the pain she's hiding, and the fear of losing one of us in the war.

Please be patient, Dominik. All will work out in the end. Aurora's voice is a breathy whisper in my mind. Her words embrace me and strengthen my resolve. We'll be okay. I know we will. I lightly place my hands over hers and remain still, enjoying the connection.

"Kids, I hate to break up this love fest, but we need to plan to train and then to depart." Like all parents, Nicodeamus has the absolute worst timing. Aurora rolls her eyes at her father before she pulls away from me. She stands abruptly and salutes Nico, then walks off in a modified march. I shrug my shoulders at Nicodeamus before I stand.

"I'll go grab some pants and make sure everyone is settled in properly for tomorrow's training push." I also decide to salute Nicodeamus, which inflates the Dragon King's ego even further. Thankfully, he doesn't realize we're being complete wise asses and that it wasn't done out of respect but sarcasm.

CHAPTER 9

Aurora

The next morning, I wake up alone in Dom's room. He and Jayce must have woken up early to get everyone started on their tasks. Silently, I return to my room and pull on a pair of leggings and a Bad Wolves T-shirt from my closet. My guitar amp is by the door, offering me solace from the pain I'm in. Yeah, I need to play something straight from the heart this morning. Pete is standing in the meeting hall, dusting my throne.

"Hey, Pete!" He jumps at the sudden noise. After realizing it's me, he smiles and approaches me.

"Morning, My Queen. What can I do for you today?" Pete is ever so eager to please me. It helps that he's an omega, and their drive to please their alpha is all-consuming at times.

"I need you to grab your bass and grab our drummer. I need to play this morning." My eyes well up with tears that threaten to break.

Pete looks panicked, then runs off to do my bidding. I walk around the main hall to open all the windows and set up my amp by my throne. I start to tune my guitar, preparing to play a song that embodies my feelings right now. Footsteps fill the hall, and I look up to see Pete and the usual crew ready to play together. To achieve the perfect acoustics, we turn our amps to face the halls. The guys look at me expectantly as I move to take my spot in the middle of the room.

"*Cemetery Gates* from Pantera. Pete, be prepared to take over vocals if I falter during the song." Pete gives me a nod before I start the opening riff of the song.

I climb onto my throne and keep the tone going. When it comes to the lyrics, they flow from me, dripping with the pain I'm feeling. My voice is almost raw with emotion. I swallow hard as I go into the riffs between lyrics, pouring my heart and soul into nailing this song and making it perfect. Out of the corner of my eye, I watch the guys move around as they play along. My guys and several others file into the hall as I sing. My eyes close as I tilt my head to the ceiling, tears escaping out of the corner of my eyes rolling freely down my cheeks.

I hear Dimitri enter and sniffle. My eyes open and I slide off my throne then begin to walk toward him. My eyes shift to that of my beast, and I feel scales ripple up my arms then recede. When I pronounce the word *gates* before the big solo, the word is growled out with the voice of my beast—its fierceness coming through strongly. At the end of the song, I practically howl out the word *gates*. My guitar cries, holding the final tone until I finally release it. I feel a little better after playing that song. It happened to be one of Andre's favorites.

Next, I decided to do another favorite of his. I choose to play *Bulls on Parade* by Rage Against the Machine. I have to say, it's hard to play this song as well as the great Tom Morello does, but I give it my all. I end up jumping around the room and jamming out as Pete tries to scream the lyrics like they should be. The song changes the room's feel from the gloom that my first song invoked to a bouncing, playful tone. It doesn't last as long as I'd like it to. Unfortunately, now I have adulting to do—damn responsibilities.

"Thanks, everyone, for coming and watching us perform! You know me by now; I needed to vent through my music." I walk over and hug Dimitri tightly. His partner for the last who knows how many hundreds of years died yesterday. I know the pain of his loss has to be hitting him harder than it's hitting me. We remain in each other's arms, silently crying.

"D..." I nuzzle his cheek like I did as a pup.

I can't help but look at him through tear-filled eyes. He's trying to be strong for me and hide his pain, but I see right through that big, grumpy bear. I kiss his cheek and attempt to smile at him. "We have a murderer to hunt, D. We will hang whomever it is by their entrails and beat them like a pinata." I get half a laugh out of Dimitri.

"Baby girl, you make me very proud of you. For once, I will not temper your rage. Release the beast and let it shred anything in its wake. We will dance on the bones of our enemies!" Dimitri's Romainian accent is very thick when he speaks. He's not hiding who he is anymore.

I felt my beast stir when Dimitri called for it. To be honest, I want nothing more than to hunt the fucker that killed Andre. I want to kill everyone and everything that had a hand in his death—my prime suspects at the moment: several high ranking Lycans and Sebastian. Andre went off to gather information on a total of five beings and died before he was able to relay what he found. I'm now positive there is a traitor in our midst somewhere. I will carry on as usual, as not to show my hand yet.

"Back to work, everyone! The war won't win itself!" Everyone scatters, and all that's left are my mates, father, and Dimitri.

I can tell by how my father is looking at me that he knows something is on my mind. "Guys—dad, Dimitri, and I need to go talk about the old days. I want to learn more about my mother and the castle." Jayce is the first to smile. He runs up to hug and kiss me. Dominik takes his time and picks me up, kissing me passionately before setting me down. Sebastian comes to stand before me, attempting to lock eyes with me—almost in challenge. My beast isn't having it and makes him turn his eyes away. I lightly grip his jaw and turn his head to face me.

"Please don't test me." Sebastian smirks and kisses me, nipping at my bottom lip for good measure. Forever the wise ass. My father approaches and offers his hand to me. The minute I take his hand, I hear his voice in my head.

I know something is plaguing you, daughter. Is this the reason for the walk? My eyes turn to my father briefly, and I barely nod my head. He squeezes my hand to let me know he saw my answer.

"Come on, D. Let's go!" I extend my hand to Dimitri, wiggling my fingers at him. He half laughs and takes my hand. I almost got him to smile.

Okay, guys, I don't know if trying to talk to both of you at the same time is going to work, but here I go. We have a traitor somewhere here in the compound. I'm not sure who it is, so don't ask. I had Andre investigate four elders and Sebastian's family." My eyes drift between my father and Dimitri as we walk out the door and head toward the stream at the property's southern edge. I know they heard me by how tense their bodies have become. As soon as we get out of range, I stop and stare at both of them. I let out a slow breath, looking at them expectantly. I can see the gears turning between the two of them.

"What made you come to these conclusions, Aurora?" Dimitri is the first to question me. All I can do is breathe in deeply.

"Some of the older Lycans questioned my bloodline, and I overheard them mention Vladimir. They were speaking as if he's still around. It kind of makes me wonder.." I look between the two of them, and I see both of their animals surge to the surface. We stand there in silence. There were suspicions that the old alpha was possibly still alive. We still don't have confirmation, and Andre would have had that answer.

"Andre was bringing me his findings. I never got the answers I was looking for." I lower my eyes to look at the ground. I miss Andre so much. He was my confidant and a mother figure. My father nods slowly, taking in all that I've said.

"The Elders could be old enough to remember the old alpha. The question is, where do their loyalties lie? Sebastian is a mate, so I seriously doubt he would plot against you; but anything could be possible." Nicodeamus rests his hand on my shoulder and gives it a squeeze. I force a smile as I look up at my father.

"I was hoping you would say that, Dad. So, we agree to focus on the Elders and try to figure out which of the four houses has it out for me." My eyes lock on Dimitri, and I watch him straighten up, his shoulders pushed back and chest puffed up.

"D, I need you to watch and listen to the ones who are training. Someone might slip and say something. You know how pups talk." I've never seen Dimitri with such a stern look on his face. He's actually quite menacing looking.

"I will do it gladly, baby girl. Anything for you." He wraps his thick arms around me and hugs me tightly to him. My arms band around his neck and I squeeze him back. I love my mates, but these are the only two that I can completely trust with behind-the-scenes things. I hate having to be suspicious of my people, but something doesn't add up. Reluctantly, I let go of Dimitri and motion for us to head back to the camp.

"Dad, I have a question for you." I turn to face him and tilt my head to the side, thinking about how to phrase the question.

"Before the ascension, why was my wolf insanely jealous of Dimitri having a sexual relationship with anyone? She pretty much claimed him as hers but didn't physically claim him." I watch Dimitri's cheeks burn flame-red from embarrassment. He wasn't the only one embarrassed, but I needed answers. After all, my animal's possessiveness of Dimitri ended the minute she smelled Sebastian. Nico simply laughs. He laughs so hard he's bent at the waist with his hand on his thigh.

"Sorry, daughter... That's a very dragon trait. You were magically bound to Dimitri, so your young animal confused it for the mating bond. It's an honest mistake. In truth, without that bond, you probably would have gone insane and took me with you." Nicodeamus slowly stands up and regains his composure, still smirking at Dimitri.

"I know the stories you told me, old friend, and I'm sorry it happened. If I was able to be with my daughter from the beginning, that bond never would have existed." Nicodeamus looks down after the words leave his mouth. He realizes what he said was a tad insensitive.

"I am grateful for all you've done for us. I am sorry if my words were cruel." Nicodeamus furrows his brows. I'm betting my father isn't used to apologizing when he messes up. Dimitri lets the comment roll off his back. It doesn't even look like it phased him.

He moves closer to my father then gives him one of those side bro-hug things with the exaggerated back-patting and everything. "We're good. We better get back before the others get suspicious."

I roll my eyes and start walking back, ahead of the guys. I listen to the sounds of battle going on in the training grounds. Yup, that's where I'm headed. Why not? I mean, seriously, I have three smoking hot mates who could potentially be shirtless. Shirtless and sweaty with beads of sweat rolling down their well-defined abdomens... Damn, I need to get laid.

I creep through the shadows, observing all the guys in their half-naked glory. Dominik and Pete are sparing, using bow staves. Dominik's muscles elongating and flexing then tightening has me mesmerized. I am so lost in my own little wet dream, I don't even notice when Elena comes up beside me. When I do notice, I scream like a little girl and claw half-way up the tree.

I'm hanging from the tree by my talons when I look down and notice it's only Elena. She's legit laughing her ass off at me. Dominik is now also under the tree, trying not to laugh, along with several others. Just to be an ass, I let go of the tree and fall, so Dominik has to catch me. What a crying shame! He's half-naked and holding me. What's a girl to do? Dominik lets out a heartfelt laugh then kisses my cheek.

"Crazy wolf! Are you trying to give me a heart attack?" He smiles and kisses my cheek again. His lips find my neck, and he nips me gently. Then Dominik lets out a primal growl and starts to walk away with me. Our forward momentum is suddenly halted by Dimitri, who steps in front of us, and my father places his hand on Dominik's shoulder.

"I know that growl, lad. I can't let you follow your instincts. We need Aurora at full strength for this journey and the battles ahead." Nicodeamus isn't budging until I'm released from Dominik's grasp. My feet hit the floor, and I look between my father and Dom. Then it dawns on me; that was a short three months. I step away from the guys, disappointed that I was denied dick. But my father is right; I will slow everyone down if I am heavily pregnant.

"Elena, I need the tea again. Dad, Dimitri, can you two watch over me?" They both smile and nod. Dimitri grabs my hand and starts leading me to his small cabin set off away from everyone. I didn't know the shack he chose was so little. He deserves better. I make a mental note to improve his living conditions when this is all over.

Dimitri leads me into a room off the main one and I freeze in my tracks. It was Andre's room. I walk in slowly. There are so many pictures of us over the years that I didn't know existed. I stare in wonder, watching myself grow up in the photographs—birthdays, holidays; they are all here. I quickly look back to Dimitri, who's in tears like I am.

"He kept a photo album of you growing up. I know he would have wanted you to have it." Dimitri reaches into a drawer, pulls out the album, and sets it on the table beside the bed. Elena's in the doorway, listening to our exchange with tears freely flowing down her cheeks. She can't bring herself to speak and offers me a cup of special tea. I look down at the contents and sniff it. Something's different. My beast surges to the surface, and I shove the tea at her.

"You drink it!" I stare at her, my instincts on high alert. Something isn't sitting right. Elena takes the cup from me and sniffs it, and all the color drains from her face.

"Princess, no! I didn't do this! Someone must have tampered with my herbs." Dimitri's bear makes his presence known as fur ripples down his arms and recedes just as quickly. My father comes up behind him and placed his hand on his shoulder.

"Old friend, we will just have to keep Aurora isolated, that's all. I will try to put her into an ice sleep. It's a state of torpor that some Ice Dragons use to leapfrog through time. If it doesn't work, I'll turn this house into one huge ice cube." My father shrugs his shoulders like it is no big deal. Then again, to him, it probably isn't a big deal.

"Before I sleep, Father, I want to try something for Dimitri." I look to Dimitri and he nods, moving closer to me.

"Please sit, D. My blood healed Sebastian quickly. I'm wondering if it would do the same for you. Perhaps slow the progression of time." I watch the idea process quickly behind my father's eyes. His dragon surges forward just before he runs out of the room. Either I had a stroke of genius, or he doesn't want to witness what I'm going to do. When my father returns, he's holding a goblet, a bottle of vodka, and a spoon. Okay, I'm really puzzled now.

"My brilliant daughter, I completely forgot about the blood bonding. Dimitri, we can bond you to the two of us. It should stop the aging process and possibly reverse it some." Nicodeamus pours about four shots of vodka into the goblet, bites his own wrist, and bleeds into the goblet. He licks his wound, sealing it before he looks at me. I bite my right wrist deeply and hold it over the goblet, making sure the majority of the blood makes it in. Carefully, I pick up the goblet and hold it out to Dimitri. He bites his wrist and bleeds into it —about the same amount as my father did. Nicodeamus looks between Dimitri and me then decides to explain.

"I know you're wondering, why the vodka? It keeps the blood from clotting, and it makes the blood taste better." His eyes turn to Elena.

"Knowledge of this does not leave this room, am I clear?" Elena nods slowly. She's obviously still frightened and sad that she almost assisted in killing me. Since I'm still holding the goblet, I drink about a third of the contents. I immediately feel the power of my father's blood in my body. Carefully, I pass the goblet to my father, and he drinks half of what's left.

Finally, Dimitri gets the remaining blood. He smiles at me quickly before drinking the rest of it. The surge of power that goes through him knocks him to his knees, and I rush over to keep him steady. I feel his muscles tense under my fingertips as they become thick and solid. Almost twenty minutes pass before he lifts his head and looks at me. It's as if I dunked Dimitri in the fountain of youth. He's absolutely handsome. I never noticed how beautiful of a man he was until just now.

"Aurora, please don't look at me like that," Dimitri says softly.

He stands to his full height and stretches his heavily muscled body. He's a mountain of a man. I know part of it has to do with his bear, but damn. Maybe my wolf isn't fucking delusional for thinking of Dimitri as hers. Perhaps it's my heat talking, perhaps not. I would have to revisit this subject once my heat passes.

I laugh softly to myself and turn away from Dimitri to look around Andre's old room. He held onto so many little things that I brought him over the years. All the small animal skulls litter the shelves in his room. Looking at them, I start cracking up. My father comes to stand beside me in front of the shelves of skulls. He starts chuckling to himself.

"I guess you took after me more than I thought. I'm guessing, by the size of these skulls, you were a little one when you started this collection." He tilts his head to look at me, the liquid mercury of his dragon's eyes focused on mine. I nod slowly and look back at my collection.

"At first, it freaked Andre out that I was bringing him my trophies. After a while, he began to look forward to seeing what I would bring him that day." I pick up a cougar's skull and hold it in my hand.

"I was ten when I killed the cougar. The guys were out hunting when it came into our yard. I had chores to get done, so I was in the garden when it attacked me. I guess it didn't or couldn't smell what I was. I felt its teeth sinking into the back of my neck as its claws dug into my ribs. Something came over me and my body went into its first full shift. Before that day, most times, I was only able to shift my hands and canines. It released me and tried to escape, but it didn't get far before I caught up to it and ripped it to shreds." I start laughing as I look over to Dimitri, who's definitely having a proud moment.

"Poor Andre had to deal with not only a freshly shifted she-wolf but cougar parts all over the yard. You know how jumpy Andre could be. He tried so hard to fight his instinct to run. In the end, Dimitri had to watch over me until I shifted back." Dimitri laughs for several moments before regaining his composure.

"She was stuck as her wolf for almost four days. That little, white hellion was like a force of nature, hell-bent on testing out her talons and her newfound strength and speed. Hell, Andre was the only one fast enough to keep up with her when she went hunting." My father beams with pride as he listens to our story. He begins to walk around Andre's room, picking up different pictures—basically catching up on the last two hundred some odd years.

Nicodeamus holds up a picture that I hadn't noticed. I walk over to my father and lean over his shoulder to look at it with him. It's a picture of Sebastian holding me as a baby. I wonder how long Andre hid this picture from me. Sebastian looks so enamored with me, like the sun rose and set with every breath I took. I take out my phone and send my baby picture to Sebastian. I manipulate the photo to have a heart frame with the caption *awe.*

Within a matter of seconds, he sends me several heart emojis and asks where I am. I tell him I'm in Andre's room and I'm being quarantined until my heat is over. He sends me several sad faces. I shake my head and put my phone away.

My father is now on the bed, sitting next to Elena, and they're both looking through the album. She tells him about the night of my arrival and the three months we spent with her and Sebastian. My dad thanked her profusely for caring for me and providing us shelter when we needed it most. I watch the exchange for several minutes until my phone goes off again. It's Jayce, and this time he wants to video chat. I walk to the corner of the room and sit in Andre's rocking chair.

"Hi, love," I say when I see his smiling face. The video changes; he must have cast it to the smart screen in the office.

"Hi, everyone! I'm currently grounded because of my heat." The guys nod, and all start speaking at once.

"Whoa! Settle down. First off, I need to let you know someone tampered with Elena's herbs. I was almost poisoned today." The guys start yelling back and forth, threatening to rip the compound apart.

"We don't need to go that crazy. There is a traitor here, and we've been aware of that for quite some time. I want you to spread the rumor that I'm very ill, and you're not sure if I'm going to survive." I watch the guys ponder what I just said.

Sebastian speaks first. "Are you sure that's wise? I mean, they could attack, and we aren't there to protect you."

"Positive. I have protection, don't worry about that aspect. Besides, I'm in heat, not fucking dead, Bash. Give a girl some credit here." Dimitri prepares to step forward, and I raise my hand to stop him. I don't need my secret weapon revealed quite yet. I look back at the guys.

"Any questions?" The twins look at each other then back to the screen.

"We'll patrol outside to keep appearances up. We need to keep this as legit-looking as possible for it to work." I agree with them and nod slowly.

"Do you want me or your father to make the announcement to the packs?" Sebastian is the next to speak. I bite my bottom lip, pondering what he said. There are very few who know about the tea's existence, and he's one of them.

"I think it's best if you and my father make the announcement together. The king and the first mate standing together makes for a stronger, united front. Say very little about what happened, just that I was somehow poisoned, and your mother is working around the clock and trying everything she can to save me." Sebastian nods then smirks.

"I'll keep the pack and the boys in line until you're able to return." He looks over at the twins and gives them a look I really don't like.

"No need, love," I state flatly.

"It would be far better if my father oversees everything. After all, he is the Dragon King. Who in their right mind would oppose him?" I watch Sebastian's face contort a dozen ways before he reigns in his emotions.

"As you wish, princess," Sebastian says with a mild inflection of a venomous tone.

I keep my eyes steady on him until he leaves the room the twins are in. I signal the twins to watch each other's backs. I carry on with casual conversation as I start writing messages to hold up to them. I'm not sure how far away Sebastian is, and I'm concerned for the twins' safety. I end the video chat and stare at Elena.

"What family do you have left in Romania? Who was your sire?" Gut instinct tells me she's related to Lycan Alpha Vladimir.

My heart hopes I'm wrong. Elena's bottom lip quivers as she looks at me. She starts shifting from foot to foot, showing her nervousness. I can scent the fear in the air—it's rather acrid. Dimitri blocks the door behind her as I wait patiently for her answer. Well, as patiently as I can.

Elena finally speaks. "We are first cousins with Vladimir. I swear, we are only loyal to you." Elena drops to her hands and knees, exposing her throat to me. My eyes narrow as I stare at her, and my hand lands on my father's arm.

I think this is the news that got Andre killed. If I'm correct, either one of the Lupi's—Elena or Sebastian—ordered the hit, or the real puppet master did. I don't bother turning to look at my father.

I feel the rage building within him. It's quite interesting that her herbs are tainted, she's dating my father, and I'm mated to her son. My eyes move to Dimitri, and he notices they have swirled to liquid mercury. He gives me a nod of understanding. He knows I'm talking to my father and that he will be filled in eventually.

I openly pose a question. "Can a mating bond be faked or forced with herbs and magic?" Elena's head whips up, and her face turns as white as snow.

"Yes, daughter, it can. It's how the alpha tricked your mother into being his mate. The elder dame made the drink and cast the spell." Dimitri's and my animal begin to growl. I want to destroy, and I don't care about the repercussions. My eyes land on Elena next. Her life hangs in the balance at this point.

"Was the tea you had given Andre for me laced with anything besides the sleeping tonic? Choose your words wisely." I can hear the guys yelling for me to stop, *don't do it*!

I'm not a pawn or a plaything. Elena is sobbing loudly, her tears falling to the floor. Her cries don't move me or stir any kind of emotion from me. The door behind Dimitri flies open, and the guys scream for me to listen to them. My arms and hands shift to armored gauntlets as I stare down at the woman I once called mother.

"Did you force the bond between Sebastian and I?" I practically roar out the sentence. My heart is aching with the knowledge that perhaps what we have isn't real. The guys all freeze as what I said dawns on them; Sebastian is the only one who is let past Dimitri. He's hesitant as he kneels next to his mother. He wraps his arms around her then looks up to me. The pain in his eyes almost cracks my resolve.

"They have my brother. We thought if I was mated to you..." He's frustrated and hurting, but how can I forgive this betrayal?

"If I knew then what I know now, I would have asked for help." My eyes remain narrowed on Sebastian. His mother is crying, and he's showing the appropriate emotions. He's trying to console her as he looks up at me, hoping for forgiveness.

"Dimitri, was there a brother when you took care of me as a baby?" I can tell when Dimitri begins searching his memory because he starts to bite his lower lip. Damn this fucking heat; I love and hate when he does that.

"I remember a wee little one running around, but I'm not sure if he was introduced as Sebastian's brother or not." Dimitri tilts his head to the side after he finishes speaking, letting me pass judgment.

My eyes fall on my father. He's clearly upset by this new information. If he's anything like me, he feels used. Slowly, my father moves closer to me and rests his hand on the back of my neck.

Daughter, I don't know what to tell you to do. If you suspect them, don't let on that you do. We can use your leniency to our advantage in the long run. They are related to the old alpha. Who knows if they believe as he did. I take his words into consideration before I look back to Elena and Sebastian. I step away from my father and glance at the twins. I know they will stand by me no matter my decision. My eyes fall to Dimitri, who nods and brings his fist over his heart.

"I have come to a decision." Heeding my father's words, I calm myself down and shift my hands and arms back to human.

"For the sake of appearances, Sebastian, you can remain in the Alpha House. You are stripped of the title of First Mate. By rights, it's now Dominik's proper title." I watch as Sebastian's beast flairs up in his eyes, turning them the white-blue of his wolf.

"Go ahead, Sebastian, challenge me! Your wolf is pissed, and rightfully so. Though, he should be pissed at you for forging a false bond." Sebastian's eyes return to his normal baby blue.

"I'm hurt, I won't lie about that. I never would have thought the two of you would sink so low. I have a lot to sort through mentally and emotionally." I feel the prince's scale warm up on my chest, and my hand absently reaches up to touch it. My eyes return to Sebastian, and they flicker between human and the mercury of my beast.

"You robbed me of the possibility of a true Lycan mate." I shake my head at him and move toward Dimitri, letting him hold me as I start to cry. My father chose this time to shove everyone out of the house, except the twins. I feel both their hands on my back as they try to soothe my pain away. I lift my head up and turn in Dimitri's arms to look at them.

"Thanks, guys, I appreciate it. I'm just very lost at the moment. I mean, my true mate is out there somewhere, and because of Sebastian, I'll never meet him." I sigh softly and lower my head. Dominik reaches up, gently grips my chin, and raises my head until he can look me in the eye.

"Princess, we love you and will support you in whatever you desire to do. As for your true Lycan mate, who knows? He might be able to break the magic placed over you. Honestly, I don't know how that shit works. I hope, for your sake, we can break it." As Dominik kisses my lips, Jayce's phone starts ringing. Dominik and I both look at Jayce, and he starts laughing.

"The prince is threatening to fly down here and burn the village to the ground. Nicodeamus, would you mind speaking to him?" My father takes the phone from Jayce and walks out of the room.

"As much as I hate to kick you out, I'm having problems keeping my urges under control." Quickly, I kiss both boys on the lips, and Dimitri ushers them out of the room.

Once the guys clear the front door, I walk over to my father while he video chats with the prince—I just can't help myself. I walk around the table to stand behind my father and rest my forearms on his shoulders to see Alaric myself. Dare I say, he's a beautiful man. He's rugged and handsome, and his beard definitely works with that Viking look he's got going on. I lower my head to be even with my father's and stare at Alaric. He blushes for a moment then clears his throat. I watch his almost golden eyes look back and forth between my father and me.

"I assume your beauty comes from your mother, princess?" He smiles and starts to laugh with my father.

"Yeah, I guess so. I never had the pleasure of meeting my mother. Apparently, I was the reason she died." I quickly drop my eyes, and my father leans the phone against the napkin holder to embrace me. Alaric, realizing his folly, clears his throat again. Smoke rings come out his nostrils. This catches my attention, and I raise my head up, watching him intently.

"My mother is a Gold Dragon. I have her fire as well as my father's fire and resistance to ice and cold." Alaric feels compelled to explain what happened.

"As for your mom, I met her several times. She was magnificent and brilliant. She was a very fair leader, unlike most of the Lycans at the time." Alaric looks down then back up at me.

"I just needed to know you were okay. I mean, I feel the turmoil." He opens his shirt to reveal my scale. He rubs it gently, and it feels like he's touching me. I look down at his scale and watch it change from golden to white. I smile, realizing the connection. I lightly touch his scale and rub it in return. His smile broadens when he feels my touch. My father starts laughing his ass off.

"Silly kids, wait until after you mate! You think that feeling is intense? It gets stronger! Only downside: Aurora's dragon half may get stronger than her wolven half." Nicodeamus looks between the two of us then stands to leave.

"I'll let you two talk for a bit. I'll be on the porch if you need me, baby girl." With that, my father leaves. My father's antics make me laugh. In the background, I hear Alaric say, "breathtaking."

"What? You act as if you've never witnessed a woman laugh before." He smiles and shakes his head at me, refusing to speak.

"I get it, it's the mate attraction. I honestly can't wait to see your dragon in all his glory. If he's anything like his human half, he must be magnificent." As soon as I call his dragon magnificent, he flares to the surface. Alaric's eyes turn the silver-gold of his dragon.

"Ah, there you are. Hello, handsome. Will you take me flying?" The slits in Alaric's eyes dilate several times. "I guess I pleased him." I can't help but smile at the thought. I pleased a Dragon Prince, and I haven't even touched him yet.

"I was concerned that perhaps my dragon would frighten you. I'm so happy you wish to meet him and go for a flight. A mating flight is a dragon tradition, you know?" Alaric states it as a question, and I shake my head no at him.

He sits back, looking shocked for a moment. "Oh! Well, um, that's a conversation for when we can sit side by side. This isn't the proper way to discuss such a serious conversation. I should go, my love. Rest well. Tomorrow will be another day that we're closer together." He kisses his fingertips and presses it to my scale. I sigh at the warmth I feel.

"Sleep well, my prince. Dream of me?" I tear up a little at the thought. I smile before I kiss my fingertips and press them to his scale. I watch him smile as he mouths, *always,* before ending the call. I hate to admit I stare at the blank phone screen longer than I should have. Slowly, I stand up and walk outside to return the phone to my father.

"Please return this to Jayce for me. I'm going to try to sleep." I kiss the top of my father's head and wave to Dimitri as he returns. I head back to Andre's room and curl up in his bed. This is going to be the longest three days ever.

CHAPTER 10

Nicodeamus

The revelations that have been made in the last twenty-four hours are borderline insane. First, we discover that Sebastian tricked Aurora into a mating. Elena more than likely doesn't love me, and she's been faking it all this time. Plus, we managed to solve Dimitri's aging problem. That, in itself, is a miracle.

I manage to get the alpha of the German Lycan pack's number from Elena. I call him and request that he sends me six of his strongest warriors that he trusts the most with guarding Aurora's life. I hope this will help cut down the possible threats to my daughter's life in the future.

Who knows, with any luck, one of the six that he sends to us might be her real mate, and we can get rid of this Sebastian bastard. I can't believe, in all these years, someone of her kind would stoop so low as to force a mating, just like old Alpha Vladimir. You better bet that I'm going to do everything within my power, with the last dying breath I hold in my chest, to take care of and protect my daughter.

I wait for confirmation of the tickets that will send the Lycans here straight from Germany. I now have to entrust the pickup of these young men to Dominik, since he and Jayce seem to be the only real mates that my daughter has.

The fate of our world as we know it is hanging in the balance. People we thought we could trust are now held as suspects in the back of my mind. Days like today make me regret my decision to trust the old alpha. We allowed him to live past the night he decided to curse us all and perform blood magic on us. Here we are, almost two hundred and thirty years later, and the repercussions of his poor choices are still felt today.

Now, I watch the American Lycan pack move amongst each other. Each one, in my mind, could be a possible threat to my child. I am fully prepared to turn this entire compound into nothing but a sea of ice. Hell hath no fury like a Dragon King scorned.

I watch Dimitri approach slowly, his great, hulking forum exuding nothing but the primal confidence of his bear. It's nice to see my old friend back in his prime, ready to go to battle and destroy the enemies before him. As Dimitri gets closer, I see that he's smiling. I wonder what the old bear's been up while we were separated. "Dimitri, old friend, where did you manage to get yourself off to?"

"Nicodeamus, I was checking on the training. Dominik and Jayce have really stepped up. Those two are really trying to pick up the slack Sebastian's absence has caused." He smirks and looks between the alpha house and his own cabin where Aurora is.

"I'm sure if Sebastian is up to something, we should know shortly. I can't see him sitting there on his hands waiting for Aurora to pass judgment on whether he lives or dies." Dimitri's observation is concrete. I just hope he isn't right.

"That's fine with me. Let Sebastian stew. I'm not concerned at all about this whelp, who would have been king." I tap my fingers on the arm of the rocking chair. I'm still watching out over the compound, ever vigilant for any signs of deception.

Aurora still slumbers, though her sleep has not been peaceful at all. She woke up several times last night, crying in her sleep, upset over Sebastian's betrayal. The deception he carried on for all this time has been eating at her something horrible. One of two things will happen: either her wolf is going to lash out and destroy everything in its path or, hopefully, if the dragon side of her nature is stronger, she'll bide her time and exact her revenge.

I rise from the rocking chair and lean on the rail of the porch, still keeping my eyes on the training circle as Dominik man-handles the American Lycans. Nothing is more enjoyable than watching a Dire Wolf fighting to prove his position within the pack. He's proving that he's the real first mate of the princess, my daughter.

Jayce is off to the side, doing what he does best: keeping records. He observes everybody's movements and interactions, taking note of anything that may or may not be significant. He is the one who's organizing the flights for the Lycans when they arrive from Germany. I can't wait until they get here. "Dimitri, what do you think we should do with Sebastian and his mother? I mean, honestly, I don't think we can trust them any further."

"I'm not sure, Nicodeamus, but I believe our best course of action is to wait for Aurora's heat to end then have her come out and pass judgment." He crosses his thick arms over his barrel chest, looking like a mountain of muscle. I can understand now why the Great Bears of the past invoke such stories of fear when they were angry. The sheer size of him is quite imposing.

"You're right, old friend. I know I shouldn't be trying to make all these decisions for Aurora. After all, he is technically still her mate, and they are still bound until a real, true mate is found or until he dies." I give Dimitri a Cheshire Cat grin that I've become so famous for.

Yes, in the back of my mind, I definitely want to rip that boy apart for the pain he's causing my daughter. But, in one sense, I almost hope his feelings for her are real and that the bond actually did some good and forged a genuine relationship for the two of them.

I remember looking at the picture of Sebastian holding Aurora as a wee baby—something I didn't get the chance to do. At that point, the look of amazement and infatuation on his face didn't seem forced. Perhaps, his wolf had fallen in love with her but may not have been a true mate like the stories they initially told.

Maybe his wolf was more in love with the idea of having a pup around versus thinking of her as a potential mate. There are too many factors involved for me to make a logical decision on the topic of Aurora and Sebastian. The whole thing is too fucking frustrating for me at this point.

I let out a soft growl and grip the railing a little too tightly—the wood beneath my hand splinters and cracks. A gentle touch is laid upon my shoulder. Slowly, I turn and see Aurora smiling at me.

"Daddy, you worry too much." Aurora looks past me to the training ring; I watch her eyes churn liquid mercury.

"I can't wait until the day death and betrayal doesn't hang over our heads." She sighs softly, then caresses the scale on her chest. Her connection to Alaric seems to have gotten stronger. In times of stress, she reaches out to him the only way she can.

"Little one, do you feel better today? I mean emotionally." I gently wrap my arm around Aurora, offering her the comfort only a father can provide. Aurora snuggles in close and rests her head on my chest. I feel her body relax as she holds onto me.

"Physically, yes. Emotionally, I feel gutted. How could he be so cruel? A true mate is a blessing, a gift. He betrayed that sacred covenant. How can I ever trust him again, Dad?" Aurora looks up at me, her sadness evident on her face. My powerful daughter is suffering from heartbreak.

"Little one, if Dimitri or I could bear this pain for you, we would do it gladly." Dimitri moves closer to us when I mention his name and rests his hand on her shoulder, rubbing it gently.

"Baby girl, all will be well. I will do everything possible to make sure all your dreams come true." Dimitri leans down and kisses Aurora's cheek, then rests his forehead against her temple for several moments before moving away.

"I'm sorry, my king. I should remain outside from now on." His eyes change to the brilliant gold of his bear, then back to his normal hazel. Hmm, interesting. My daughter's heat calls to him. Perhaps, her wolf wasn't off base with Dimitri. Aurora pulls away from me and heads back to the cabin door.

"Prepare the troops. Once my heat is over, we leave for Alaska. No more waiting, no more stalling. If, by accident, several traitors don't make it, oh well. Not my circus, not my monkeys." Aurora's animal surges to the surface, and the wave of power that comes off her is impressive.

The fighting stops in the ring, and everyone turns to face the cabin. Aurora shifts quickly and lets out her death howl, its tone haunting and summoning. Every wolven being within earshot of her was forced to shift by the power of her will alone. She stands there for several seconds before shifting back and walking into the house. My eyes pass over all the wolves now as they prowl the compound. I'm not sure what's more frightening: the power my daughter wields or the fact she can wield it.

~Later that night~

Dominik returns to the compound with the six Lycan warriors from the German pack. These men are stout, unlike the American Lycans who still do physical work. Dimitri is the first to greet them and catches them up on what has been going on. Then I notice the alpha's sons, Klaus and Kaden. Another set of twins have arrived. It would be comical as fuck if my daughter started a collection of twins.

Klaus is the first to approach me. Instinctively, I hold out my right forearm to show him the brand of the royal house. Klaus, in turn, shows me the brand of his father's pack. Once our identities are confirmed, we embrace briefly then head toward the cabin Aurora's staying in. Risky, yes, but I need to have them meet so he sees who his people are fighting for.

We arrive at the cabin's door, and I mentally reach out to Aurora. Several seconds later, she opens the door and her jaw drops and nostrils flair, inhaling his scent deeply into her lungs once she sees Klaus. She blinks several times before she moves out of the way to allow us to enter. I've never seen my daughter speechless before, so this is quite impressive. Aurora's eyes churn liquid mercury, and I feel her reaching into my memories.

Aurora clears her throat and speaks to him in German. "Thank you for making the long journey here. Please forgive my appearance. I haven't been myself lately."

She motions to the couch and waits for both of us to sit before going into the kitchen. She returns with three beers. Aurora sets the beer bottles on the table, then shifts her right hand into her armored gauntlet and uses her talons to open all three bottles. Carefully, Aurora picks up the first beer, and we watch the frost move across the glass before she offers it to Klaus. His eyes go wide, looking between Aurora and me. Apparently, stories of her ability haven't reached his pack yet.

Aurora continues to speak in German. "I am sorry if my grasp of your language is lacking. I recently learned it." She hands me my beer then sits down in Dimitri's favorite recliner in front of us.

Klaus looks completely gobsmacked as he stares at her. Neither of us expected her to conduct business in his native tongue. As if it just dawned on her, she shifts her right arm back and shows her royal brand to Klaus. Klaus immediately drops to his knees before her and rests his forehead on her knees.

"You are the last true ruler of my people. We serve only you from now until death and beyond." His German flows like the Rhine River, smooth and sure. Klaus looks up to Aurora, his eyes golden like that of his wolf. I watch him try to stare her down and fail.

"Forgive me, princess. I had to make sure you were the one." Aurora reaches down and threads her fingers through his thick, medium-brown hair. She seems very interested in him, which could be a death sentence for Sebastian. Quickly, Aurora pulls her hand away like it touched fire.

She draws in a shaky breath, still speaking to Klaus in German. "I forgive you. If you wish to call your men inside, I shall shift for you; let you see what exactly you're dealing with. No secrets."

Aurora climbs over the back of the couch and begins to shove furniture out of the way. Klaus goes to the door and shouts for his men to come in. Aurora's eyes fall on me and, in the back of my mind, she says to stop her if I need to. She's not sure how her beast will react to strangers in her temporary den.

I place myself in front of Aurora, who decides to stand in the house's dining area. She's wearing a simple robe that will tear easily. I listen to Klaus explain to his people that she's the true heir. Aurora raises her right arm and shows the guys her mark before she begins her shift.

She does it slower than usual, allowing them to watch each bone break and reform as her thick, white fur slowly blankets her muscular Lycan form. Frost begins to coat her fur just before her white dragon scales ripple up her fingertips to her elbows. Scales slowly form on her muzzle and around her eyes. Her wolven head is broader and longer than the average Lycan's. I can actually see some of my dragon's features in her animal. For instance, her eyes are almond-shaped, and she has a boney ridge up her muzzle like my dragon. Aurora's beast has grown in size as well. She easily stands nine feet tall. Klaus and his men stare in amazement, looking at Aurora's impressive beast.

"Gentlemen? Do we have your allegiance?" I state. All six men fall to their knees before Aurora. I watch her study them for a few moments before she turns and walks to the back of the house.

"Now that's settled, I have an announcement to make to the

pack. I need you guys to stand with me. The pack hierarchy has been shifted, and we must settle the masses. I know you've been briefed on what's going on here, so let's make haste." I lead Klaus and his team of men toward the porch of the Alpha House.

Sebastian stands there with his arms crossed over his chest like the self-important fool he is. Klaus moves forward, lets out a low growl, and locks eyes with Sebastian. Both are alpha's sons, but there's one huge difference: Sebastian's title was handed down. At the same time, Klaus's was earned through repeated battles over the centuries.

I look between the two males; Sebastian, even though he's built heavy for the Americans, is considerably smaller than Klaus. Is it wrong that I hope they fight? Eventually, Sebastian backs down, and whispers move through the pack because of how quickly he submitted to the new male.

Without warning, the temperature plummets and frost begins to race along the ground. Aurora emerges from the cabin, the unease of the pack bringing her out of her self-imposed isolation. Her alpha power blankets the pack and drives the weak to their knees. The only ones left standing are the Dires, the German Lycans, Dimitri, and myself. The entire American pack is on their knees, whining from the pressure of her influence.

Sebastian is also on the ground. From what I was told, he was once able to withstand Aurora. Now, he's on the ground like the rest of his birth pack. Oh, how the mighty have fallen. With a flourish of her right hand, she cuts the oppressive power that blankets the compound.

"Dominik, summon your pack to the meeting point I gave you earlier. The North American Lycans shall remain here. It will be lambs to the slaughter if we bring them with us." Aurora's voice is commanding, leaving no room for questioning her authority.

Sebastian moves to approach Aurora. She quickly shifts her hand and points her talons at her once first mate, she bares her canines at him. Her yellow-green toxin starts to drip from her exposed canines as she stares at Sebastian.

"You forced a mating by magic. It's going to take a long time to regain my trust. You cost me the chance at a true Lycan mate. For all I know, he could be right here," she motions at Klaus and his packmates, "and I wouldn't know because of your betrayal." Her words are growled out, her body shakes with the effort to restrain her beast. I rest my hand on her shoulder, trying to stay her hand.

"Baby girl? Daughter? Consider this: he can fight alongside us and earn his place back at your side through battle. Or he can die trying?" I'm trying to appeal to my daughter's logical dragon side. It must have worked because she lowers her arm and shifts it back to human.

"You owe my father your heart, Sebastian. He just saved your life," Aurora says, devoid of any emotion.

Then her eyes flicker to Klaus and Dimitri. She speaks in German for Klaus and his men. "We leave in an hour; be ready. Klaus, you and the twins are with me. Dimitri, take the other truck with father and Klaus's men. Dominik, give your men the keys to the other four-by-fours so we can fuel up and depart. I'm done waiting." Aurora finishes with her instructions, flipping back and forth between English and German depending on who she's speaking to.

She shoves past Sebastian, heading into the Alpha House to go pack. Klaus and I look at each other, then to Dimitri. The big guy is trying so hard not to laugh his ass off over Aurora's latest antics. We turn and start heading toward Aurora's truck.

"Guys! Wait up!" Sebastian is yelling and trying to catch up to us. Right now, I wish I had both wings. I'd be gone. Then I'd fly over him and shit right on his head; just cover the bastard in molten dragon shit. I must have what he perceives as a friendly smile on my face.

"Thanks for waiting up! Where are we going, and who do I ride with?" Sebastian says hopefully. I raise an eyebrow at Sebastian. Can this fucker be serious?

"I suggest you wait for Aurora and ask her. This is, how do you say it? Her rodeo?" I'm not sure if I'm using the phrase right. I glance at Dimitri, and he gives me the thumbs up, so I change my expression to a serious one and stare the whelp down. Sebastian double blinks and looks back at the Alpha House. He visibly pales, thinking about dealing with Aurora in her angered state.

"Um, okay? I mean, you are still King Nicodeamus. I'm sure you can tell me where I should be going." In my mind, I'm screaming, "*go to hell and rot.* Or, better yet, *go visit your ancestors and not come back.*"

"Yes, I am still king. My daughter out-ranks me by birthright. So, yes, I know where you should go. It's Aurora's job to make sure you get there." I smirk at him.

Cocky mother fucker has finally been knocked down a peg. Sebastian heads back to the house and enters. We can hear Aurora clear as day when she yells that he better find his own ride because he wasn't riding with her. Dimitri and I can't help but laugh; they sound like an old married couple. Sebastian comes running out and heads toward his Jeep. Once inside, he pulls up to where the other vehicles are waiting.

Aurora steps out of the Alpha House with a duffle bag over her shoulder. She takes her time heading to her truck, where the twins and Klaus are waiting for her. I watch my daughter climb into the bed of her truck and look out over all the gathered vehicles.

"Roll out!" she yells before jumping down and firing up Black Betty. Plumes of black soot shoot from the diesel stacks as she begins to roll. We fall in line behind Aurora and so on down the line. Sebastian chooses the rear. I start to laugh; this isn't a regular wolf pack where the alpha leads from the back. My daughter is the soon to be mother fucking queen when she takes back the throne. Strigoi, beware: you have one pissed off hybrid coming for you.

CHAPTER 11
Jayce

The last forty-eight hours have been hell on my nerves. We discover Elena and Sebastian manipulated the most sacred of bonds for their own ambitions, and Aurora accepted a Dragon Prince before even meeting him.

Now, she seems more powerful than ever. Andre, my best friend, was murdered because he must have found something important. The American pack was deemed unfit to fight once Aurora saw the German Lycans. I have to admit, they are huge in comparison to the American pack.

Personally, I understand why she left them behind; they can all turn on us in a second. Strategically, it's brilliant and dumb. I mean, we would have had higher numbers for the battle. On the other hand, if they turned on us, our odds would be far worse.

"Klaus? Can you tell us what you know about the fortress?" I watch Klaus turn his heavily muscled frame so he can face all of us when he speaks.

"It's heavily fortified but has developed flaws over the years, which we plan to exploit." He studies Aurora's side profile while she drives. I notice he seems appreciative of what he sees. "

The flaws have to deal with the lower levels. They are flooded, which means the Strigoi are somewhere on the first level." Klaus looks between the three of us. His English isn't bad, which is a pleasant surprise. Aurora receives word that some of the smaller vehicles need to refuel, so we pull up to the diesel pump to top off the tank. Aurora turns to look at all of us.

"If your information is correct, that means they are more than likely in the throne room." Aurora's grey eyes slowly examine Klaus. He has medium-brown hair that's longer on the top, and his eyes are grey like Aurora's.

They seem to stare at each other forever before Sebastian breaks the spell by knocking on Aurora's window. I've never seen her go from zero to demon bitch so fast. She's snapping and growling at Sebastian.

Gently, I touch Aurora's shoulder in an attempt to calm her. She turns to look at me, and I notice her beast is close to the surface. Dragon scales line her eyes like eyeliner. The silver shimmer makes the grey of her eyes look ethereal. Her head tilts left then right as she studies me.

My wolf chooses now to come to the surface. Through my wolf's eyes, I see Aurora with a bright light behind her. My vision has never been like this before. The world is in tones of grey and black with lights behind the objects to outline them.

"Aurora? Is this how you see when you shift?" I look around in wonder; everything is so sharp. If I really concentrate, I can see the blood flowing through my brother's veins. Aurora starts laughing.

"Apparently, both you and Dominik got the same gift from me. Yes, I can tell by your eye color you gained my vision. It's most helpful when a species can use glamours. Now, you can see right through them," she says so matter-of-factly, like it's no big deal. To me, it's a total game-changer.

I smile broadly and start examining the world around me. I hear Aurora lower the driver's side window. "Yes, Mister Lupi? What can I do for you?" Oh shit, he's really redefining being in the dog house. My vision goes back to normal, and I watch Sebastian cringe at Aurora's tone.

"Aurora, please love, can we talk?" Sebastian says in a pathetic tone. Hell has officially frozen over. Sebastian I-don't-give-a-fuck-about-anyone Lupi is begging. I start videoing it. I'm positive Dimitri and Nicodeamus would love to see this.

"LOVE? LOVE! You don't even understand the meaning of the word!" Aurora screams at the top of her lungs. We barely made it into Canada, and I think she's going to kill him. Out of nowhere, Dimitri's hulking form rises up behind Sebastian.

"I suggest you leave, boy. She's not interested in talking to you right now." Sebastian doesn't even attempt to argue with Dimitri; he just turns and leaves. Dimitri faces Aurora and kisses her forehead.

"Anything for you, baby girl. Anything." He gently caresses her cheek then heads back to the truck he was in.

Aurora shakes her head then fires the truck up again, getting the caravan back on the road. Klaus is pondering talking to Aurora. Part of me wants to warn him; the other part wants to watch the explosion. Klaus gently rests his hand on her arm. I watch Aurora glance at him but doesn't swipe his hand away.

"I was filled in on what happened. On behalf of the German Lycans, we are sorry." He furrows his brows and removes his hand from her arm.

"We still treasure and honor the idea and dream of finding a true mate." I watch Klaus interlace his fingers as he stares at his hands in his lap. Aurora reaches over and rests her hand on his knee.

"Thank you, Klaus. It hurts so bad to be betrayed and to realize my true mate is out there somewhere waiting for me." I watch a single tear roll down her cheek.

"He's out there somewhere, praying to Morrighan to find me, and I'm here..." Aurora's voice cracks as she's overcome with emotions. Dominik and I both lay a hand on her to soothe her. "I'm here with a false bond, all because Sebastian and his mother are self-serving assholes."

Through the bond, my brother and I push our love for our mate the best we can. Aurora rests her cheek on Dominik's hand and then reaches up to touch mine. She keeps her eyes on the road and sighs softly. My eyes turn to Klaus; so many emotions flicker across his face. I can't tell if he's empathetic or he knows what she's going through.

I lean forward and kiss Aurora's hand before I speak. "Love, we are here for you. Your father and Dimitri are here for you. From what I can tell, you have the full power of the German Lycans and the Dire Wolves behind you. You do not walk alone." I see Klaus hesitate before resting his hand on Aurora's thigh. I watch her look down briefly, then back up to the road ahead.

I can tell Aurora is deep in thought. She sits up straighter and removes her hand from mine. Aurora hits a button on her steering wheel. "Betty, play my playlist," she says, her voice wavers and almost cracks as she utters the simple command.

A few seconds later, the truck responds by saying, "Playing playlist." The opening notes to Shinedown's *How Did You Love?* starts filling the truck. Aurora begins singing along with the song. I watch her lips move almost hypnotically until I notice her canines have descended. Klaus gives me a look of concern, poor man has no clue what the fuck he got himself into.

Gently I tap Klaus's shoulder to get his attention. "She's like a force of nature unleashed upon the world."

Dominik nods along with my words. His phone goes off and it's the prince. Quickly, Dominik brings the prince up to speed. I look back over at Klaus. "Right now, we're sitting in the eye of the hurricane. Her rage and pain aren't focused on us. She's battling between her logical side and her beast's desire to royally fuck up what's hurting her."

I lower my eyes briefly before looking back up at Klaus. "Aurora works through her pain with music. We've almost figured out when she's going to explode by the songs she picks."

Dominik decides to cut in at this point. "What Jayce is trying to say is this: if we say run, do it. It's not going to be pretty when she finally loses the battle with her beast's instincts." Dominik rubs the center of his chest, indicating the pain we are both feeling from Aurora. We all watch her; she's so focused on singing it's like we're not even here.

I turn away from my brother and watch the scenery outside my window. The miles blow by like dust in the wind. Aurora shows no sign of fatigue after driving for the last nine hours. We pull into a rest stop somewhere in the middle of Canada to refuel. Aurora sits on the tailgate of her truck once it's fueled. Dimitri approaches her cautiously while Klaus and I watch them from a safe distance. Dimitri holds out a bag of food and shakes it to break Aurora from her trance. She takes the food and pats the tailgate beside her, Dimitri joins her. I can't decide if that's the bravest or dumbest thing I've ever witnessed.

Klaus returns to his pack mates and brother to update them. I spot Dominik over by Nicodeamus, so I decide to join them. As I approach, I notice Sebastian with his head in his mother's lap, looking distraught.

"What's going on over there?" I motion toward Elena and Sebastian. Nicodeamus wins for best resting bitch face today. He looks at Elena and Sebastian, then back to me.

"Old laws dictate death for betraying the ruling family. Forging a false bond is grounds for execution." Nicodeamus raises his right hand to rub where his left arm used to be.

"Their lives are in Aurora's talons—literally." He turns to watch Klaus with his pack-mates and motions toward them.

"Their pack is the last of the true Lycans. I had and still hope Aurora's mate is there in their pack somewhere. A true mate can break the false bond." Nicodeamus looks almost sad as he turns to

Aurora and Dimitri. "I just have to wonder, was there magic cast to keep those two apart?"

I watch Aurora and Dimitri interact. They do act like a mated couple; they're perfectly attuned to each other. Is their comfort level due to the fact he raised her, or is Nico correct in saying she's his? Nicodeamus then yells for Dimitri and Aurora to join us. They meander over; Aurora hugs and kisses her father, then snuggles into me, suppressing a yawn.

"Something wrong, Dad?" Aurora asks before yawning into my side again. Dominik moves to my side and kisses Aurora on the top of her head. She looks up and smiles at Dominik, then snuggles into his side.

"Nothing is wrong, sweetheart. I just have a few questions." This catches Dimitri's attention, and he looks around to see if anyone is within earshot of us. When he's sure it's clear, he gives Nicodeamus the all-clear.

"The question is actually for you, old friend. Did Elena send you and Andre regular care packages?" Dimitri looks puzzled by the question then looks between Elena and Nicodeamus.

"*Da*, why?" Dimitri answers quite tersely. Nicodeamus taps his finger on his chin for several moments, then looks to Dominik.

"Aurora looks exhausted. We'll stop here for the night. Secure enough rooms for everyone." Dominik nods then leads Aurora off.

Once they are out of range, he places his hand on Dimitri's shoulder. "What if I told you I think you're a victim of Elena's tea as well?" Nicodeamus backs up and looks at me, then back to Dimitri, waiting for it to dawn on the Great Bear.

Several moments passed before you can tell when it hit him. Dimitri falls to his knees, and his hands fly up to cover his eyes. Is the big guy crying? Holy hell, he is crying. The atmosphere changes radically and, in an instant, Dimitri shifts to his bear, and that hulking beast is out for blood. His bear stands on its hind legs and roars its pain and anger into the night, shaking the very ground we stand on. Those golden orbs lock onto Sebastian and his mother.

Over a half-ton of enraged Great Bear thunders across the field between the rest stop and the motel. Sebastian's and Elena's faces visibly pale as they watch their death approach. With his full force, Dimitri hits their Jeep, sending it flying through the air. The metal of the Jeep is twisted upon impact, and we all watch the attack in horror.

Nicodeamus raises his hand, halting anyone from interfering. Dimitri launches the Jeep once more before a blur of white and frost stands before him. Aurora's hybrid beast roars at the Great Bear. He slowly lowers his head and swings it from side to side.

Aurora's beast looks back at the Jeep in time to watch Elena and Sebastian crawl out of the wreckage. They look like they barely survived the attack. Aurora's beast moves forward and presses her forehead to Dimitri's bear's forehead. They stand like that for what seemed like forever before they turn and head our way. The whole event played out like an action movie crossed with horror. It was very surreal; I still can't wrap my head around it.

As they walk side by side, Aurora's beast has its taloned hand resting on Dimitri's neck. Usually, it's her animal that needs to be reined in. This is fucking backward as all hell. She stops several feet in front of us and shifts back to her human form. Quickly, I remove my flannel shirt and help her slip it on. Aurora doesn't move far from Dimitri, her fingers running through his thick fur.

"I don't know what was said to Dimitri, but whatever set him off... I almost wasn't able to stop him." Aurora looks at the three of us. Nicodeamus waves off the approaching crowd.

"I wouldn't," he cautions the group. Once everyone leaves, Nicodeamus looks back to Aurora.

"I have reason to believe that it's possible you and Dimitri may be mates. But something Elena put in her care packages blocked it." Nicodeamus studies Aurora's reaction.

You can watch as the rage moves over her face. Scales erupt then recede just as quickly. She takes off my shirt, shifts back into her beast's form, and howls her rage into the night. Dimitri's bear bellows right along with her. I move quickly and place my hands on Aurora's chest, trying to stop her. Aurora drops her muzzle until she's at eye level with me. She rests her forehead against mine and does the happy growl she likes to do. I feel the moment her body shifts back, and Dominik helps her slip my shirt back on.

"They have a lot to answer for tomorrow," Aurora states, then grabs my hand and heads toward the motel. "I need a shower and sleep." I turn Aurora to face me and kiss her on the lips.

"Go with Dominik. I'm going to help your dad sort things out." Aurora nods and follows my brother inside. Nicodeamus approaches me with Dimitri in tow.

"It's obvious that Elena lied about knowing the old magics. The real question is, what else did she do?" Nicodeamus turns to look at the remnants of Sebastian's Jeep. We stare at the crumpled, twisted remains. How in the world did they walk away from that wreck? Dimitri eventually shifts back to his human form and looks between Nicodeamus and me.

"I regret losing my temper, but I do not regret attacking them." Dimitri crosses his thick arms over his chest, looking at us. Apparently, he doesn't care about his dick swinging in the wind either.

"I'm impressed that Aurora was able to stop you," Nicodeamus states, studying Dimitri. Dimitri looks down, his brows furrowed.

"I would never hurt Aurora." He looks up and at us each in turn. "However, you fuckers wouldn't make out so well." Dimitri flips us all off then walks toward his room at the motel.

"Jayce?" Nicodeamus says as he watches Dimitri walk off.

"Yeah?" I tilt my head to the side, looking at Nico. He moves closer to me and puts his arm over my shoulder.

"We should go see what Elena and Sebastian are up to." He's got that mischievous look in his eye. It's almost like he's saying, *let's just kill them now and surprise Aurora with the heads.* I raise my eyebrows, looking at him after reading between the lines.

"Let's go get'er done." I might not be as bulky as my brother, Dom, but one bite from me and it's a death sentence.

That knowledge makes me smile as I follow Nico into the night. We creep around the motel exterior, trying to catch their scent. Two laps around the building and nothing. I text Dom and ask for their room number. He responds quickly and says it's room thirty-five—the one right in front of us. Nico places his hand on the door and freezes it solid. He makes a fist, busts the frozen knob off, and pushes the door open. There's no evidence they were ever here. Nico growls, and his dragon's eyes are visible.

"They're on the run." Nicodeamus darts to the parking lot and starts counting cars. No vehicles are missing, which means one of two things: either they ran off into the night or they were picked up somewhere. We stare at each other for several moments.

"Use your phone and tell everyone what happened. Alert Ellis as well; we need to change our route and plans. I will not give them an opportunity to ambush us!" Nico storms off to points unknown. Well, this trip just got more interesting.

CHAPTER 12

Dominik

It's sometime after midnight my phone dings, letting me know I received a message. It's from my brother, Jayce, who alerts me on what has occurred while Aurora and I slumbered. Apparently, shit went down after we went in to relax.

Now, Sebastian and Elena are on the run and missing, henceforth proving they were the rats. According to my brother, we have to amend our original travel plans and change our course of action. Aurora's father is looking over the maps and plotting which roads we should take and which ones we should avoid in case of an ambush. It's quite suspicious that they left without any kind of vehicle. They were apparently prepared in case of discovery.

Now, I wonder exactly how much information they've already passed on to the other side. Nicodeamus is handling all the planning from this point on, only allowing us knowledge of it within moments of his adjustments to the course. He's trying to eliminate any possible threats or leakage of information between here and our destination in the northernmost part of Alaska.

I sit up in bed to shoot a message off to my brother, letting him know I understand the necessity for all these extra preparations. My eyes slide over the sleeping form of my mate, and I watch her in her restless sleep.

Aurora's skin occasionally ripples with fur or scales —depending on where the ripple occurs. I know her subconscious mind is working overtime, wanting to plot how to kill and destroy all those that stand against her.

The betrayal of her mate runs deep, and it cuts her so profoundly that our hearts ache with her. Going forward now is going to be like walking around with a ticking nuclear bomb, never knowing exactly when she's going to explode.

I text my brother again to let him know about Aurora's rippling scales and her skin shifting in her sleep. I warn him that we have to be on guard. He replies quickly, saying her father knows of a way to help her sleep without dreaming. He'll figure out something within the next day to help us, so we don't have to worry about her disappearing in the middle of the night.

I know previously, long before us, her beast took advantage of her deep sleep. Somehow, it put her human thoughts to the back of her mind, allowing her to run on instinct alone. This knowledge causes me great concern, and it's why I don't sleep soundly tonight. I heard the stories of what happened before her awakening, how her beast had hunted a woman down just because Dimitri came home smelling like her.

I listen to the doorknob turn, and a little ray of light comes into the room. Slowly, my brother pokes his head in and looks around. As silently as possible, Jayce closes the door and locks it, then comes into bed and crawls on Aurora's opposite side.

At least this way, we could possibly sleep in shifts to make sure both of us get some semblance of sleep. I nod to Jayce and allow him to curl up and slumber first. I feel a bit stalkerish watching them. Let's face it, taking these kinds of precautions isn't normal. But then again, our situation is anything but typical.

~Several hours later~

Dawn breaks over the horizon, painting the sky in blues and purples. As the morning progresses, the colors change to hues of oranges and reds until finally, the sun nears its apex and changes the sky to blue. I leave the room early and grab breakfast for the three of us. Nicodeamus and Dimitri are organizing our caravan and letting them know what transpired last night.

I return to our room to find Aurora and Jayce screaming from their climaxes. Well, at least someone is having a great morning. I wiggle the bag full of breakfast sandwiches. The first to turn around is Aurora, and she's off Jayce before he even has a chance to look at me. Aurora takes the bag from me and pulls out what she wants, then sits at the table to eat.

Jayce is the first to speak as he grabs his breakfast. "What's the plan?" I hop up to sit on the tabletop and look between Aurora and Jayce.

"That's a great question. Unfortunately, I don't know. After yesterday's debacle with Sebastian and his mother, Nicodeamus isn't telling anyone shit. He's going to take point when the caravan gets rolling. Nicodeamus is concerned that there might still be spies." I shrug my shoulders and dig into my breakfast sandwich. There's almost an uncomfortable silence that I have to break.

"All I know is they bailed after Dimitri launched them last night." I ponder that for several minutes.

"Now I know why Great Bears are beasts of legend. Fuck, remind me to never piss Dimitri off." My brother and I nod in agreement, and Aurora shrugs her shoulders. She lowers her head and sets her sandwich down. I've never seen Aurora look so broken. I don't know what changed in her internal monologue, but I notice the minute that fire sparks back to life within her.

"I'm going to fucking destroy them all. I will tear them limb from limb and put their heads on spikes in my yard." Her voice is mostly the growl of her beast. Her mercury eyes have an eerie glow, and her hair is blanketed in frost. We can feel her rage building. Quickly, she jumps off the bed and runs out the front door. Nicodeamus meets her halfway in the middle of the parking lot.

"Father," Aurora says in a rather hollow tone.

"They have stolen so much from me." Aurora's hands shift into armored scales, her long white talons lightly dusted with frost.

"They will die by my hands. I will make their entire bloodline extinct." She bares her canines at everyone who gathered. Aurora is so enraged that she's not calming down for anything.

My phone rings, and it's an unknown number. I stare at it for several seconds before I answer it. It's Ellis, and apparently, Aurora's mood is sending Alaric's dragon off the deep end. Ellis instructs me to go near Aurora and put it on speaker.

I do as instructed, then I shout, "Okay, NOW!"

Alaric's dragon bellows and forces Aurora's shift. Her beast whines and whimpers before she shifts back to her human form. I give Aurora my hoodie, and then she snatches my phone from me and goes to sit in her truck. I look back at Nicodeamus; the cocky fucker is just smiling. Nicodeamus looks at the truck then back to us.

"Alaric's dragon just forced Aurora's beast to submit." He shrugs his shoulders like it was nothing.

"How in the Nine Hells is that possible?" Dimitri's Romanian accent is definitely more pronounced when he's angry. Nicodeamus huffs like we just asked him to perform a miracle.

"Male dragons only choose powerful females. Aurora is probably the most powerful female born in generations. His dragon basically said, *if I am worthy, you will stop.* Her shift and whining was her beast's way of telling him he was." Dimitri, Jayce, and I look between each other. Something is definitely missing in translation. It looked more painful than a romantic conversation.

Nicodeamus huffs again. "Load up! We need to get rolling; we're burning daylight." My brother and I head back to Aurora's truck, and Klaus is right behind us.

When we get back to her truck, we find her in the backseat with her headphones on, still talking to Alaric. Jayce grabs the keys off of the center console and fires up Black Betty. Nicodeamus reaches over in front of Dimitri and honks the horn.

Off we go again. This time, I sit in the back with Aurora and position her so her head lays in my lap. I've always hated road trips because my wolf hates being trapped in a vehicle. Every five to six hours we stop and refuel, switch drivers, then move on. We've been traveling like this for almost a week already. Our food is passed around while we continue our journey.

Something must have happened that spooked Nicodeamus because we suddenly take a hard right. We all snap to attention as we watch what unfolds around us. A truck comes out of nowhere and sideswipes the truck behind us, the one holding all of Klaus's men. Two more come from opposite directions as they try to box us in. Klaus cuts the wheel hard and turns our vehicle around. The rest of our caravan stops to assist. We are within one hundred yards of the impact zone when we all jump out. The shift takes us all quickly as we move as a single unit.

Klaus's Lycan is definitely heavier built than Sebastian's. His fur is grey and black, and he looks like the devil himself. He roars into the night and charges toward his pack's truck. A van speeds into the scene out of nowhere and twenty unknown Lycans pour out of the back. They head straight for the other truck and begin their attack. Klaus springs into action, clawing the back of their necks and severing their heads.

A great, white mass leaps into the fray, joining in on the action. Aurora's beast is larger and faster than Klaus, and her rage is palpable in the air. More Lycans file out of the trucks, but we outnumber them two to one. In the back of my mind, I realize this is a setup.

We fight valiantly and obliterate the opposing forces. Nicodeamus stands on the tailgate of his truck like a brigadier general. I can see him scanning the horizon for any more enemies. After we all shift back to our human forms and get dressed, we head back to Nicodeamus. He looks at all of us as we gather around. Not a single loss on our side and every one of our attackers have been killed.

"They are testing us, trying to find a weakness." Nicodeamus begins to pace before speaking again, "Check all the trucks and look for anything that may give away our position." Dimitri taps Nicodeamus on the calf, and he bends down to listen to what Dimitri has to say. "Dimitri says it's called a tracker or a GPS thing. Find it and destroy it."

We return to Aurora's truck and Jayce, who already shifted back to his wolf, walks beside Aurora as she inspects her vehicle. Jayce stops by the left side of her bumper. Quickly, Aurora slips under the vehicle and we hear something snap. She slides out and holds up a small, black box. Nicodeamus and Dimitri come over with three other trackers in their hands.

"We need to send a decoy with the trackers in it," Dimitri says in a very calm tone. I pull out my phone and look at the map program I have. There's a rather large truck stop up ahead. I show Klaus and Aurora, and she nods before taking my phone from me.

"Dad, Dominik found a truck stop about fifteen miles ahead. We can hide the trackers on trucks preparing to leave to send them in different directions." Aurora shows her dad what she's talking about, and he smiles.

Nicodeamus approaches me and gives me a hug. "I am proud to call you one of my daughter's mates." He gives me a brief nod before he turns to address the others. "Roll out! We stop at the next rest area!"

Jayce, Klaus, Aurora, and I look at each other before running back to the truck. Aurora grabs a pair of leggings and a sweatshirt, then hops into the driver's seat. Several moments later, we arrive at the rest stop. Nico sends everyone out in different directions to look for trucks that seem to be ready to depart. Everyone moves quickly, hiding the little black boxes on unsuspecting tractor-trailers.

Aurora sits on the roof of her truck's cab, eating a smorgasbord of tacos. Her mercury orbs scan the surrounding area, watching everything that comes and goes from the yard. It's moments like this where I feel the loss of Andre the most. Usually, he would be the one on the lookout, but it looks like Aurora tasked herself with remaining vigilant.

Nicodeamus and Dimitri are having a heated debate as they lean over a map that's spread out over the tailgate of Dimitri's truck. Neither one is speaking English, and I can only assume it's Romanian. Earlier this week, I learned that Dimitri's people were one of the proud Romani tribes of Gypsies. I clear my throat so as not to startle either of them.

"Ah, son, perhaps you can settle this for us. I want to take this route, which is about fifty miles longer. Dimitri wants to take this one because he's concerned about snow. Which do you think is better?" Shit on a shingle. Now I'm being pitted between my father-in-law and Aurora's possible new mate. I'm so fucked, and not in the good sense. Lucky for me, mother nature makes the decision easier because large snowflakes begin to fall. I look up to the sky and silently thank the wolf goddess for saving my tail.

"In light of the most recent developments, I believe the shorter route will be to our benefit. We're over three-quarters of the way to our port. We need to get as close to that land bridge as we can before we have to shift and travel by foot." Dimitri and Nicodeamus both look up at the sky. I want to tell them staring at the snow isn't going to stop it.

"He's right, my king, we may not have that much time left. We've been traveling for what seems like forever. Only four hundred miles to go and we are at the Wales port." Dimitri is trying his hardest to get the king to see reason. Our animals are getting restless from being caged in the trucks. I can only imagine what his dragon is feeling. Nicodeamus shakes his head and smirks.

"Ok, the snow wins; we take the short route. Get everyone loaded and ready to roll in twenty minutes. We don't stop until we hit the port." Nicodeamus heads back to the passenger side of the truck and gets in to wait. Dimitri and I shake our heads before heading off in different directions. I make it back to the truck to find Aurora asleep and curled up in a little ball. I furrow my brow and look at Klaus, who is standing watch over her and the truck.

"She crawled in the back, grabbed your sweatshirt, then went to sleep. She grumbled something about Ellis meeting us at some port." Hmmm, makes sense. I guess he's going to introduce us to his group. That way, we can catch their scent to prevent us from accidentally attacking them.

"Alright, we need to load up. We're driving straight through to the port. No more stops between here and there. Grab extra provisions and whatever you need to eat before we remain shifted until after whatever ambush we're walking into." The look of surprise on Klaus's face is entirely worth it. I look over and see my brother, Jayce, coming back from a different store. It looks like he bought every protein bar they had in stock.

"I've got enough to sustain the shift and then some. Aurora's going to need a lot, so we need to keep her fed." Jayce is funny when he goes all mother hen on us. I grab two of the bags from him and watch as the others walk out with similar bags in their hands—time to gorge ourselves. While we cross over to Siberia, our animals will burn more calories from trying to keep us warm through the blizzard-like conditions.

With one of the bags of protein bars, Jayce slides in the back and lightly rocks Aurora. "Love, we need to start eating. We're not far from the port. You need to start storing the carbs for the crossing." Aurora pops one eye open, revealing the liquid mercury of her beast.

Slowly, Aurora sits up and rubs her eyes before rooting through the bag to grab what she wants to eat. Klaus climbs in the driver's seat and fires up Black Betty. While he is distracted, I watch Aurora's hand slide forward and snatch the cheesecake flavored bar that Klaus left on the center console. He acts like he didn't see her do it and just laughs to himself, watching her eat it in the back seat.

"About five hours before we make it to the port. Make sure you eat." Klaus's accent is heavy as he addresses us. He pulls out behind Dimitri and we're off again. I text Ellis and let him know our approximate ETA. He warns us about the storm and says it's whiteout conditions at the port. I forward the message to Klaus's brother, who's in the truck with Dimitri and Nicodeamus, to let everyone else know what happened.

The next three hours are the longest hours of my life. It gets to the point where we have to stop at a town about fifty miles from the port. Ellis and his group are en route to the village before heading back out to the islands. We found an abandoned farm on the outskirts of the town and set up camp inside the barn.

Several pack mates scouted the town beforehand. Apparently, the townspeople head further inland this time of year. Every building and store is devoid of people. Our scouts return with boxes of pasta and rice; you know, the heavy carbs we need for the remaining part of our journey.

A knock sounds at the barn door, and we all fall silent. Dimitri and I move toward the door and open it slightly. Ellis stands at the entrance with about twelve other men behind him. Dimitri gets out of their way, and they all file in, dragging a caribou behind them. Aurora remains in the shadows and watches as the strangers enter the barn. Ellis has another small box in his hand and refuses to hand it to anyone.

"I have a present for the princess from her future mate!" Ellis projects his voice, knowing full well he is being watched.

Klaus keeps his eyes on Aurora as she moves across the barn's rafters above Ellis. She drops down silently behind him, and her eyes are pools of liquid mercury as she stares at him. Aurora lightly taps his shoulder and holds her hand out to him.

Ellis almost jumps out of his skin when she touches him. He spins around and leaps back, terror evident on his face. Once he realizes it's Aurora, he holds the box out for her to take. Aurora gently takes the box from him then leaps back up to the platform—which is about twelve feet off the ground. All eyes are on Aurora as she opens the box. Inside is a hunk of meat and a large canine tooth. I watch Aurora smirk then devour the offered meat.

Aurora steps back out of sight and strips herself of her clothing. She shifts into her beast's form and leaps back down from the platform. The Polar Bear clan quickly backs up after seeing that monster of a Lycan hybrid move toward them.

Jayce brings a frightened Ellis up to speed as Aurora examines the caribou. The upper lip of her beast curls up for a moment just before she sinks her canines into the rump of the caribou and uses her talons to cut a hunk off. She drops the chunk of meat into the box and pushes it to Ellis.

"You dragons are fucking freaky. Damn, what happened to chocolates and flowers? But no, y'all send dead things and hunks of flesh. Fuck man... Now, I have to bring this back." Ellis visibly shivers then freezes when Aurora gets in his face. She breathes frost on him —just a light coating—before walking off.

Nicodeamus steps forward and says, "I suggest you return her offering to the prince before she gets mad." He looks up to the platform where Aurora sits, still shifted, watching everyone moving around below her. Aurora backs into the shadows, and the glow from her eyes can still be seen. Then suddenly, it disappears.

"That's just fucking freaky." Ellis grabs the box, and he and his men disappear quickly out the barn door. Aurora moves from the shadow, shifts back to her human form, and fully dresses. She looks around and then jumps back down to join the rest of us.

"Silly bears." She shakes her head and giggles, looking back at Dimitri.

"You can easily beat their fuzzy asses." We watch Dimitri closely, and his eyes glow the golden hue of his bear, then fade back to his human amber.

Slowly, he nods and smiles broadly at Aurora. She dips her head lightly to him, then moves back to the caribou and rips off a chunk of flesh. According to Ellis, the caribou is a gift from the prince. The fat content of this animal will help sustain our energy. Someone in the back asks what he sent Aurora.

"The prince sent me a hunk of walrus. He figured I'd need the extra energy to power my gifts." A soft smile graces her crimson lips, thinking about the thoughtful gift she had received.

Aurora moves around the barn, watching everyone interact and eat. I'm honestly not sure what she's looking for, but something is apparently off to her and she wants to check it out. She stops at another food dump, grabs several protein bars, and starts eating as she moves about. I look around quickly and—well, I'll be damned—Nicodeamus is doing the same damn thing. It's got to be a dragon trait to prowl around and make people uncomfortable.

Aurora stops and tilts her head to listen, and Nicodeamus does the same thing before moving to the door. Aurora moves to follow, but he raises his hand to stop her. A frustrated growl can be heard from her as she stares at the door, waiting for her father to return. I move forward cautiously and hug her from behind. Aurora sighs softly and leans back against me.

"A dragon landed. I feel that it's the prince. Father doesn't want me out there for some reason." Aurora sighs again and leans a bit more against me. Her heat has just about passed, but that delicious scent still lingers on her flesh.

"We need to organize our people. We will depart early in the morning. It's going to be a long, cold walk." Aurora moves away from me and starts to break the groups up. She encourages them to sleep as their animals to keep warm tonight.

Dimitri's Great Bear comes up alongside Aurora and begins to herd her toward the food, encouraging her to eat more. She shakes her head and laughs before jumping on Dimitri's back and riding him around the barn like a horse. I haven't heard her laugh that hard as he starts to swing his head, making his whole body rock.

The barn door pops open and a Viking-looking man stands in the doorway. Nicodeamus moves in front of him to stop him from going much further. Aurora is still playing with Dimitri and doesn't notice the prince enter. Aurora leaps off Dimitri's back, and shifts before her paws hit the ground.

She charges Dimitri as he rears up and tosses her. Aurora lands on all fours, tail whipping back and forth before her talons dig into the dirt. She launches herself at Dimitri again, but this time her beast rolls his bear and sends him flying. Aurora just threw over a half-ton bear. I watch the prince's jaw drop, and Nicodeamus smiles broadly like a proud peacock.

The prince whispers, "Holy fuck," which catches Aurora's attention. She growls as she turns her head to see who spoke. Instantly, her demeanor changes.

Aurora's beast tilts her head left then right, studying the prince from a distance. Dimitri moves alongside her and offers her a robe to wear. She looks down at the offered robe then looks at her talons and whines. She knows her talons will shred the material. Jayce moves forward and takes the robe with him, leading her into one of the stalls so she can shift and get dressed in private. I walk over and introduce myself to Alaric and wait nearby just in case.

Hesitantly, Aurora steps out of the stall with Jayce. I can tell he helped her brush her hair and made her look presentable. As she approaches, her eyes flicker between steel-grey and the liquid mercury of her beast. The prince isn't doing much better as he shifts his weight from one foot to the other.

When Aurora is about five feet away, she lets loose all the power she could manage to test him. Her alpha power magnified significantly since the last time she unleashed it. Everyone is driven to their knees, including Jayce and me. Only three remain standing: Aurora, Nicodeamus, and Alaric. She had to test him and had to test us too, I guess.

Aurora releases her grip on the room and stares at Alaric. He smiles broadly. It's apparent he sees her like we do, like the sun rises and sets because of her. He starts to laugh and moves his hair aside. Weaved into one of his braids is her stark, white braid. Aurora closes the distance, looks up into his eyes, and then reaches slowly up into his hair to touch her braid. I can tell from where I'm standing she is holding her breath, waiting for rejection.

"You, princess, are more than I could have ever dreamed of. I can only hope to be the mate you deserve." He gently takes her hand from his hair, kisses her knuckles, then drops to his knees before her.

"I am yours to command. My army is your army; my dragon is yours." He holds her hand as he looks up to her. There's nothing but love there for her. I know in my heart that my brother and I approve.

Aurora first looks to Nicodeamus, and he gives her a nod of approval. Then her eyes find both Jayce and me. We smile at her and do matching, sweeping bows. Aurora giggles as she watches our antics. Lastly, her eyes find Dimitri; his opinion means so much to her. He bows his head and raises his fist over his heart. Aurora mimics Dimitri's move, placing her fist over her heart. Out of character for Aurora, she lowers her head to Dimitri then looks up to him. Although shocked, the big guy gives her a shy smile, embarrassed by the level of respect she has just shown him.

Aurora turns slowly and looks down at the prince, who is still kneeling before her. Her slender fingers gently cup his bearded cheeks, threading through the coarse hair. Ever so slowly, she leans down and tenderly kisses his full lips. As she kisses him, the rumble of approval from his dragon makes her smile. They open their eyes simultaneously, and their beasts can look at each other up close.

It is said that when our beasts surface, they can see each other's true form. We are technically one entity, but it's almost an out of body experience when mates meet. The world around them does not exist, and time stands still.

Aurora and Alaric continue to look deeply into each other's eyes. Eventually, Nicodeamus decides to move forward and lightly touch Aurora's shoulder. She growls at her father for interrupting her. Aurora's eyes widen in horror at her actions, and she backs away quickly.

"I'm sorry, Alaric. I got lost for a moment." Aurora's eyes dart to her father then back to Alaric.

"Will we be safe crossing? Our numbers are few due to the betrayal of the American Lycans." Aurora looks back at the fifty that we brought with us. According to the last message I received, the other two hundred from my birth pack will be arriving in the morning.

"My love, two hundred Dire Wolves will be here by sunrise as requested. We will march with two hundred and fifty at your command." I raise my fist over my heart and bow my head to look at Alaric.

"Any suggestions, M'Lord, would be most helpful and appreciated." Alaric looks at the force we travel with and then back to Aurora.

"My mother's people are with us. I am in command of fifty Gold Dragons and another twenty Ice Dragons that are loyal only to me. Ellis has about twenty Polar Bears loyal only to him on the ground." Alaric moves forward and offers his hand to me.

"Brothers in arms and bond mates to Aurora, you and your family have my protection." I shake his hand firmly and watch him shake Jayce's hand as well.

"I speak for my birth pack when I say we are grateful for your help and protection." I look to my brother, Jayce, and he's smiling like a fool while looking at the prince. Well, I know who's going to be ogling the new mate together.

Alaric moves forward and hugs Aurora once more, then goes to shake Nicodeamus's hand before heading to the door. He pauses in the doorway and looks back at us. "Ellis will let me know when you arrive in the danger zone. My team and I will keep the dragons off you. Destroy anything that isn't a part of your or Ellis's group. There's a pack of Lycans on the move to the islands. Be Careful."

He stares at Aurora when he speaks his final words. Surprisingly, she nods and waves at him. As soon as Alaric was out the door, Aurora runs as fast as she can after him. If I know Aurora, she wants to see his dragon. However, Nicodeamus blocks Aurora's path.

"No, daughter, not right now. He needs to focus on tomorrow, not you running out into the snow." Aurora growls at her father and walks away, pouting. It's going to be a long night.

We slept in shifts last night just in case of a surprise attack. I wake up the next morning and I can't find Aurora, and I realize that Nicodeamus is also missing. Shit, what the fuck did I miss? Jayce is by the fire making the last of the rice and pasta for all of us to eat. I walk over to the barn doors and shove one of them open.

About a foot of snow fell last night, which blankets the ground for as far as I can see. We are now in whiteout conditions. I concentrate and shift my eyes to be like Aurora's. After doing so, I'm able to make out the outline of Nicodeamus's dragon and Aurora's animal together. She is standing on top of her father's head, watching the countryside.

I turn my attention to where she's looking, and I can make out the outlines of my pack-mates on the horizon as they come up from the south. Good, we will be able to leave as planned. I return to the barn and rally the troops. Everyone eats quickly as they wait for the Dire Wolf pack to arrive.

CHAPTER 13
Dimitri

Great Goddess Callisto, help me. First, I spend years fighting my feelings for Aurora. Then, her wolf kills because she believes I'm hers. Then all of a sudden, I don't rank, and my feelings for her are squashed. Bloody hell, Nicodeamus is right! We were drugged so our bond wouldn't grow—a thousand curses upon the Lupi family and their heirs. By my Romani blood, I will have vengeance for what they have stolen from me.

Mate after mate, I watch Aurora gain in power. The theory that Nicodeamus presented seems valid, but the real question is, what can I do to break the spell? I watch Aurora assemble the troops in preparation for departure. The way she rallies everyone reminds me of her mother on the battlefield.

Nicodeamus's dragon roars and begins walking toward the Bering Land Bridge. My bear lumbers along toward the back of the pack. What I lack in speed, I more than make up for in strength. We know we're walking into an ambush, so it's just a question of when.

We walk for miles, following the path that Nicodeamus's dragon blazes for us. We walk in this endless sea of white, not able to see more than a couple of feet in front of our faces. If it wasn't for the strong scent of Nicodeamus's dragon, our sense of direction would be thrown off by the lack of landmarks. However, I can faintly make out the glow of Aurora's eyes as she sits on her father's back. I pick up my pace to get closer to his dragon so I can see exactly what's going on.

Aurora sits statue-still on her father's back, watching the pack behind him. Her eyes slowly scan the horizon, watching for any signs of the impending attack. The Dire Wolves and I are having no trouble whatsoever moving through this heavy snowfall. Our only disadvantage is that, unlike Aurora and her father, we cannot see much further ahead of ourselves than maybe a couple of feet.

Howls erupt in the distance, coming from multiple directions ahead of and alongside us. Here it is the moment of truth. This is precisely what we've all been preparing and training for. Now we get to see how good Nicodeamus and my training is as the Dire Wolves aid us in battle. Aurora issues several short barks, and the pack splits into three equal units. These units end up splitting off: one going left, one going right, and the third still lagging behind Nicodeamus.

Aurora leaps off her father's back and comes up alongside me. Her eyes focus on the Lycans walking with us, and she issues several more barks at them, sending them off in their own direction.

The wind shifts, and several different scents hit our noses. I pick up the first scent from the Polar Bears, the second scent—that bastard Sebastian. Aurora begins to growl deep in her throat. With that tone, you know someone is going to die.

She separates from her father and starts walking about seventy yards to my left. Nicodeamus then goes another sixty yards to my right. Divide and conquer is the order for today, apparently. To keep everyone safe, I just hope we switched up the training enough after Sebastian left.

Nicodeamus roars loudly as the crunching of the snow becomes louder. I see Aurora's glowing eyes look back at me briefly before she takes off toward the masses. The spray of blood is a stark contrast against the bright, white snow. The scent of copper and blood fills the air as bellows of pain and anguish echo all around us.

A pair of Polar Bears charge at me. Finally, I get a chance to prove myself. I don't think they were expecting to see a bear of my size in existence. When they get close enough, I swipe at them with my long, hooked claws. His white fur is painted crimson, and the snow is littered with droplets of blood. The second Polar Bear pisses himself when my next swipe rips the head right off his companion.

Another skull for Aurora's collection. Too bad we're on the ice; it won't be here in the spring. Without a second thought, I charge the second bear and roll him onto his back. Quickly, my massive maw snaps down around his throat, and I shake my head violently until every tendon and blood vessel is severed.

It's a great time to be alive; I live for moments like this. With each Polar Bear that I dispatch, I feel more like my old self. Briefly, I look up and see Aurora running toward me. She sails through the air over me to take out a Lycan who had snuck up behind me.

His head goes flying past me and hits a Polar Bear's face, knocking him out cold. I casually walk up and use my claws to rip his throat open. By the time I look back to where Aurora was, she's long gone. How many fucking Polar Bears live out here? Damn. I mean, seriously, it seems like a never-ending supply. On a more positive note, they can't fight for shit.

I see the blue glow of Nicodeamus's fire raining down on the mass of bodies in front of him in the distance. I watch in horror as Aurora launches herself off her father's head, through his flames, and into the fray below. I did not teach that girl to fight like that!

I make a newbie mistake and stop paying attention to what is going on around me. I feel the pressing of a sharp blade against my left rib cage, too close to my heart for comfort. Slowly, I turn my head to find Sebastian holding the knife.

"Shift back and live, remain as a bear and die," Sebastian says in an ice-cold tone. I shift back to my human form. He still has the tip of the blade pressed to my chest.

"Coward," is all I say to him. He doesn't fight with honor.

For all I know, that female, Ravenna, was his real mate and he had forsaken her for power. If I remember correctly, he only gained Aurora's speed and talons and nothing else. I look down at the blade again; it's tinted green, which means Dire Wolf venom. I can't survive that, so I decide to play along and see where this rat bastard takes it. He starts pushing me toward Nicodeamus and Aurora.

I walk with my hands up in the air to show there's an issue. One minute I see Aurora's eyes; the next, I don't. She just went all ghost on us. This is about to get seriously interesting.

Suddenly, Sebastian's left arm is severed at the elbow. He screams in pain as he backs up, trying to escape. Aurora manifests out of what seems like thin air, and she stands there in her human form. Her hands and forearms are shifted, her heavily armored gauntlets covered in blood.

"Betrayer! False mate! Coward!" Aurora continues to call him names as she stalks closer to him, herding him back toward the edge of the ice.

The beating of wings can be heard, but Aurora is too focused on moving in for the kill. Flames rain down from the sky between Aurora and Sebastian. I leap into the air and tackle Aurora to the ground before she is burnt to a crisp.

The ice chunk Sebastian is on starts to float off to sea. A large, Red Dragon swoops down to grab Sebastian off the ice and flies off with him. My body tenses, prepared for another attack, but nothing comes. It's almost eerily silent except for the giggling I hear under me.

"D? I think you can get up now." Wait, shit… I look down, and I still have Aurora pinned under me.

She's laughing almost hysterically, and tears are rolling down her cheeks from how hard she's laughing. I remove myself carefully from her then realize I have the boner to end all boners. How embarrassing! I try to cover myself with both hands. I feel my cheeks flush as Aurora just keeps staring at my cock. FUCK! Nicodeamus—thank the gods—comes up behind Aurora and slaps his hand over her eyes.

"Dimitri, get yourself under control. You can kill someone with that thing!" Nicodeamus is half-joking, I think.

Jayce is in a state of shock, staring at me in all my aroused glory. Fucking cock has a damn mind of its freaking own. Death and destruction litters the field around me, and here I am with a rock-hard, throbbing boner. Just fucking wonderful.

Now is the perfect time to go for a swim. I jump into the arctic water and instantly regret my decision; it's much colder than I was anticipating. I crawl back out of the water, and thankfully, my cock calmed down. I shift to my bear and decide to remain in this form until after catching up with Ellis.

Everyone returns to their animal form and begins to walk toward the first of the islands, which we can now see. Ellis comes out onto the ice to greet us and lead us back to headquarters. There's a single cavern visible on the island, so we follow Ellis underground.

Ellis starts passing out blankets and clothing as everyone shifts back to their human form. Aurora waits until Dominik secures her something to wear before she allows him to lead her into an alcove to shift and get dressed.

Once she's done, she emerges from the alcove wearing a full-length gown. It's a pale, powder-blue and fits her like a glove. It must have been left there for her by Alaric. I wrap a blanket around me like a toga before approaching the group. They are already in an in-depth discussion about what happened and what's yet to come.

Nothing new has been discussed since our last meeting before the mission. However, we gain further information from Ellis when he tells us that fire dragons, otherwise known as Red Dragons, have joined the fight. When we go for the second half of this journey, the Gold and Ice Dragons will await our signal to join in on the attack.

Now, Aurora sits next to her father as he looks over the maps with Ellis and Klaus. The battle strategy is being amended since we now know Sebastian is on the field. He knows way too much and can make this battle way too dangerous for us, so the original formation has been changed. Ellis is dividing his bears up into four groups to match our four groups of troops.

Everyone's mulling around the cavern, eating, drinking, and generally getting to know each other so in the heat of battle, we can recognize who is friend and who is foe.

Ellis is about to make a phone call to Alaric when Nicodeamus stops him. He is concerned about Alaric's phone going off and giving away his position. We ponder his suggestion for a moment and then agree that he's probably correct. It's not safe with how close we are to the enemy.

I can tell Aurora is quite distressed. Even with her sitting on Dominik's lap, scales still ripple up and down her forearms. I understand her distress level; a male she once considered her mate is now trying to attack and kill us.

Jayce reappears, bringing Aurora a tray of meat and some sort of spicy drink with it. Usually food and drink is an excellent way to cheer Aurora up, but she doesn't appear to be hungry at the moment. Nicodeamus has the look of a concerned father as he watches his poor child deal with all the revelations that have happened in such a short time.

I know the level of betrayal that she and Nicodeamus feels runs bone-deep. I don't know if there's anything I can do to help her deal with everything. As a young pup, when she would get stressed, I used to give her rides on my bear and purposely toss her and roll around with her.

I start to laugh a little as I think about that memory. Aurora gives me a strange look because I'm almost laughing my balls off in the middle of a serious discussion.

"Aurora, do you remember when you were a little girl, and you would get upset or stressed out over what was going on around you? What would I do?" Aurora slowly stands up, looks around the room, and then snatches a drumstick off Jayce's plate and begins to pace.

I can tell she's now searching her memory for all the crazy, little things I used to do just to make her smile. I can also tell the moment she figures out the answer to my question. Her smile slowly broadens, her eyes light up, and she looks almost ethereal.

"That's an easy one, D. You used to sit there and tickle the hell out of me. When that didn't work, you would shift to your bear and roll around on the floor with me, tossing me in the air with your paws." A melodic giggle escapes her lips as she looks deeply into my eyes, reliving the memory.

"Or you'd lay down so I could climb onto your back and grab onto your fur, and we would go running through the forest while Andre would scream at us to slow down." Aurora is almost laughing hysterically. Slowly, she turns to look over at Nicodeamus. She smiles and sits down next to her dad, snuggling into his left side, still very protective of him.

"Dad, Dimitri deserves, like, national honors for dealing with me. My mood swings alone deserve hazard pay. I was stubborn and pig-headed and probably a royal pain in his ass." I try not to laugh as Aurora perfectly sums up her childhood for her father.

"I definitely didn't make their lives easy, nor did I even attempt to. I had all this speed, strength, and agility, and I just wanted to go. Poor Andre. I'm surprised he still had hair when you saw him last. That poor man would be terrified and frantically searching for me while I clawed halfway up a tree, staring down at him and trying not to laugh." Aurora's gaze lands on me as she smiles and points at me.

"Damn, Dimitri and his sneaky bear with his sense of smell

would find me every flipping time. I know one thing, between those two, I learned how to hide, I learned how to evade, and I learned that you cannot trick a bear's nose for anything." The way she is smiling at me makes me feel like the king of the world—like the sun rose and set around me for once in my life.

It's moments like this when I hope and pray that Nicodeamus is right and she's really mine. She has me so elevated upon a pedestal, it's like I can do no wrong. I've loved that girl since she was born, and I love her still, though it's changed. The rest of the guys are watching me as I smile like a lovesick pup.

Of course, while we're all jovial and laughing, remembering the past, Ellis gets a text message. The message is from Alaric, who informs us the German Lycan pack was attacked. Everyone survived except for the alpha. Klaus and his brother Kaden are so distraught that both of them want to go back to their birth pack to keep everything under control.

Shortly after Alaric's text message, Klaus's phone starts ringing. He answers quickly and receives a report from his younger brother about the attack. Klaus gives detailed directions to his younger brother as to what to do. He decides to video chat with his brother, so it's projected for his entire pack to see. He reassures them that all will be well and he is on a mission of utmost importance to return the last living Lycan heir to the throne.

Aurora chooses this time to stand up and take the phone from Klaus, and she looks down at the phone itself. Aurora slowly raises her right arm to show his pack that she bears the royal house's mark.

You can hear the chatter erupting on the other side with shouts of joy and excitement. They all begin to rally behind her, pledging their undying loyalty to her and to the remaining people of her house. Aurora stands perfectly straight, shoulders back, looking like the future queen she is. She addresses the pack in their native tongue, reassuring them she has the drive and ability to regain her mother's throne.

She looks up and scans those who are assembled before her. Aurora gives them a nod and acknowledges her forces before addressing the Lycan pack. She tells them she will be returning to the throne, she will remain in the castle after the war is over, and she will reunite all the packs and call them home. Then she issues an open-ended invitation to anybody who wishes to challenge her upon her arrival on Romanian soil. No one dares to speak.

Aurora watches the Lycans drop to their knees and lower their heads, submitting to her. Aurora lets them know she's going to hand the phone back to Klaus, and she allows him to handle the daily duties in her place. Slowly, Aurora walks back over to Klaus and hands him the phone. Aurora gives him a kiss on the cheek and tells him she's sorry for his loss. She creeps back over to where Dominik and Jayce are, and she sits between them and starts to eat.

Her drive for vengeance has been stoked, and the fire is burning much brighter than it was before. Hell hath no fury like a woman scorned. And I am damn sure Aurora is going to rain hell on Earth upon those who stand against her.

Nicodeamus chooses this time to speak with Aurora about the weaknesses of each dragon species. We all listen carefully, making mental notes of where would do the most damage—with hits that we may or may not be able to rain down on them. Let's face it, dragons are a hundred times larger than any of us, except for maybe Nicodeamus.

I can see the gears turning behind Aurora's eyes as she starts to contemplate what her father's telling her. She tilts her head to the left then back to the right again. She scoots closer to her father and stares him right in his eyes, grabbing his hand with both of hers. Both of their eyes become that of their beasts.

We can tell they're having a deep conversation, privy only to them. The way they are sitting stock still, barely even blinking, we can tell whatever is passing between them is of vital importance. The tension in the air starts to increase as the moments tick by. Nicodeamus is the first to break off.

"I am not a fan of this idea, baby girl. But if the opportunity presents itself, I will be more than happy to assist you in making it happen." Nicodeamus, like Aurora, does tilt his head left then right after he finishes speaking to assess whether his answer was enough. I decide to question them since his response makes no sense to me.

"M'Lord, what do you mean? What opportunity are you speaking of?" You know that look somebody gets when they are absolutely up to no good? Well, right now, Nicodeamus looks like the cat that swallowed the canary. That's usually the look he gets when something really reckless is about to happen.

"Well, I'm kind of happy you asked because it'll be much easier to explain it now than during battle. My crazy-ass daughter wants me to launch her into the air using my wing. That way she can sink her talons into a dragon flying overhead and rip out its throat. Honestly, from a logical standpoint, it should work perfectly. My only concern is the landing." I'm really starting to hate how Nicodeamus says everything so matter-of-fact when it has to deal with life or death.

Thankfully, Dominik speaks up next and takes the words right out of my mouth. "Hold up, you mean to say you're going to send Aurora flying through the air to sink her talons into a dragon's hide? Then, we have to be concerned about her getting to the ground safely after she kills the dragon? Just fucking wonderful!"

Dominik throws his hands up into the air and begins to pace. I look over at his brother, Jayce, and he is a ball of nerves. He's definitely very anxious about the possibility of his mate getting injured. Ellis is going back and forth, shaking his head no while saying, "Aww hell no, that bitch is crazy," under his breath.

I've decided that I'm in the middle of some sort of crazy rom-com that's gone horribly wrong. Aurora has lost her mind, and her father's not far behind her. Her two Dire Wolf mates are the only ones making any sense. The poor Polar Bear is beside himself. And I'm sitting over here, thinking what the actual fuck just happened?

I know Aurora can be reckless at times, but this absolutely takes the bloody cake. How does she expect to get to the ground without killing herself? I mean, seriously, these dragons are what, ten to twenty thousand feet in the air when they're flying? Even if she gets lucky and one swoops down close enough for her to launch at it, Who's to say he's not going to gain altitude to try to shake her off?

Between Aurora and her father, once they have their mind set on something, it's virtually impossible to get them to change their course. Tomorrow is going to be a shitshow. If we make it out of this in one fucking piece, I will be absolutely amazed. For now, I have to try to figure out a way to talk some sense into that girl before she ends up becoming a dirt torpedo.

Klaus walks over, listening to Aurora and her father discussing ideas for her to become a Lycan projectile. Poor Klaus ends up face-palming and starts shaking his head in disbelief at the lunacy he's listening to. I really can't blame him right now. I'm still pondering how the fuck I got myself into this shit. I've lived almost two hundred years—past what my species should have lived—and now I'm probably going to die because the princess lost her mind.

Aurora runs over to the fire pit, grabs a few charcoal pieces that have cooled, and then heads over to the cavern wall. She starts drawing pictures of flying dragons, her father on the ground, little circles and stick figures that are supposed to be us, and then a giant smiley face flying up toward the dragon.

I thought her homicidal tendencies were kind of frightening, but this absolutely takes the cake. She explains that when the timing is right she's going to run toward her father, he's going to lower his wing, she's going to stand on his wingtip, and he's going to launch her into the air like a frisbee. I really can't see this working; no way, no how.

But if I start thinking a little bit left field with this, I can almost see it working. Shit, just like that, I'm beginning to see the brilliance in her insanity. Both of her mates are attempting to talk her out of her hair-brained scheme, but it ain't going to happen. We'll just have to wait and see what happens tomorrow. Hopefully, she stays in one piece, and we can all go home happy little campers.

CHAPTER 14

Aurora

I have no bloody clue what time I went to bed last night. But shit, if I could get about three more hours of sleep and a giant pot of coffee, I'd be golden. I look at the assembled group in front of me; we are well-rested and fed. None of us really know what we're walking into today.

What I do know is that Alaric is quite anxious this morning. I raise my hand and start rubbing his scale, trying to soothe him like he's done for me so many times already. I feel him relax, and I honestly think, somehow, he knows what I'm planning to do. It really doesn't matter though. It needs to be done. Without air support during the attack, we're sitting ducks.

I know my strengths and weaknesses. I don't think the boys understand entirely how strong I truly am. And I don't mean physical strength, I mean strength of will, drive, and integrity.

After everything, my father has shown me about attacking the dragons. I know their weak spot is their neck—especially if I can get up close to the head just under its jaw and sink my talons in there. The scales there are so tiny and spread out that it'll be easy for the tip of my talons to get in and start ripping. I just have to figure out how to land the fucker. I wonder if I can make dragon surfing a sport?

I better not say anything about that to the guys because they'll really start to panic. It's bad enough I slept in a twin taco last night, neither one of them wanting to let me move. I really do understand their level of concern, but if I have the opportunity, why not take it?

Through my dreams last night, when Alaric visited me, he said he wouldn't be far away. I'm counting on it. But again, if more dragons than what he's expecting shows up, then dang, I guess I'm going flying. Either my father's going to have to launch me into the air, or Alaric will have to carry me. That way I'll only have to dive-bomb off Alaric and onto the dragons below him. Either way, I fully intend to get the job done.

That fucking rat bastard Sebastian... I swear to the gods if I see him, I am ripping his fucking head off. His head is going on my goddamn wall right beside his fucking mother's. Between the two of them, they have stolen way too goddamn much from me, and I will never forgive them for that. They better hope and pray I'm not the one who finds them first because unlike the others, I'm going to make it fucking painful.

I growl as I work through my inner monologue, and everybody's head whips to look at me and see what exactly is going on. I smile and wave and start to laugh. Yeah, I just had a Harley Quinn moment. Oops.

I find my twins standing together and talking by the fire. Gently, I touch Jayce's shoulder and get him to turn to me. I kiss him deeply and passionately, making him growl. His fingertips dig into the meat of my ass as he lifts me off the ground.

I smile against his lips and whisper, "I love you."

He returns the passionate kiss and tells me he loves me too. Slowly, Jayce lowers me to the floor. I don't even have both feet on the ground before Dominik twirls me around and aggressively kisses me. Damn, I love when he tries to get all dominant with me. I growl and bite his lip before I start giggling.

I whisper against his lips, "I love you." In no way am I saying goodbye. In my mind, I'm just making sure they know they are loved. Hesitantly, Dom lowers me to the ground.

I smile at both of my mates before I head off to find my father. When I find him, he's in an in-depth discussion with Dimitri and Klaus. I run my fingers up Klaus's back as I pass him on my way to my father.

Klaus makes a soft growl in the back of his throat. I stop and turn to look at him. His wolf's eyes are beautiful; they're gold in color. I break eye contact and move to my father and hug him tightly. I'm not sure who needed it more, him or me. Gently, I place a kiss on my father's cheek and tell him I love him. In turn, my father kisses my forehead and tells me he's proud of me and loves me.

Just to fuck with Dimitri, I go to Klaus next to hug him and kiss his cheek. I thank him for coming to our aid and being there for me. He smiles at me then gently kisses my cheek. Klaus's hand slides through my long, snow-white hair, his smile radiating affection. Does he wish for more than just my allegiance? It doesn't really matter right now; Sebastian's false bond won't let me find my real mate. I break away from Klaus and move toward Dimitri.

Dimitri appears nervous, which isn't like him. I move slowly toward him and circle around him, looking him over. He's definitely a handsome man. His shoulders are so broad and thick, and I can't help but run my fingers over them.

Dimitri's frame tenses the minute my fingers make contact with his shoulders. It's not fear that makes him tense, so what could it be? When I move to stand before Dimitri, he's not looking at me like he usually does. That fatherly look of adoration is gone. Now, his hazel eyes move over my frame, almost caressing my flesh. Quickly, my eyes dart to my father, and he just smiles at me. I seek out the twins, and they're smiling too.

What the fuck is going on around here? I start to back up, and Dimitri wraps his large hands around my elbows to stop me. I stare at his hands and notice how gently they grip my arms. I draw in a deep breath then look up to meet his eyes. Dimitri slowly raises his left hand to cup my right cheek, and I lean into his touch.

"Aurora," he says in his deep husky voice.

I can't help but feel like my insides are on fire with how he's looking at me. "Your father and I suspect that Elena cast a spell to keep us apart. We believe she used blood magic to stop our bond from forming." Dimitri gently rubs my cheek as his eyes beg me to understand. I stop breathing the moment everything Dimitri says clicks. Frost begins to spread from the spot I'm standing and starts to coat the entire cavern.

"I wasn't crazy? My wolf was right?" I start crying; I can't help it.

The tears flow freely down my cheeks, and all I can do is stare up into Dimitri's eyes. I have loved this man before me for the better half of a hundred years. All that time, I thought I was insane, that my wolf was wrong and tricked by the binding. Dimitri quickly pulls me flush with his chest and holds me tightly. I feel the rumble of his bear in his chest, trying to soothe me like he used to. I push back lightly so I can look back up at Dimitri again.

"I swear you will have Elena's head. I will give it to you." I feel my canines descend, and my eyes churn to liquid mercury.

Dimitri chuckles just before he kisses me on the lips for the first time ever. I can sense Jayce and Dominik approach, but they don't interfere. My hands slowly slide up Dimitri's broad chest, and I rest my palms on his cheeks and hold him to me. I can feel him smiling mid-kiss, then I slowly pull back to look at him.

"Kill the witch, break the spell. Easy enough. Then, off to storm the castle!" Poor Dominik facepalms again and complains it's not going to be that easy. I tilt my head to the right then give Dominik the middle finger.

I start to turn away from Dimitri before I make my announcement. "I am the Poke-master! I have collected them *all*!" I scream *all* because Dimitri slapped my ass, hard. Quickly, I spin to face him as I rub my poor ass cheeks.

"Remember, princess, you collected the others. I've been right here waiting for you." Dimitri's dominant attitude is kind of a turn on, and I start laughing as I look at him. He went all cheesy on me by quoting one of my favorite eighties songs: the Richard Marx song about the guy waiting for his love to return.

Damn emotional wolf; fucking tears start rolling down my cheeks. What the fuck? I'm starting to turn into a freaking wuss. I roughly wipe the tears away, then look to the pack, who's trying to act like they didn't see anything.

"We leave in ten minutes, so be fucking ready!" I head off to my part of the cavern.

I can still hear the guys congratulating Dimitri. I slowly turn around to look at him, and he has a giant grin on his face. I haven't seen him smile so much in so long. He deserves to be happy. Several moments pass and I decide it's time to shift. Quickly, I consume the last of the rations I hoarded away for myself before I head to the gathering point.

We have our marching orders from Nicodeamus, and we break off in our assigned groups to head toward Siberia. The larger one of the two Diomede Islands separates our forces. I feel Alaric's anxiety spike just as our groups pass the second island.

I clamber up my father's back and start to watch behind us, keeping an eye out for any enemies. Knowing those sneaky scum bags, they'll attack from behind. Through the pack link, I order the group to converge and form a circle. Once everyone is in place, we have eyes in all directions.

What we didn't account for was a Red Wyvern swooping down to snatch me off my father's back. Stupid move grabbing me. The wyvern continues gaining altitude; I'm guessing it's planning on dropping me. Without warning, I reach up and cut the tendons on one foot. Once it loses its grip on me, I reach up and grasp onto the remaining foot. With my free hand, I slash at its exposed abdomen. The wyvern screams in pain as I continue to disembowel it. Blood and intestinal contents coat my scales as I continue to rip. In the distance, I sense Alaric gaining ground. He should reach me once I start to fall.

Now, I grip both legs of the wyvern and hold on tight. It's only a matter of time before it bleeds out. In my head, I start singing Limp Bizkit's *Break Stuff*. It seems entirely appropriate right about now. Suddenly, the wyvern begins to fall from the sky. I use my talons to climb up onto its back and hold its wings open to slow our descent.

I feel Alaric before I see him. His giant, taloned dragon hand comes down and gently grips me, and I release my hold on the wyvern's corpse. I gently rub my muzzle on Alaric's scales as he carries me. Then I notice he has a group of dragons flying with him in formation. Once the wyvern corpse reaches the ground, we watch it take out some of the enemies' Lycan forces. Yes! Two for one! Alaric's nest mates break off to fight the remaining wyverns.

We gain speed as we approach a Black Dragon. This thing is fucking huge—it dwarfs Alaric's dragon. I pat his hand to get him to drop me onto the monster's back, but his dragon only shakes his head *no* at my idea. Through the bond, I push my plan to him. Hopefully he sees it's the only way to take out that acid breathing monster. I can hear him huff before he changes course. Honestly, I can't believe I won that discussion.

He aligns himself over the center of the Black Dragon's back. While a small Gold Dragon keeps him occupied, I drop down from twenty feet above him. The Black Dragon keeps circling the battle below, yet he's not interfering. Ever so carefully, I walk along the spines on his back, making sure to remain on his armored plates.

In the back of my mind, I start humming the *Mission Impossible* theme song. This dragon is much larger than I was anticipating. I begin to get concerned until I notice missing scales at the base of his skull. Mentally, I reach out to my father, and he confirms what I'm thinking: dig quickly and sever the spinal cord. Alaric and his group are close, making sure no one gets close to me.

When I feel the time is right, I sink my talons into the exposed flesh. The Black Dragon roars and starts to whip his head from side to side, trying to shake me off. I hold on for dear life and sink my talons into his skin as I wedge myself between his spines. He stops whipping his head around, so I go back on the attack. I rip out several more large chunks before he starts thrashing his head around again. My once white fur is now covered in blood and flesh chunks from the Black Dragon. This is getting irritating; every time I start getting somewhere, he starts thrashing.

The good news is I can see two decent-sized blood vessels and vertebrae. As the thrashing slows down, I lunge quickly and easily slice through one of the blood vessels. Blood goes everywhere! It covers me as well as the dragon's scales. His blood is coagulating almost the second it hits his scales and me. I'm a big, gloppy, blood-covered mess. The only bonus to this gory mess is that he's slowly losing altitude. The dragon's roars are getting weaker, and he's not thrashing as hard.

Seizing the opportunity, I sever the second blood vessel. I feel as though I am swimming in a sea of blood. I have to sink my talons deep into his flesh just to keep from sliding off. I carefully move to stand after I notice the ground is approaching fast. Thankfully, he's headed right toward his own reinforcements. I grab on to the crown of horns that adorn his head and brace for impact. Just as I sense the impending crash, I jump up to lessen the blow to my body. The Black Dragon's body slides for several hundred feet before stopping.

I jump off the dragon's corpse quickly. Alaric's dragon lands close by and observes me. I'm cold, wet, and feeling gross. The blood in my fur is coagulating and freezing at the same time. I can't shift to my human form, or else I will turn into an ice cube. Alaric lowers his massive head to my level and starts blowing his hot breath on me. I'm just thankful he has enough sense not to try his flames on me. One great wing comes forward and shelters me from the wind.

There's a war going on about two thousand feet from us, but Alaric's only concern is my health and well-being. After about his fifth or sixth heated breaths, I'm defrosted, and the blood chunks have started falling away. I rub my muzzle against his dragon's nose, and then I lick it affectionately. Alaric forgets his strength when he tries to nuzzle me back. I end up on my ass in the snow, shaking my head at him. If a dragon could look sorry, he was doing it. I dust myself off and start walking back to the battle.

Apparently, I'm not allowed to walk anymore because Alaric's dragon scoops me up, flies me over to my father, and drops me on his back. With my arrival after the Black Dragon crashed, the remaining forces retreat quickly.

Without a second thought, I leap off my father's back and give chase. My mates come up alongside me as well as the rest of the Dire Wolves. One by one, we hunt down and slaughter the remaining Polar Bears and Lycans.

The only unanswered question I have: where the fuck is Sebastian? I stand there and watch as the last of my enemies fall around me. All this bloodshed and for what? The Polar Bears didn't need to die; they were lied to and misled. The Lycans that fought, I wonder which pack they were from? I stand here in the middle of the tundra, surrounded by corpses, and all I can think about are the pups back in America.

My father's dragon comes up behind me and bathes me in his blue flames. All the dirt and grime from the day is gone. I nod my wolven head at my father before I start walking.

Alaric's dragon lands before me and opens his taloned hand, revealing a wooden box. I tilt my head left then right, studying it. Carefully, I use my talons and open the box. Within it is clothing; a heavy coat and boots. I look up at Alaric and motion to his wing. Taking the hint, he drops both of his wings to block me from the cold winds. I get dressed quickly in the clothes provided. My gloved hand lightly touches Alaric's wing, and he lifts it. The clothing he picked out for me fits beautifully, and I step out looking like a princess for the first time in my life. The twins and Dimitri come to stand before me. I gently rub my face along their muzzles.

"Alaric and I are going to fly to his summer chalet." I look over to my father, and his dragon is smiling—well, he's showing his teeth, so I assume he's smiling.

"I know you remember where the chalet is. Please lead our forces there." Nico nods his great dragon head and roars, assembling the troops. They turn and start heading south as they follow behind Nico.

I look back to Alaric's dragon, he lays down in the snow and extends his wing. Carefully, I step on the scaled bone of his wing and begin climbing toward his back. Once on Alaric's back, I remove my glove and press it to his scales.

"Where should I sit?" I look around his dragon's back, puzzled.

I'll lower my head. Sit directly behind the ridge of horns. It should protect you from the wind. I look toward Alaric's head where he indicated. He turns his body so his head is close to his back. I carefully climb onto his neck then move to sit behind the ridge of horns. It's a perfect fit for me, and I feel safe and secure where I'm sitting. I pat Alaric's neck, and we take off.

It's interesting sitting here with a dragon's eye view of the world around me. I shift my eyes to that of my beast, and I get to see the world how Alaric sees it. Everything looks so amazing up here above the clouds. It looks like we are flying over a field of cotton balls. Through the bond, I can feel that my joy from flying with him pleases him and his dragon.

Carefully, I reach down and start scratching at his scales under the horn ridge. It seems like there's a build-up of dead skin in some spots, so I carefully remove it. I keep working on his scales while I'm back here. Soft rumbles can be felt from his dragon as I preen his scales. I know I love the feel of my father's fire through my fur, so I assume Alaric is enjoying the attention.

In the distance, a castle on a cliff face comes into view. It looks like it stepped right out of a fairy tale story. Without warning, two Gold Dragons flank us. I shift my arms and hands quickly, ready to fight.

Through the bond, I hear Alaric's voice. *Settle, my love. It's my mother and sister escorting us home.* His words offer me a little comfort and reassure me that we're safe for the moment. However, I have trust issues now, and it's hard to relax when I'm surrounded by strangers. *Love, my life is tied to yours directly. I would never put our lives at risk. I have too much to live for now.*

Without a second thought, I shift my hands back and rub his scales. I attempt to relax and enjoy the remainder of our flight to his castle.

The castle is one that you would expect to hear about in a fairy tale novel. Tall spires adorn the four corners, and a tall wall surrounds the main structure. We fly in lazy circles, gliding on the thermals around the castle grounds so I can get a good look at his home. I can tell he and his dragon are very concerned if I approve of their nest because his anxiety is spiking. I gently rub his scales.

"Your nest is beautiful. Can we land so I can get a better look at you and your home?" No sooner do the words leave my mouth than his dragon banks and lands softly in the courtyard. Alaric lowers his head, allowing me to slowly slide off his neck to land on his foreleg. My hand rests on his dragon's cheek as I step down. Once I'm safely on the ground, he sits up and spreads his wings, and roars. My inner beast stirs at his call, and I feel compelled to howl along with him. We roar and howl several times until my human throat is sore from the effort. I smile up at him and shake my head as I laugh. His large dragon head lowers to my level.

When I'm this close, I notice the blues mixed in with the white. His scales also slightly change color depending on the angle I look from. Alaric stands perfectly still as I continue to touch his scales and look at his dragon form. His large, golden, serpentine eye follows my movements.

Out of the corner of my eye, I noticed movement off to my right. I quickly duck under Alaric's lowered wing. I remain firmly pressed against his body, slowly working on climbing up his leg to get my feet off the ground. Alaric's dragon huffs, and I guess he's laughing for some reason.

I remain perched on his leg directly under where his wing attaches to his body. If he chose to stand up now, I would surely fall. A woman's voice reaches my ears and I start to growl, not happy another female is near what's mine. Slowly, Alaric lifts his wing and turns his head to face me. I stare into his dragon's eyes, my own churning liquid mercury; every move I make, Alaric mimic's.

My love, Mother wishes to meet you. That's the female you heard speaking. No threat, I promise. Alaric's voice echoes in my head. I gradually calm down and nod to him. I slip carefully back to the ground and straighten my hair back out. I draw in a deep, measured breath and make sure my eyes are back to normal. I adjust my stance to how Dimitri told me I should carry myself at court. My hand rests on Alaric's side just before I step out from under his wing.

His mother is a vision of beauty. Her hair is long like mine but is the color of spun gold. Her skin is the most perfect of porcelain, with lips the color of blood. She rushes forward and embraces me tightly. My look of apparent panic causes Alaric to make a rumbling noise, which gets his mother to back off.

"I'm sorry, my dear! I never thought my boy would find a mate. When he said it was you, I just couldn't contain myself! Oh, where are my manners? My name is Katherine. I guess you can say I'm Queen of the Ice Dragon Court." She smiles while looking at me and slightly bows her head.

Two men come forth, one carrying clothing and the other with a dressing blind. The men start to herd Alaric's dragon to an alcove close by. I watch the men for a moment, then turn my attention back to Katherine. I move the ripped sleeve of my coat and show her the royal mark on my forearm.

"I'm Princess Aurora Marelup, last of my name, first of my kind —future queen of the Lycan packs." I curtsey to the queen and she returns the gesture. Her hand gently comes out to touch mine.

"I knew your mother. She was such a kind and caring soul. But gods help you, if you crossed her, she was downright ruthless." Katherine smiles as she speaks about my mother. It warms my heart to know someone besides my father and Dimitri is left alive that knew my mother. I smile and laugh a bit.

"I have a lot of my mother's tendencies and my father's black or white view of the world. Though, thankfully, I have a much better grasp of technology than he does." I watch his mother's visage pale considerably when I mention my father in the present tense.

I straighten up my stance a bit more, my resolve as hard as steel. "I rescued my father from the Dire Wolf camp in the Nankoweap Ruins. Apparently, their alpha—who was the beta in my mother's time—chopped off his left arm and took him hostage." I tilt my head left then right, assessing her reaction.

Before I can speak again, Alaric wraps his arms around my waist and kisses my cheek. "My father should be here tomorrow with the rest of my troops. That's not going to be a problem, is it?" I watch my scales ripple across my hands then recede just as fast. My eyes lock on Alaric's mother's eyes—there's a definite fear there. Katherine begins to pace in front of us before she turns and looks at her son.

"Alaric, you know what this means for all of us?" Tears are threatening to break free from her eyes. Katherine's flesh flushes from the effort of trying not to cry. Alaric kisses my cheek then locks eyes with his mother.

"I do. It means dad isn't the rightful king, and we no longer hold any title. Nicodeamus was next in line for the throne, but with him not wed to another dragon or dragon kind, he cannot sit upon the capital's throne. Aurora, however, can and will sit upon the throne— she is dragon-kin and my mate. If Aurora allows it, I wish to wed her before we dethrone father." I watch Alaric talk to his mother. It feels very surreal, like I'm watching some reality TV show. I have a prince, who's really not a prince, who wishes to be my husband and mate. I turn in Alaric's arms and look up into his grey eyes.

"Make the preparations. As far as my father is concerned, he will see the value of having not only our mating but our marriage to solidify the alliance between the Lycans and Dragon houses." I stand on my tippy toes and kiss his lips.

"Besides, I think you'll look pretty damn fine in dress clothes." I feel my father reach out to me mentally, and I bring him up to speed. Alaric's grip on me tightens as I widen the connection, allowing both of them in on the conversation. I personally suspect anyone who gained power after my mother's house fell. Both my father and Alaric agree. I look at Alaric's mother over my shoulder, and my mercury orbs frighten her some.

"Father says hi, and the wedding will happen tomorrow at dusk. The Dragon Star is at its apex tomorrow, and he wants it to bless our union. Plus, it's my birthday." His mother's fear is clearly visible.

She's shaking, which proves to me that she knows something about the attack. "Alaric, love, please show me to our chambers. I wish to freshen up." Alaric studies his mother's reaction to what I said before he leads me off.

CHAPTER 15

Alaric

Today has to be the absolute best day of my life! My mate flew with me, and she tended to the scales my dragon can't reach. Aurora even sought shelter under my wing when my mother approached. I feel like I'm king of the world right now.

Now, I'm only concerned about my mother's reaction when Aurora said her father is still living. She seemed to get very nervous after that. Maybe there was betrayal on my father's side? I'll ponder this later, but for now, I'm supervising the construction of my bride's wedding dress—nothing but the best for Aurora. I don't care if I don't have a title. I don't care if we have to walk through the fires of Hell to secure her birthright to her mother's throne.

I stand back and watch the seamstress work on Aurora's dress. Honestly, I don't think any fabric will ever be good enough for her. It's my own opinion, not how she feels. She doesn't care about finery or any of the usual court bullshit.

I receive news that Nicodeamus was spotted on the horizon with the rest of the packs. He's way ahead of schedule. Good, it gives me time to get them all settled, bathed, and fed before tomorrow. I tell the one manservant to prepare enough robes for their arrival. He bows and leaves to complete his task.

The second seamstress shows me the suit she's preparing for me. It's a beautiful compliment to the dress I commissioned for Aurora. I can't believe she agreed to marry me on such short notice. Our bond is different than that of her wolf mates.

Our bond is bone-deep; no bite is required or even a mating. We were matched on the most primal and genetic level. If we were not a match, our scales would have died the moment they were implanted. I gently rub Aurora's scale on my chest, and I can instantly feel her joy. I wonder why my parents never swapped scales. Perhaps I'll ask my mother later.

"Alaric?" Speaking of the devil, here's my mother now.

"Hard at work, I see," Katherine says in a bored tone as she looks over the suit. She plays with the lapel, examining the stitch work closely.

"What do you need, Mother?" I tilt my head to the side and examine her body language, looking for a clue as to what her motivation is.

"I don't need anything. Why would I need anything? I'm the Queen, after all." She looks at me and tries to hold my gaze. She couldn't do it for long. My mother starts fiddling with the hem of her sleeves instead of looking at me. I slowly cross my arms over my chest and lean against the wall, watching her.

"Let me guess, either you're bothered by the fact that Nicodeamus is still alive or the fact that his daughter is my mate," I smirk as I watch her eyebrow twitch, a dead giveaway that I hit the nail on the head. My mother bites her bottom lip and continues to stare at the hem of her sleeve. Katherine begins to walk around the room until she reaches the window.

"Your father knew about the attack before it came. That's why we didn't attend that night. He admitted to the knowledge a few months ago. He said those horrible Strigoi were sent in search of the last true heir. A puppet master is pulling their strings. Tomas is not the true leader; someone else is giving the orders." My mother looks frightened. I slowly move to embrace her.

"Mother, we will protect you. Aurora is quite strong; she took down Nexus all by herself." I smile broadly after seeing my mother's shock at the news.

"Besides, I believe we can take back the throne, usurp my father, and assemble the nest to take back the main castle. Aurora is alpha enough to force every wolven creature to shift. I've seen the video that proves her power. Hell, I've felt her power for myself." I release my mother, and she breaks away to spin around and face me.

"Are you absolutely sure, Alaric? You know your father is a powerful male. I don't want to see my only son die." Katherine is practically in tears as she thinks about the possibility of me dying.

A knock at the door makes both of us look at the sliding bolt lock. A single long, hooked, white talon makes its way between the doors then slices down, cutting the beam in half. A thud is heard as the door flies open. Aurora stands on the other side, partially shifted. She must have sensed my inner turmoil. Her eyes are fathomless orbs, the churning mercury not giving away where she's looking.

"My love, I know the mid-shift is exhausting. Why don't you take your full form?" I smile, looking at Aurora as she smirks then fully shifts.

Her great, white hybrid beast looks down at us. I can feel my mother's body trembling beside me. "Mother, I told you she can defend herself." I smile as I look at Aurora's hybrid up close for the first time.

I slowly approach her and caress the heavy scale-like armor on her forearms. I raise her arm to look at how her scales form into gauntlets to protect her. Where the wolven claws should be, long, white, curved dragon talons exist. Aurora remains still as I touch her beast's form. I guess it's only fair; she did examine my dragon closely before. My mother's eyes widen as she watches me manipulate Aurora's talons. My eyes move to Aurora's head; it's a unique mix of Lycan and dragon features. Her muzzle is broader with a ridge up the nose plate like a dragon. Tiny scales adorn her eyelids, almost like eyeliner. For a moment, as I stare at her mercury orbs, I can see a slightly darker shade of grey in the center of her eyes—the darker area in the shape of a dragon's slit. I simply smile at her and stroke her muzzle.

"I can see your eye slits," I say in a teasing tone as I look up at her. Aurora's ears flicker before she tilts her head to look at me, then rolls her eyes. Her long, white tail whips from side to side in irritation. I'm guessing I'm right; I can see where she's focusing her gaze.

"Are you sure that's safe, Alaric? She could be unpredictable," Katherine states from her spot near the window. She looks like she's ready to jump at any moment.

Aurora growls and begins to freeze the room. Her alpha power is unleashed, driving my mother and the seamstresses to the ground. In the distance, we can hear Nicodeamus's dragon's roar. Aurora answers back in a mixed sound that can only be explained as a howling roar.

Then she approaches my mother and shifts back to her human form. "What do you know about the night my mother died?" I can see a fine line of scales ripple down Aurora's spine all the way down to her tailbone. This happens several times before my mother speaks.

"My husband knew and kept us here. He knew about the attack and didn't let our clan attend or even think about leaving the nest." Katherine lowers her eyes and puts her hands over her face as she begins to cry. Aurora looks back at me. I can see she's struggling for control.

I unbutton my dress shirt and wrap it around her. Her oppressive alpha power slowly diminishes, and everyone else can start moving about again. Aurora looks up at me with tears in her eyes. I can't tell if they're rage or pain tears. She slowly lowers her eyes, just staring at my chest. I gently kiss her forehead and hold her. What else could I do? I mean, the twins were right; she's quite scary when she's dealing with an emotion outside of rage. For all I know, she could lose her shit and take out everyone in this room in a few seconds. My mother seizes this moment to escape out of the room as quickly as possible.

Aurora, completely uncharacteristic, speaks in a soft voice. "You know I'm going to kill him, right?" She doesn't bother to look up at me. I rest my head on top of hers and just smile.

"Consider my father's head a wedding present." Aurora backs up and looks at me, my shirt barely staying on her shoulders. Her smile rivals the sun. I haven't seen her this happy since she went flying for the first time. Aurora's smile turns mischievous as she tilts her head to the left.

"Do you really mean it, Alaric?" Her hands slide down my chest to rest on the edge of my pants. Her fingertips slowly slip under the waistband and slide back and forth, touching my lower stomach. I can feel my cock come to life, quickly becoming almost painfully hard. Her scent has changed. In the back of my mind, I know her heat recently should have ended, but there's always that slight chance she's still fertile.

"Aurora, we should be careful. It's still so close to when your heat should have ended." I'm trying to be responsible. I don't have condoms here, and I don't want her to regret our first time together.

Aurora's fingers make short work of my belt, my button, and then my zipper. My trousers fall to the floor, leaving me bare for her inspection. Aurora's eyes slowly roam over every inch of my body. Her mischievous grin turns into one of appreciation.

I'm now very thankful for all the extra training sessions I did every single week. Aurora shrugs my dress shirt off and tries to herd me to the desk behind me. She's got another thing coming if she thinks I'm going to allow myself to be dominated by my mate.

When we get close to the desk, I grab her by her waist and spin her around. Aurora's palms slap down hard on the desktop. I wrap her thick, white hair around my left fist and pull back so her neck is exposed and her back is arched. I press my body flush with hers, and my cock rests between her plump ass cheeks. My right hand comes up to lightly grip her throat as I growl softly. "We do this my way, love. I can't promise to be gentle. Your scent is driving me insane."

Through our bond, she responds, *Anything, my love, I need to feel you!* Aurora's breathless voice echoes in my head, making my cock leak with anticipation.

I slowly move my hips back and feel my cock slide down her ass crack to her dripping folds. Once I'm lined up, I thrust into her roughly. Each stroke out is agonizingly slow, but my thrust back into her is fast and hard. Aurora's moans are music to my ears.

The soaking wet slaps of flesh on flesh drives me to start fucking her harder. I tighten my grip on her throat as my thrusts start to become erratic. All of a sudden, Aurora's powerful cock-crushing orgasm rips through her. My balls begin to tighten, begging for release. A fresh gush of Aurora's cum spurts out of her pussy, drenching my cock and balls. I'm too close to my own orgasm to hold back any longer. I use Aurora's hair to move her head to the left.

I roar as my orgasm rips through me, and my canines descend just before I sink them into the muscle of Aurora's shoulder. I feel my seed pulse in waves into her womb, every shockwave rippling through me. Instinctually, I know what's happening. I keep making small thrusts, milking every last drop of seed I have into her. I carefully withdraw my teeth from her flesh and lick the wounds clean. I release my grip on her throat and hair and start kissing her skin. "I love you so much. I hope I wasn't too rough?"

Aurora lays her chest on the desk and stretches. "Fuck no! That was phenomenal!" She turns her head to look at me over her shoulder. I withdraw from her slowly then slide her whole body onto the desk. I crawl onto the desk beside her as she rolls onto her back. Aurora bends her knees and places her feet flat on the desk. I lightly run my fingers over her soft abdomen.

"I have to say it's a first for me to have fucked here. I'm just glad everyone had enough sense to leave." I chuckle softly as I watch Aurora look around.

"You know I need to return the favor." Her fingertips trace where I bit her.

She raises a single eyebrow and looks at me before she covers her mouth to yawn. I carefully extract myself from the desk. I gently scoop her up in my arms and carry her to my room. Aurora seems so happy and peaceful when she sleeps. Lucky for me, a maid is cleaning up in there.

She looks up, startled by my arrival. A knowing smile graces her lips, and she turns down the bed so I can tuck Aurora in. Once she's settled, I go and take a quick shower. When I'm done, I leave my room and make arrangements for Aurora's dress and appropriate jewelry to be left for her to choose from. I handpick attendants to help her dress for the wedding.

The castle herald announces the arrival of Nicodeamus and his army. I run downstairs as fast as I can to greet everyone. "Welcome home, everyone!"

I approach Nicodeamus first and embrace him. In a whispered tone, I speak to him. "We need to talk. Gather the twins and Dimitri; we'll meet in the library." Nicodeamus nods then moves off into the crowd. I finish greeting everyone, then make arrangements with the servants to get the troops fed and food and drink to be brought to the library.

I wait for the guys to arrive in the library. My hand rests on the decanter for a moment before I lift it to pour a few glasses of well-aged bourbon. Once the guys arrive, and everyone is inside, I lock the doors, pass out the drinks, and turn on some music to prevent anyone from listening in.

"I have news," I blurt out the first thing that comes to mind.

"Apparently, my father knew about the attack, and that's why there were no dragons present at the festivities. The second bit of news is Aurora and I are getting married tonight, so her claim to the dragon throne is stronger." The guys start talking among themselves then Dominik speaks.

"Aurora agreed to go along with this? She doesn't believe in putting one mate above the others." Dominik looks pissed, and so does his brother. There's a soft knock at the door and through the bond I know its Aurora. Quickly I open the door and let her in, I'm thankful, our angel decided to make her appearance.

"You're right, Dom; no mate is above the other. The very public wedding tonight is part of a two-fold plan." Aurora holds up one finger.

"It appears to be a political marriage since mates don't need a wedding. Our enemies will believe I haven't gained power from him. Without a true dragon mate, they will believe me to be weak and a target." A sadistic grin creeps across her vermillion lips as she holds up the second finger.

"Then, I will kill them all and add their skulls to my throne." The way Aurora says it so matter-of-fact is kind of scary. I'm starting to understand why Nicodeamus said her dragon side is quite strong.

"Daughter, what would you have me do? I'm supposed to be dead." Nicodeamus smirks, then looks to me and bows his head for a second.

"That's easy, Father. You're walking me down the aisle. Let those fuckers gawk all they want. The first to raise a hand will die by my talons." The minute the word *talon* leaves her lips, she shifts both arms, displaying her weapons. I notice her scales have changed. The ridges are more prominent and now have sharp edges. Nicodeamus is the first to take notice as he reaches for Aurora's hand.

"What's the word? Upgrade?" He carefully twists Aurora's gauntlet in his hand, admiring the change.

"I see you two had time to work on your bond." Nicodeamus smirks as Aurora looks between me and the twins, then finally Dimitri. Her eyes fall to her own arms, looking at how the scales changed. Her eyes light up and churn liquid mercury, except they're now adorned with dragonic slits. I'm guessing her vision is also altered by the way she's studying things.

"Are you okay, my love?" I move closer and shift my arms like hers.

My scales are just as rough looking. They have shades of mostly blues and whites with the occasional fleck of gold. I lightly touch my talons to hers to get her to look at mine. Aurora has a look of wonder as she lines one of her arms up with mine. Almost identical in every way, except color.

"Wow. I guess I know what gift I got from you, Alaric." Her father almost chokes on his water.

I can see the guys' noses working as they catch her scent. The change in it is subtle, but it's there. I watch Nicodeamus huddle the twins together and bring them up to speed. Shock isn't even the word to describe the look on the twins' faces. Poor Dimitri just shakes his head and throws his arms up in the air. It's too soon to alert Aurora of the possible cargo she may be carrying. We'll know more in a month if it's taken root.

"What the actual fuck is wrong with you four? This is cool as shit, and y'all are over there measuring your dicks in the corner. Where's the damn food? I'm starving!" Aurora practically growls out. Dimitri and Jayce bolt out of the room to get more food while Dominik, Nicodeamus, and I deal with a heavily armored, hungry hybrid. Lucky bastards made it out. I'm almost jealous.

Epilogue

Night of the Wolf

November 30, 2019

The local elite from surrounding clans have all gathered for the social event of the winter. A full string orchestra is playing in the foyer, and drinks are being passed to arriving guests. I stand on the balcony overlooking the festivities below in my full royal regalia.

Tonight's wedding is two-fold. First, it's the Night of the Wolf, which is also Aurora's birthday. Second, we are luring all of the traitors to one location to completely clean the house.

Queen Katherine, my mother, moves gracefully through the crowd, greeting all of the dignitaries. My father, King Bane, his arrival is met with full fanfare. The king's eyes lock on mine as he motions toward the library to speak to me in private. Once inside, I lock the door and put music on to hide our voices.

Bane speaks first. "You know, Alaric, I disapprove of this marriage. Our benefactors will not be pleased with this move." I pour two bourbons and pass one to my father.

"I believe it to be a brilliant move. If indeed Aurora is the only heir to the Lycan throne, then marrying her secures us two provinces and three wolf packs. The smartest way to build an army is to conquer it—that's what you taught me." I slowly raise the bourbon to my lips and sip it. Bane starts to stroke his thick white beard, contemplating what I just said to him.

"Brilliant strategy, Alaric. You're a chip off the 'ole block. Perhaps after she gives you an heir or two, we'll attempt to oust the Strigoi. Then we will have a true winter retreat." Bane briefly embraces Alaric before heading to the door.

"Do you need me to walk your bride down the aisle?" Alaric smiles and sets his glass on the desk.

"No, Father, we have it all under control. I believe the bear, Dimitri, is escorting her down the aisle." I move to the full-length mirror in the corner of the library and adjust my medals and ribbons. "I'm just waiting for the steward to tell me it's time to take my place and get this show on the road."

"Very well, son. I'll do my kingly duty and walk in the procession with your mother. The only thing that wench did right was produce a strong son." Bane practically snarls the last part out. Gritting my teeth, I make sure my poker face is perfect; not a single indication of the rage that boils below the surface is given.

"Thank you, Father, for this boon. I'm sure the princess will produce strong sons for me. After all, there were no stronger Lycans than Anca and Vladimir." I smile at my father, watching his reaction closely. Bane looks back at me and smiles.

"Yes, they were the strongest of their kind. I'll make arrangements to introduce Vladimir to his daughter very soon. Rumor has it that her hair is white, and she is dragon-kin." Bane studies me, both of us posturing for each other.

"Rumors..." I pull out my phone and show my father an image of Aurora with long, black hair.

"She's almost an exact replica of Anca; gods rest her soul." Bane takes my phone from me and sends the photo to himself. He scrolls through my pictures, but every single one shows Aurora with black hair.

"I wonder why rumors of a white Lycan would surface," Bane says as he hands me my phone back.

"All the mates other than Vlad were castrated before Anca went into heat. Which reminds me, I have the herbs for you to make your mate obedient. Even if she's the last Marelup heir, we can't allow her to gain in power." I accept the satchel and tuck it into my inner coat pocket.

My dragon is roaring, wanting to roast my father to ash for speaking about his mate in such a way. I smirk as I refill my glass, attempting to remain calm. "You know how the peasants are. They need a savior to believe in." I laugh to myself, thinking about my mate rending the flesh from her enemies.

"A white Lycan, how absurd. It's like saying your scales are Easter egg color." We both enjoy a hearty laugh before exiting the room.

~On the other side of the castle~

Aurora

I stand before the mirror, my black wig pinned in place with a dainty tiara in the middle of my curls. Nicodeamus moves up behind me to look at us in the mirror.

"You look exactly like your mother with this wig on," Nicodeamus says softly as his fingers lightly touch the curls. Dimitri watches from the bench near the window.

"*Da*, except Aurora is a wee bit taller and has more muscle tone." Dimitri's tone is almost reverent as he compares me to my mother.

"I still hate that Vladimir named you, though the name does fit you. You are a beacon of light and hope, with so many facets to who you are." Nicodeamus smiles at me and kisses my cheek before he moves away. Dominik comes walking into the suite with a scroll. Jayce follows closely behind, carrying a tray of food.

"Alaric sends food before the ceremony. He said to only eat this tonight because he's not sure if anyone will try to poison us," Dominik says calmly as Jayce sets the tray down.

"I have the processional line up. Traditionally, we all wear hooded cloaks until we arrive at the pulpit. Once we're up there, the friar will instruct us to lower our hoods. Aurora is the only one not required to wear a hood." Dominik turns and starts passing out cloaks to everyone. I touch my own face as I look in the mirror.

So this is what my mother looked like, I say softly to myself as I examine my features over.

"Let's get this over with. It's all bullshit anyway. It just sucks that this stunning dress is going to get ruined." I move around the room, adjusting the guys' cloaks and hoods to make sure their faces are completely covered.

I look down at the flair of the sleeves of my gown. Alaric made sure I would be able to shift my arms without destroying the gown. The sleeves are long enough that no one will see until it's too late when I do shift my arms. The gown itself has a sweetheart top, which purposely exposes Alaric's scale on my ample chest.

For strategic purposes, I move several locks of black hair over Alaric's scale to hide it for now. Three handmaidens approach me, fastening the train into the back of my gown as well as the embroidered veil. I roll my eyes, absolutely hating being handled this much. The handmaidens finally leave, and I finally get to look at my family.

"Our forces outnumber those in attendance three to one, so I'm not overly concerned. I still want to move in formation. Jayce, you and Dominik enter first, then Dad and I. Dimitri, you watch our backs." Nicodeamus and Dimitri start laughing at the same time. I can't help but growl at them.

"I'm sorry, daughter, you set the procession the same way your mother did when she married Vladimir. We found it funny. It will cause flashbacks for those who were present for your mother's wedding." Aurora smiles, canines bared, and her eyes are the liquid mercury of her beast.

"When did you gain the dragon slits in your eyes?" Nicodeamus says. I move back in front of the mirror to look at my eyes.

"Hmm, nice upgrade. I look really freaky now!" Purposely I do that maniacal Joker laugh as I look at the guys. At least I'm in a good mood, which means the bloodshed shouldn't start too early.

A knock sounds at the door and I go on high alert. That was a five-minute warning. Everyone settles down and double-checks their appearance. I have the most glorious last-second idea and pull out my favorite lip stain. Untwisting the top, I stare at the rich, deep-red color of the stain that I have chosen. Carefully I paint my full lips making sure to accentuate my perfectly pronounced cupids bow. As the stain dries, it takes on the appearance of dried blood, and I feel it's the most fitting color for tonight's festivities.

"Time to reign in blood, boys." I start humming the song *Heathens* by Twenty One Pilots. Oddly enough, my song choice is quite fitting as I start walking in the line-up's third position.

My group moves as a single unit down the hallway, passing Ellis and his bears. I maintain my resting bitch face as I move. My steps are silent and calculated; the only sound from me is the soft humming of my chosen song en route to the pulpit.

My group arrives at the double doors of the throne room. The steward is waiting to receive word that it's time to send us in. It's so quiet that you can hear the opening prayer in the throne room. We hear three knocks, and the steward opens the double doors. *It's show time*, I say through the bond to those who can hear me just before our group enters, walking in time with the music.

Whispers erupt throughout the throne room. Most are commenting on how much I look like Anca or that the Lycan Queen still lives. King Bane is the most shocked at my appearance—the blood-red lipstick was apparently my mother's signature color.

Once we're at the pulpit, I gracefully curtsey to King Bane and Queen Katherine. Next, I turn to Alaric and lower my head submissively to him, playing the role I'm in perfectly. Alaric reaches out and places his hand under my chin, allowing me to raise my gaze.

King Bane's ego gets the better of him as he moves to inspect me. He grips my jaw tightly and examines my eyes and then my teeth like I'm some sort of broodmare. Bane quickly raises the right sleeve of my gown to reveal my royal brand. Bane raises my arm for the entire throne room to see.

"Aurora is Anca's heir!" Bane shouts to the gathered dignitaries.

My mates can easily feel the aggravation through the bond. Alaric does the only thing he knows to calm me and rubs my scale, acting like his shirt is bothering him. That thoughtful action soothes me, and I calm down, remaining in Bane's grip.

"My son has chosen wisely for this political alliance. This bitch will birth powerful sons," Bane speaks with such detachment, it's unbelievable. It's getting harder for the guys to maintain their silence as the king practically bashes and degrades me in front of them. I flood the bond with how much I love them trying to ease their concern. Bane finally releases me into Alaric's hands, and I instantly calm down. Now, the friar raises his hands and begins the ceremony.

"Lords and Ladies, we have before us tonight, on the Night of the Wolf, two powerful bloodlines. Though it is a political marriage, we pray for their love to eventually grow. We ask the Elder Gods for strength and fertility. That Anca's heir produces strong sons, who will be able to ascend the Ice Dragon and Marelup Throne." The friar takes out a piece of red silk and lightly binds Alaric's and my hands together. "This sash represents the blood that shall be shared between bloodlines when the first heir is born."

Next, a silver sash is wrapped around our hands. "The silver represents the prince's dragon's sight. May he always see the best solutions in the future." The friar places his hand on top of mine and Alaric's hands.

"If anyone present has any reason these two should not be bound, speak now or forever hold your peace." The friar looks around the hall at all the attendants. He didn't, however, look to his left at my witnesses.

The guys move as one and rip off their cloaks and flinging them aside. Before their cloaks hit the floor, I reach up and rip off my black wig; my long, snow-white hair cascades down my back. In an instant, Alaric and I shift our arms, so our gauntlets and talons are at the ready. Nicodeamus steps forward with Dimitri at his side.

"I am Nicodeamus, true mate to Anca Marelup and the true Ice Dragon King!" My group and I stand at the ready for the battle ahead.

To Be Continued.....

Book 3: Fight

Made in the USA
Middletown, DE
08 July 2022

68808355R00121